Also by Scott Reintgen

Talespinners #1: *Saving Fable*

Escaping Ordinary

~ Talespinners Book 2 ~

SCOTT REINTGEN

Crown Books for Young Readers
New York

Text copyright © 2020 by Scott Reintgen
Jacket art copyright © 2020 by Maike Plenzke

All rights reserved. Published in the United States by Crown Books for Young Readers, an imprint of Random House Children's Books, a division of Penguin Random House LLC, New York.

Crown and the colophon are registered trademarks of Penguin Random House LLC.

Visit us on the Web! rhcbooks.com

Educators and librarians, for a variety of teaching tools, visit us at RHTeachersLibrarians.com

Library of Congress Cataloging-in-Publication Data
Names: Reintgen, Scott, author.
Title: Escaping Ordinary / Scott Reintgen.
Description: First edition. | New York: Crown Books for Young Readers, 2020. | Series: Talespinners; book 2 | Audience: Ages 8–12. | Audience: Grades 4–6. | Summary: Rather than rest after saving Fable, Indira must begin a teamwork tutorial that leads to a quest filled with dragons, unlikely allies, and threats to all of Imaginary.
Identifiers: LCCN 2019040424 | ISBN 978-0-525-64672-3 (hardcover) | ISBN 978-0-525-64674-7 (epub)
Subjects: CYAC: Books and reading—Fiction. | Adventure and adventurers—Fiction. | Heroes—Fiction. | Cooperativeness—Fiction. | Fantasy.
Classification: LCC PZ7.1.R4554 Esc 2020 | DDC [Fic]—dc23

The text of this book is set in 12-point Cochin.
Interior design by Ken Crossland

Printed in the United States of America
10 9 8 7 6 5 4 3 2 1
First Edition

To Thomas,
wake up, little one.
There are worlds to conquer.
Love, Dad

Contents

1

The Story House

"And for the first time in weeks, the sun began to rise."

It took several seconds for that booming voice to fade. Indira stood at the center of a bright living room. The light glanced off her one-handed war hammer as she extended it. The Axel twins—also known as the Thunder Brothers—stood on her right and left, holding out their own matching weapons. Indira kind of felt like they looked like a soccer team in the middle of a halftime huddle. The three of them held the pose for a few stretching seconds. Indira could feel heat creeping up her neck until another voice broke the silence.

"Cut! That's a wrap!"

Indira sighed with relief. They'd been working on the final scene of her first story for weeks. Just offstage, she saw matching relief on the face of everyone who'd been working with them. David came grinning onto the set as the other workers started clearing out equipment.

"Great job, everyone!" he called. "Seriously! What an accomplishment! Can you believe it? We're really done. The Story House is finally finished!"

Indira gave her brother a side hug. The Axel twins nodded their thanks. Indira knew David had been a little disappointed by his role. After hearing the title of the story—*Indira Story and the Thunder Brothers*—he had assumed that *he* would be one of the brothers in the book's title. I mean, he was *her* brother, after all. But the Author had gone in a completely different direction. David had turned out to be a minor character in the story. Mostly there for comic relief. He'd put on a smile about it, but she knew him well enough to know that it hadn't been easy on him.

"What now?" Indira asked, looking around. "Do we start the sequel?"

James Axel shrugged. "Are we even *in* the second book? I couldn't tell from that ending."

All of them looked around. It took a few seconds for one of the bookmark stagehands to come bustling forward. "Casting announcements to come! Indira, you're headed back to Fable. It's standard in-between-books protocol for protagonists. There's a dragoneye waiting outside."

The Axel twins nodded in unison before heading back through the nearest hallway. Some of the other characters involved in the final scene followed them. Indira wasn't sure she was ready to go. It felt like they'd arrived just a few weeks ago to start working on the story.

"Can I walk around the Story House? One more time?"

The Mark smiled. "Of course, dear. It's *your* house, after all."

"I'll meet you out front," David whispered. "You did great, baby sister."

When Indira and the rest of the cast had arrived six months ago, their Story House had been a single-level, one-room building. She had learned that each room represented a new scene or chapter in the story the Author was telling. After they'd performed the first scene, another door had appeared. Inside? A second room that represented the *next* scene.

Every new idea the Author came up with made their Story House bigger. Now Indira walked back through the mansion their crew had created together. She ran a hand along the banister before peeking through a door on her left. It was one of the bigger rooms.

Sensing her presence, the room activated. The boring wallpaper vanished, replaced by a clearing in a forest. Indira watched an image of herself running forward, the Axel twins close behind her, all of them ready to face their nemesis in the story's climactic fight scene.

Indira made her patient way back through each room, watching highlights as she did. So much of her time at Protagonist Preparatory had been spent in fear that she'd never make it into a story at all. But here she was, walking through one that had been written just for her.

It still didn't feel real sometimes.

She'd learned a lot since then. Her Author—Darby Martin—had made plenty of tweaks along the way. A part of being a protagonist was learning to adjust. Being quick on your feet. Indira had slowly started to trust her Author to write the very *best* possible story. Not that she didn't put in the occasional suggestion or two.

As she made her way back through the house, she watched happy moments and sad scenes and hilarious misunderstandings. She couldn't help feeling proud. They'd done their job and they'd done it well. The story was complete now. Indira arrived back in the very first room.

It was called the Seed, dear reader.

Writers have them every day. Little seeds of ideas that—given light and water and room to grow—can blossom into something more. Indira paused there to watch.

A slightly younger version of herself fell through a huge hole in the ground. She landed in a dark and forgotten cavern. It was there that she discovered her hammer for the first time.

"Thanks for believing in me," she whispered to the walls.

No one knew if the Authors could *actually* hear them, but Indira felt grateful all the same. It was such a joy to be chosen. She walked out the front door and closed it carefully behind her.

A small, circular park waited. It was surrounded by other Story Houses that were still in progress. Characters from those stories were taking their breaks between scenes, chatting excitedly. Most of the houses on this block were still under construction. Some were no bigger than shacks. Others were even larger than her own house, and nowhere close to being done.

David strode forward. "Take a look at that Story House. It's all yours, baby sister."

She looked back. There were three levels, a pair of balconies, all covered in storm-gray bricks. Above the house, a huge cable extended up from the chimney and ran up into the clouds, out of sight. Indira had been told that that cable represented the house's connection to the Author's imagination. It was a source of power that fueled the story forever.

"Remember at the beginning?" she asked. "The connection was just a thin little thread."

David nodded. "And look at it now. Pretty healthy-looking to me."

The thicker the cable, the deeper the Author's connection to the characters. Their link had only grown since the beginning. Everyone kept saying it was a great sign.

"And now . . . ," Indira whispered. "The readers."

Both of them looked farther up the road. Their Story

House sat in a section of the neighborhood reserved for new stories. Around the block, though, were other, more established tales. Some were actually quite famous. In the air above those houses, she saw thousands of little strings attached to the roofs. Each one represented a connection to a reader.

It was hard not to look a little longingly in their direction.

"Readers will come," David said calmly. "Let's focus on what we can control."

She allowed her brother to sling an arm around her shoulder and lead her off in the other direction. The dragoneye portals were waiting at the far end of the little park. Indira snuck one more glance back over her shoulder. *Every cage has a key.* Her First Words whispered into the air. She'd been through so much since she'd first heard them. Looking at her Story House, she smiled one more time. It was hard to imagine that she and the other characters had actually *built* it together. As she turned, though, she set her eyes firmly on what was *next*.

Fable was waiting.

2

Home

Indira's feet set down with a familiar *whoosh*.

The dragoneye had delivered them to the outskirts of Fable, and in that moment there was nowhere else she'd rather be. There was something about seeing the city from a distance that felt right. She led David down a row of particularly nice houses until Fable burst into view.

Once again, the city wore a new costume. And this costume was *sleek*.

"Whoa," David said. "Looks like a science-fiction setup!"

Indira found herself grinning. The city looked as if it had leaped five hundred years into the future. She stared up at towering skyscrapers, each infused with bright light. Flying vehicles darted in and out of view, leaving little blue streaks behind them. The entire side of one building flashed massive advertisements. Like moths to a flame, Indira and David were drawn into the electric city.

"I missed this place," Indira whispered.

The city walls winked back at her. As the two of them entered, more surprises waited. The city's usual populace swirled in the streets, and it took Indira a few seconds to realize the Marks had all transformed into robots. Most of them were still tall and thin—able to slip between pages at a moment's notice—but many now sported spinning wheels, while others had silver antennae or brightly painted buttons. The dying sunlight reflected off their metal bodies like sparks.

Indira looked toward where she knew the Talespin coffee shop was located. Her heart beat a little faster. It was the first place she'd seen her Author, but also where her standoff with Brainstorm Ketty had happened last semester. The city's new costume had temporarily relocated the coffee shop, though. Indira's eyes scanned upward.

"Check it out, D. A flying coffeehouse!"

The entire building hovered in the air above them. Indira saw engine burners glowing blue beneath the structure, each one working hard to keep it afloat. A girl sitting along the outdoor patio noticed the two of them looking up and waved. Indira smiled back.

"Let's head to Protagonist Prep," she said. "We can explore the city after we check in."

It took a lot of effort to keep walking and to ignore all the distractions. Bright lights flashing here, loud voices booming there. The streets felt more packed than ever, but Indira walked confidently forward. It was just one of the many spells that Protagonist Preparatory cast. Any character who'd attended the school had a knack for finding their way back to the front doors again.

Rounding a corner, Indira found the building waiting in the distance. Her first thought was that the school now looked like a grounded alien aircraft. The upper section was shaped like the top of a gigantic mushroom. The lower sections tightened into more structurally sound cylinders, and the exterior was lined with perfectly even glass windows that ran the entire length of the building. One detail remained the same, however: the front doors of the school stood open. They were massive blast doors now, but they still stood as open as they had when Indira first arrived.

Have you ever gone on a long trip, dear reader? Maybe you took a car ride down the coast, or a plane across the country. Other places can be so exciting. Almost like trying on a pair of new shoes for a time and walking around to see how they suit you. But there's no feeling quite like returning to the place you know best, the place where everything began. There's a word we use for such places, and it never quite captures our love for them. Indira said that word anyway.

"Home."

New Assignments

The interior of Protagonist Preparatory had transformed to fit Fable's science-fiction theme. Industrial lighting filled the halls. It pumped through the floors and ceilings like blue veins. Indira maneuvered through little pockets of students. She saw a mix of golden jackets and blue ones. The sight had her stomach turning.

Golden jackets for protagonists. Blue jackets for side characters.

The school hadn't fully done away with its old classification policies. Brainstorm Underglass and Brainstorm Vesulias had agreed to eliminate classes that were just for one group or the other, though. It was a nice first step.

Indira led David down a familiar hallway and was struck once more by dueling emotions. This was where she'd first learned that she'd be in a story of her very own. It was also where Brainstorm Ketty had started her efforts to sabotage Indira's career. The door into Ketty's old office was open. Indira glanced inside and saw a red-haired woman with her back to them.

She hadn't met the newest brainstorm, but rumor was that the woman was a big-time advocate for *every* character. Indira thought that was another step in the right direction.

A quick knock at Brainstorm Underglass's door was followed by an even quicker call to enter. Indira and David walked in together. The brainstorm looked busy, but the second her eyes landed on Indira, a smile surfaced.

"As I live and breathe! Indira Story has returned. It is so wonderful to see you, dear."

Underglass glided across the room. The woman surprised Indira with a hug instead of a handshake. She smiled once again before shifting back into her more typical business mode. The effect was complemented by the woman's crisp suit and the fact that every single item in the office was set precisely in its proper place.

She took her seat and raised a single eyebrow. "I want a full report."

Indira felt like a soldier relaying news back to a general. It didn't take long to walk through the whole experience. How quickly their Story House had grown. How some of the rooms had taken much longer than other rooms.

Underglass asked a few questions, but mostly listened. When Indira arrived at the end, the brainstorm nodded and pressed a button on her desk.

The magical blackboard behind her swirled with movement.

"We've monitored the initial response from beta readers," Underglass announced. "Those are the earliest readers, kind of like test subjects. Not that we were worried. It's just standard protocol for characters with series potential. And so far? It's been great. The beta readers really like you. Full marks for adventure. Some high scores in humor. A *really* promising result in the 'everyman' category. A lot of readers find you very relatable."

Indira could feel herself blushing. Why had she been so nervous?

"That's such a relief," she said.

Underglass held up a finger. "But there is *always* room for improvement."

"Improvement?" Indira echoed.

"For both of you," Underglass clarified. Another swipe brought up a new blackboard with detailed information about David. "Ultimately, there's a very thin line between a series that never lifts off and one that nestles into the hearts of readers forever. David, you're a likeable character, but you didn't exactly fly off the page in the first novel. The majority of reviews don't mention you. And those that do claim you're a little flat."

"Flat?" David repeated. "Like . . . a pancake?"

"Pancakes are *supposed* to be flat," Underglass replied. "Characters are not. Most of your lines were there for comic relief. Some great moments, of course, but a character should be more than *one* thing. You want to be real enough that you cast a shadow."

David stared at her for a second. "But I like pancakes."

Underglass pointed. "See what I mean? Straight to the joke. You have to be more than one-liners. Indira and the rest of the cast need you to come into your own as the series progresses. Every character playing their part, so to speak. That's why you've been enrolled in our side-character boot camp."

Indira watched David's playful grin vanish. *Boot camp* brought a very specific idea to mind. Indira could see a whistle between the lips of an army captain. She half imagined David in a uniform attempting to do push-ups. She wasn't sure if she should feel bad for him, or laugh.

". . . it's not the end of the world," Underglass was saying. "Aragorn is running this one, and he's not nearly as strict as some of the other captains. It will be hard work, but we signed you up because we think it's *exactly* the kind of thing that will sharpen your skill set."

David's eyes widened. "You mean the dude from *The Lord of the Rings* will be there?"

Underglass bristled. "That *dude* was a king. Show some respect. You'll be reporting at six o'clock tomorrow morning. Don't be late." The brainstorm turned to Indira. "And that will also allow Indira to pursue the training we've assigned for her."

She blinked back to life. "Wait. What? You said the readers liked me. I thought I was going to get a vacation or something! I've been working day and night!"

"Room for improvement," Underglass repeated. "General consensus showed one glaring weakness in your first story. We've designed a training assignment that will help solve it."

Indira's cheeks went red again. This time her blushing had more to do with anger than embarrassment. "Weakness?" she repeated. "I don't have any weaknesses."

"That's actually the problem," Underglass answered. "The Author made you a little too flawless in the first book. Several readers noted that you didn't exactly *need* the other characters, especially during the climax of the novel. We have to fix that. You need to have a little more vulnerability. Not to mention it'd be nice if you relied on your teammates more. Not everything should be solved with the smash of a hammer. Our tutorial will focus on the art of complementary teamwork. It's called the Hero's Journey."

Indira started to protest again, but Brainstorm Underglass held down a button. There was a little robotic beep. "Melody. Could you bring in that paperwork? Thanks."

A few seconds later a familiar-looking assistant came bustling into the room. Indira nodded politely to the woman, still holding back the frustrated words that were piling up in her mind. Melody hummed to herself as she handed David and then Indira their own individual folders.

"These detail your assignments," Underglass explained. "Indira, your packet includes a rendezvous point, as well as a profile of all your teammates for the mission. I highly suspect some of the names listed there will have you feeling a little more positive about your mission."

Indira lifted a curious eyebrow before opening the folder. There was a slightly blurred picture of a boy in a dark blue jersey. The initials *JW* glinted at the top of the page. Indira scanned down, reading some of the notes, but couldn't make sense of any of it. She turned the folder back toward Underglass. "I've never seen this kid before."

Melody gasped. "Oh no! That's the wrong file!" The assistant scuttled across the room, exchanging folders with Indira, scolding herself as Brainstorm Underglass watched with hooded eyes. "I was sorting through some of our recent Author research. Apologies!"

Indira opened the new folder, and this time she *did* recognize the face staring up at her.

"Allen Squalls?"

Underglass nodded. "You might recall that Allen went missing last year, before you arrived at Protagonist Preparatory. He was your Author's first potential protagonist. Brainstorm Ketty targeted him the same way she targeted you. Only her methods of bullying actually worked on

Allen. She drove the boy out of Fable entirely. He ended up down in Plot Hole, a nervous wreck. We found him and explained what happened. This mission is important for his recovery. He's excited to get a second chance."

Indira's initial annoyance faded a little. She'd first seen Allen's face on the missing posters last year. It was hard to stay mad about a mission that would help someone who'd been tricked out of his chance at being in a story.

When she turned the page, Indira's heart jumped a little.

A familiar boy looked out from behind a curtain of fire-red hair. His irises smoldered, and the picture showed a flame summoned in one outstretched palm. It was Phoenix.

Indira felt like she hadn't seen him in a really long time, but she knew less than a year had passed. She'd met Phoenix before ever setting foot in Fable. Even then she'd thought him mysterious. The two of them had become best friends. Their bond was only made deeper by the fact that she'd saved him from Brainstorm Ketty last semester. Her stomach fluttered at the thought of joining up with him again.

"Our selection of Phoenix was no accident," Underglass noted. "At the risk of embarrassing you, Phoenix is a potential romantic interest in your next story."

Indira actually choked. The noise that came out of her mouth could most accurately be described as a squawk.

Her eyes darted over to David, who burst out laughing. Indira sputtered.

"I don't—he doesn't—there isn't . . ."

Underglass grinned. "Exactly the point. You're not sure how you feel about him, or how he feels about you. Your Author is apparently wrestling with that same problem. Our records show that Phoenix is one of *two* characters in consideration for the role."

Indira slumped into the nearest chair. "Two?"

Underglass nodded. "After considering your history with Phoenix—all the connection you've already developed to this point—we decided to include him in the Hero's Journey tutorial. We thought it might give him a slight edge over the other potential romantic interest. Normally we try to avoid bias in these situations, but let's just say I have a soft spot for you and what you did to save the school. So unless I was mistaken about your feelings . . ."

"No!" Indira blurted. "Yes. I mean no. What?"

Underglass practically beamed. "Very good. I do not intend to pressure you at all, but if Phoenix doesn't fit this role, it's likely he'll remain unfinished."

It took Indira a moment to realize she was trying to sink down even lower, but the chair was holding firm and wouldn't allow her to actually hit the floor. She couldn't have heard that right. "Did you say *unfinished*?"

"I'm afraid so," Underglass replied. "The Author has

been *brainstorming* possibilities for each of them. And once they start dreaming up scenes for a character, it's difficult for us to link them with a new Author. Sometimes a character can survive being set aside by their Author and make it into another book in the future, but the most common outcome is that a discarded character remains discarded. If he isn't the romantic interest, he'll likely remain unfinished."

Indira choked again. "No pressure? How is that *no* pressure?"

"It's no more pressure than normal, dear. This is simply how the world of stories works. It is my belief that you and Phoenix are a natural fit. I think that's how you feel as well. This Hero's Journey is simply an opportunity for the two of you to put that to the test."

Indira's cheeks reddened. "Do we have to . . . kiss?"

Underglass laughed outright now. "I doubt that would be the worst fate imaginable, but no, you do not have to kiss. You simply have to have fun being the dynamic duo you've always been."

David cleared his throat. "Maybe we should move on?"

Indira could not turn the page any faster. She hoped to find Maxi waiting there, but the next face wasn't one that she recognized. The girl had short hair that spiked slightly in the front. Indira thought she looked tiny, but wondered if it was because of all the random gear she was wearing. Three different necklaces, a thick pair of glasses, and earrings shaped like rockets.

Indira read the name aloud. "Gadget."

"A promising student," Underglass said. "Unfortunately, Gadget has been with us at Protagonist Preparatory for four years now. She's wonderfully talented, but she has a tendency to focus too much on the tech available to her, and not enough on the story itself. We're giving her one more chance. A Hero's Journey tutorial at your side might just be the answer."

Indira frowned. "Great. So her fate rests on my shoulders too?"

Underglass raised an eyebrow. "Am I to understand that you no longer have an interest in bringing the best out in others? Do you not wish to be a hero? That is not the Indira Story I remember."

Indira wanted to be annoyed by that. She was being handed what felt like a very needy team. One character was recovering from the same torment she'd been put through last semester. Another was a good friend who might end up as an unfinished character. And the last one was getting one final shot at making it into a story. Definitely not the vacation she'd been imagining.

A reminder echoed in the back of her mind, however. Hadn't other people spent time making sure *she* became the best version of herself? Didn't she owe it to each of these characters to do the same? Underglass was right. Indira wanted to be a hero.

Even in the small things.

"So . . . ," Indira said. "We just travel somewhere?"

Underglass looked pleased that she had come around. "You are heading to Plot. It's north of the city. We've designed a Hero's Journey for you there. It's a quest tutorial. Can I assume that you're not too angry with me for signing you up? Do you see the purpose for yourself and the others?"

Indira nodded stubbornly. She didn't hate the idea of more adventures with Phoenix. Besides, she knew how important practice could be. Last year, practice had been the one thing that had saved her from giving up completely. "I guess it won't be so bad."

Underglass smiled. "I knew you'd be up for the task. You report tomorrow morning. The address is in your brief. Keep an open mind, all right? And have some fun."

With a satisfied nod, Underglass pressed another button on her desk. An electric current shot through the air and left Indira's hair standing on end. It was followed by an explosion.

All three of them ducked in terror. Indira's hand went instinctively for her hammer. Her eyes found a spot in the room where a general haze of smoke was rising.

Exactly where Melody had been standing.

David shouted, "You fried Melody!"

Underglass rolled her eyes. "I didn't fry Melody. It's all this *technology*. I keep forgetting which buttons do what. It's madness. Melody will be fine. I just teleported her. Again."

Indira couldn't help laughing. "You're sure she's okay?"

"I'm quite certain. She always gets teleported back."

Indira stood. "That's a relief. We'd better get moving. Wouldn't want you to teleport us. Thanks again for everything, Brainstorm Underglass."

She nodded over to David—who still looked a little stunned by Melody's disappearance—and the two of them started toward the door. She was turning the handle when Underglass spoke.

"Oh, Indira. I really meant what I said. It is great to see you again."

Indira smiled. "You too. It's really good to be home."

They walked back through the hallways. Indira wanted to be annoyed by the idea that she had a weakness to work on. She wanted to feel overwhelmed by all the responsibilities she was taking on with the other characters, too. Instead, a thunderous beat was drumming to life inside her chest. Her fingers settled on the grip of her hammer.

She was ready for more adventure.

She couldn't help grinning.

This was going to be fun.

4

Reunion

Indira and David were both given temporary boarding assignments in one of the local townships, but after a quick tour, Indira led him out of Fable proper.

"I've got a better idea."

Their primary focus over the last six months had been finishing the Story House. Whenever she'd had spare time, though, Indira had been very intentional about keeping up with old friends and family. Mrs. Pennington had all but demanded weekly calls. Indira's adopted family had been chosen for their own story, but Indira knew the launch had been delayed several times now. She hoped that meant the two of them would be right where she'd left them.

The Skirts hadn't changed. Fable's outermost neighborhood featured rows of identical townhouses, all pressed tightly together. Indira turned down her familiar street and was a little sad to see the place she'd called home unlit. "Oh man. Guess they're not here."

David shrugged as Indira ducked down the narrow passage between the Penningtons and their neighbor. She reached down and lifted the gutter spout. Lying right in the middle of the flattened grass was a silver key. Indira snatched it up and headed for the front door.

"We'll just wait inside and surprise them," she said with a grin. "Come on."

Everything in the Skirts was old, so it took a little wiggling to get the key in, and a pretty hard slam of her shoulder to actually wedge the door free of the latch. Indira was fumbling for the light switch when an extra sense tickled down her spine. Instinct told her that something—or someone—was inside.

She reached for her hammer, eyes searching the shifting shadows, before flipping the switch to on. A thunderous shout answered.

"SURPRISE!"

The echoing noise came at her from every direction. Indira nearly struck the closest person with her hammer. Detective Malaprop stumbled back in fright as the rest of her friends and family came laughing forward. It was a surprise party. A room full of people she loved!

Indira glanced over and found David grinning.

"Were you in on this?"

Mrs. Pennington was the first one forward. She

wrapped Indira in a huge hug before spinning her toward the others. It was not hard to see that her adopted mother had orchestrated all of this. Gavin Grant stood to her left. He had the same military-style haircut, but now he looked at least a few inches taller. Indira wondered if that change had come directly from working with his Author.

Maxi was leaning against the wall beside him, sporting a pair of thick sunglasses even though the room had been pitch-black just a few seconds before. Indira recognized them as the unique sunglasses that only the Editors — even those in training — wore. Those dark-framed glasses couldn't hide Maxi's squeal of excitement.

Detective Malaprop wasn't the only unexpected attendee. Some of her teachers were there too. Her escape-class professor, Alice, waved from the crowd. Professor Darcy stood near the food, leaning unromantically over a bowl of chips.

It took Indira a long second to realize she'd taken three steps inside and stopped moving. David gave her an encouraging shove. There was a flash of fiery light near the back of the room, and as Indira made her way forward, little Patch marched out of the kitchen with an absurdly large cake balancing precariously in his arms. Phoenix followed, snuffing out the flame he had just used to light the candles. Her heart leaped a little. She squinted at the lettering on the cake:

CONGRATS ON YOUR FIRST STORY!

"I made this all by myself!" Patch declared.

Indira smiled because the letters were all different sizes, some slightly crooked. Her adopted brother smiled proudly as he set the cake down on the table between them. Maxi started a chant from the back of the room. "Speech! Speech! Speech!"

The others took up the cry (although she could distinctly hear Detective Malaprop chanting the word *screech* instead of *speech*). Indira tried to blush her way out of it, but when the chanting continued, she held up a hand for silence. She pointed to the encouraging words on the cake.

"I'd never have made it without your help," she said. "It's so good to see you all again. Now eat some cake and stop embarrassing me."

Everyone laughed. Smiling, she leaned in and blew out the candles. Patch used the distraction to steal some icing from one corner. Indira winked at him as the group swirled back to life. She felt overwhelmed and thankful and hungry all at the same time. The first person to corner her was Detective Malaprop. She learned that he had received a surprisingly big role in a series called *The Right Word*. Through his own hilarious errors, Detective Malaprop helped children figure out the right word to use in every situation.

Alice curtsied in for a quick hello and wished Indira the best of luck on her next book. Professor Darcy was too busy making Mrs. Pennington blush at the back of the room to greet her. Indira gladly plunked down on the couch between Maxi and Phoenix with her cake in hand.

"You've been gone *forever*," Maxi lamented. "It's been so boring here."

Phoenix pointed his fork in her direction. "Hey. I thought you said that you had fun last week when we visited the Imaginary Sports Hall of Fame."

Maxi's expression was carefully hidden behind her sunglasses.

"Oh yeah. Except for that. That was . . . a lot of fun."

Phoenix—who had always been on the quiet side—leaned forward with a grin. It was a different side of him than Indira was used to seeing. "Oh really? What was your favorite part?"

Maxi shrugged. "The thing with the teams and the ball."

Phoenix and Indira exchanged a look before bursting out laughing.

"You didn't pay attention to any of it," he accused.

Even through the sunglasses, Indira could tell Maxi was rolling her eyes.

"Please. Our tour guide was like not even cute. And I'm amazed that a place could have that many brooms hanging around and still have such dirty floors."

Phoenix shook his head. Indira settled back into the couch and could not have felt more at home. This had been her refuge during that difficult first year of school. Mrs. Pennington's meals had fought off the bitter taste of her hardest days. Patch's accidental jokes had made her laugh when the rest of the world didn't seem very funny at all. It was home in a way that her Story House had never been. She thought about the past six months. The Story House had been more of a game, every room acting like a piece of a larger puzzle. It was still one of her favorite places, but it could not hold a candle to the Pennington house in that moment.

Those feelings only doubled as she watched Professor Darcy say something to Mrs. Pennington. Her adopted mother was so shocked that she dropped a pie onto the floor. The moment echoed, reminding Indira of the time that *she* had accidentally been the reason for Mrs. Pennington dropping one of her famous desserts on the floor of the Adoption Agency.

"I'll be right back," Indira said.

She crossed the room to help Mrs. Pennington clean up. Her adopted mother tried to shoo her back to the others, but eventually gave up and handed Indira a second rag. The two of them wiped the whole mess away before returning to the kitchen and starting in on the ingredients of a new one. They worked silently for a few minutes before Mrs. Pennington stopped what she was doing and looked up.

"We've missed you terribly, dear."

Indira smiled. "It's really good to be home."

Mrs. Pennington dusted her hands on an apron before pulling Indira into another hug.

"I'm glad you came when you did. I'd have been too busy to see you otherwise."

Indira was surprised by that admission. Mrs. Pennington had *always* made time to see her, no matter what. It wasn't like her mother to let anything get in the way of family. Indira was about to say something when she noticed the grin on Mrs. Pennington's face. The pieces finally clicked together. There was only one reason Mrs. Pennington would be "too busy" to see her.

"Your story is starting!"

Last year, she'd learned the Penningtons were going to be in a short-story collection about life in Chicago. Indira knew they'd been waiting around for it to finally begin.

Mrs. Pennington did a little dance. "Tomorrow!"

Indira wrapped the woman in another hug and they danced around the kitchen together.

"Honestly," she said, "that's why Patch wrote the letters on your cake! I knew if I did them I'd be a mess. Figured I might as well just blame the sloppy lettering on him instead."

"Do you know what kind of story it is?" Indira asked.

Mrs. Pennington blushed. "Well . . . there's supposed to be a *romantic* interest. I'm afraid I'm a bit out of practice. It's nice that Mr. Darcy is here. I've been brushing up on my technique."

The words *romantic interest* made Indira's stomach churn. Not for long, though, as she looked back and found Mr. Darcy trying to lock eyes with Mrs. Pennington from across the room. It was like watching a bad scene in a movie. He considered her seriously before sweeping off dramatically in the other direction. Indira couldn't help laughing.

"Well, you deserve it, Mom. I can't wait—"

Indira's sentence was cut off as Patch went sprinting past with a still-lit candle. Mrs. Pennington hustled after him. Left alone for a moment, Indira's mind drifted to the task that was waiting for her. Underglass's words echoed: *Always room for improvement.*

She knew she had work to do. Training would improve who she was as a character. It was nerve-racking and exciting all at once, but all of that could wait for tomorrow.

Tonight she'd enjoy the family she couldn't ever dream of improving.

Gavin Grant convinced the group to play board games. David and Phoenix argued the whole time, both of them too competitive for their own good. Maxi wisely played them off one another and ended up winning the game in a landslide.

The rest of the night was measured in cake and laughter.

Indira couldn't seem to get enough of either.

5

The Cast

David's alarm woke Indira up. She was still half-asleep as he rolled out of his trundle bed and stumbled toward the bathroom. When he returned, his whisper of a mustache was clean-shaven and his clothes neatly ironed. Indira wondered if he was taking the boot camp idea a little too literally.

"Looking sharp," she mumbled.

He shrugged. "Just trying to make a good impression."

"Don't worry, D. You will."

He nodded. "What about you? Shouldn't you get ready?"

Indira glanced at the mirror hanging on the opposite wall. She adjusted the collar of her shirt before looking back at David. "Ta-da! I'm ready."

He rolled his eyes, but the two of them descended the stairs together. Mrs. Pennington fussed over them for a few minutes, even forcing bag lunches into their hands. Indira gave her mother one more massive hug. It was harder than expected to walk out the door.

On the porch, she paused and took a deep breath.

Adventure was in the air.

The sun hadn't risen, but the futuristic version of Fable glowed brightly enough for them to find their way. Everything hummed and blinked and buzzed with digital life. Indira led David back to the front doors of Protagonist Preparatory. He was quiet. She could see him chewing his bottom lip nervously, and she thought she knew how he felt. Last year, she'd been a nervous wreck too.

"You're going to be all right, D."

He looked down at his feet. "I know I sounded confident, but what Underglass said hit pretty hard. It made me feel like—I don't know—like I've been holding your story back."

"Hey. Not true." She set a hand on her brother's shoulder and waited until he looked up and met her eye. "I was there, David. We both heard Underglass. It's a team deal. I get better. You get better. If we both improve, there's nowhere for the story to go except *up*. You've got this."

He nodded. "Right. You're right. Okay. Do me a favor and don't get caught up in any world-altering conspiracies. Maybe have some fun instead?"

"Trust me," Indira replied with a smile. "I'm all about keeping a low profile this time."

The two of them hugged. David slung a bag over one

shoulder and headed for the front doors. She thought she saw added confidence in each step. Seeing that was like a weight slipping off Indira's shoulders. He was going to love boot camp. She could just feel it.

Besides, she had enough to worry about on her own adventure. She glanced through her papers to find her assigned pickup location. She had some time, but it never hurt to get there early. Maybe she could even sneak in a nap.

The location listed on the document was GROUP PORT B33.

Indira found it in the upper corner of her map. After tracing the route, she tucked the map back in her bag and started walking. It felt surprisingly nice to be alone. Her time in the Story House had been so chaotic. One scene after the next. Most of her breaks were spent getting to know the other characters or rehearsing lines. It was re-laxing just to walk and breathe and exist for a second.

Eventually, the path led to her assigned location. At a distance, Indira noted it wasn't an actual building. Instead, she walked into an open park that was sectioned off by a circle of black spheres. Each one was about the size of her shack back in Origin, the town where Indira had lived be-fore being invited to Protagonist Preparatory. The spheres were raised slightly in the air by a framework underneath, almost like massive golf balls on equally massive tees.

Indira had never seen anything like them.

It took a few seconds to figure out that the spheres were numbered. She followed the natural sequence and realized her assigned number would lead her nearly all the way back around to the beginning. She cut across the park and made a line for the sphere labeled B33.

The sound of her approaching footsteps was masked by the rather loud banging of tools. Someone had popped open the side panel of the structure that held the sphere in the air. Indira saw that the person's entire upper body was wedged underneath like a car mechanic. She heard something that sounded vaguely like a swear word, a loud metallic rattle, and finally a relieved sigh.

Indira stared down, a little distracted by the stranger's odd-looking boots. She thought maybe she was losing her mind, but the longer she watched . . .

"Are those your *bones*?" Indira asked.

The person let out a yelp of surprise. It was followed by a bang. Indira winced as the stranger struggled out from underneath the sphere. The girl had short hair and a sharp look to her. Black streaks stained her face and hands. Her narrowed eyes examined Indira like one might inspect a strange zoo exhibit. After a moment, the girl tapped her boots.

"These?" The color of the boots flickered before flashing an image that Indira could only assume was an X-ray glimpse of the girl's feet. "These are my X-boots. More for show than anything. I made them for a project last year."

Indira nodded, impressed. "So is the portal broken or something?"

The girl shook her head. "Nah. I got here a few hours ago so I could take the whole thing apart. Wanted to look at the guts, you know? I'm almost done putting it back together. It'll be just a few more ticks."

Indira watched the girl snatch a metal part and disappear into the underbelly of the machine again. She stared in confusion. "So you just . . . took the whole thing apart. For fun?"

"Of course," the girl replied. "How else was I supposed to figure out how it works?"

"Why does it matter *how* it works?" Indira asked. "As long as it works."

The girl made a frustrated noise. "Until it breaks and you're stuck in enemy territory without a clue. Why risk *not* knowing how something works? That seems silly."

Indira supposed that was true. She'd gotten into the habit of just kind of rolling with the punches. Her instincts had always worked well enough. Why bother with schematics or blueprints or machine parts? Indira could hear the girl rotating some kind of tool that made a loud clicking noise. After a few more seconds, she slid back out into the open, looking pleased with herself.

"Good as new." Her eyes landed on Indira's lunch. "I'm starving. You mind?"

Indira blinked once before offering her bag. "Sure."

The girl snatched the lunch out of Indira's hands. It

took her two seconds to find the BLT wrap that Mrs. Pennington had hand-rolled. She waved the wrap at Indira, who nodded permission. She'd barely removed the tinfoil before digging in. When she noticed Indira staring, she shrugged.

"Sometimes I forget to eat," she said. "Too focused on work. This is pretty good. Could use some more lettuce, though. Hey. Who are you, anyway?"

"I'm Indira Story."

The girl's jaw dropped. She pointed at Indira with the remaining half of the BLT.

"You're Indira Story. *The* Indira Story?"

Indira nodded politely.

"Wow." The girl took another bite. "I'm eating Indira Story's sandwich."

Indira nodded again. "You're pretty much devouring it. I'm guessing you're Gadget?"

It had taken her a few minutes to piece that together, but after getting a good, long look at the girl, Indira had figured it out. She wasn't wearing all the fancy hardware she'd been wearing in the photo Underglass had provided, but she definitely acted and talked like someone named Gadget would. Plus, she was wearing the earrings shaped like launching rockets that Indira had noticed in her file. She'd found the first member of her team.

"You know my name," Gadget said, still shocked. "And I'm eating your sandwich."

Indira laughed now. "It's nice to meet you."

Footsteps sounded. Indira turned in time to see the other two assigned members of their group enter the park. Phoenix came first. She couldn't help noticing that he looked a little taller, a little more confident. Her plan was to act as normal as possible. Things didn't need to be weird between them just because of the secret mission Underglass had given Indira. Her plan to play it cool was a little more difficult when she saw that flash of fire in his eyes.

The other boy walked in Phoenix's shadow. Indira recognized the golden curls and wide eyes. The first time she'd seen Allen Squalls had been as a picture on a missing-person poster. Back then, he'd sported a wide and crooked grin. Time under the thumb of Brainstorm Ketty had thinned out that smile into something far more nervous. Indira waved at both of them.

"You're at least forty-five seconds late," she joked.

Squalls nearly yelped. "It's totally my fault. I *knew* we should have been walking faster. If you want to send me home, that's totally understandable. My bag is already packed. I can just head back right now—"

Phoenix shook his head. "She's just kidding, Squalls."

"Definitely kidding," she said quickly. "I'm Indira."

She held out a hand at the same time that Allen offered her a fist. Both of them awkwardly switched and the final result was Allen holding Indira's fist and shaking it up and down. Phoenix grinned at the exchange before nodding past Indira.

"I'm guessing that's Gadget?" he asked.

The girl had set Indira's lunch aside and was carefully positioning tools back in her utility belt. Indira grinned. "I can't imagine what gave her identity away. . . ."

Once introductions had been made, Indira realized everyone was waiting for her. She'd kind of forgotten that she was the leader of the group.

"Oh. Right. Do we just get inside?"

"What does your packet say?" Phoenix asked. "Mine ended with meet here."

"Same," Squalls added. "No directions after that."

Indira rummaged through her bag and flipped her own informational packet open. Naturally, there were more directives on her sheet than theirs. The additions were reminders from Brainstorm Underglass. *Lead them.* She eyed the next step on the outline and read it aloud.

"'Your team will board the B33 device. You will set your destination for the town of Ordinary, located in the southeastern corner of Plot. Upon arrival, you will receive more information about your mission.'" When the rest of the crew didn't react, Indira decided to take charge. "Well. You heard the instructions. Let's get moving. Everyone inside."

But the final piece of advice from Underglass echoed. *Lead them, but don't forget that you're on a team.* That was the reason why this tutorial had been created for Indira. She needed to invite the rest of the team to be heroes too. She took a deep breath before looking around at her new crew.

"Gadget." She pointed at the girl. "You know how these machines work. Why don't you get us all loaded up and set our destination to the right location?"

Gadget looked a little surprised. "Right. Of course. I'm on it."

It took her a few seconds to open a hatch in the sphere. Allen made a careful inspection of the interior and muttered something about safety regulations. Phoenix gave him a playful shove inside. Indira was glad to see a connection already forming between the two of them. Spending time with someone like Phoenix wasn't the worst way to kick-start Allen's recovery.

Indira crawled in after them. The interior reminded her of a ride she'd been on in her own Story. The scene had taken place at a county fair, and Indira had accepted a dare to ride a roller coaster known as the Terminator. She hoped this ride would be smoother than that one. There were six seats in total, all arranged in a circle that faced inward. Indira reached overhead to pull a harness down, which clicked neatly into place. Gadget was leaning over a central console, tapping buttons rapidly, as the others pulled their own harnesses down.

"Sequence initiated," Gadget announced. "Our coordinates have been set for Ordinary. Who's ready to be chopped into a million pieces and reassembled in a new location?"

The girl raised her own hand excitedly. Phoenix just stared at her. Allen actually let out a horrified groan.

"Chopped up? What do you mean *chopped up*? I thought we were teleporting!"

Gadget nodded. "Well, that's how teleportation works. The Illusion of Continuity states that when memory—"

Indira cut the girl off. "Maybe just hit the go button?"

Allen Squalls was searching for a way to undo his buckles. Indira heard Phoenix trying to calm him down as Gadget took her seat. The moment her harness clicked into place, the entryway sealed. Allen covered his face with his hands. Indira couldn't help throwing Phoenix a little grin as the entire device hummed with energy. Adventure was waiting for them. Her eyes flicked back to the lone window. It offered a view of the square they'd just been standing in.

Indira realized this was a good time to say something leaderish. Should she make a speech? The machine rumbled louder and louder. She was trying to think of something profound to tell the others when her eyes landed on the one detail she hadn't noticed before.

A small piece of metal sat on the ground outside.

Sunlight glinted across its surface. Indira's eyes widened.

"Gadget!" She pointed. "Please tell me that's one of your tools."

The girl was shorter than Indira and had to crane her neck to get a good look outside. Indira saw a flash of panic on her face. The noise in the cabin grew to a deafening volume. Gadget looked like she was running mathematical equations in her head. A moment later she lunged for the central console. But her harness was fastened too tightly. Her fingers fell just short of the controls. Desperate, the girl shouted across to Indira.

"That's one of the location stabilizers!"

"How do we stop—"

Maybe you know the feeling, dear reader. If you've ever sat on a roller coaster as it approached the summit. That sickening lurch as you realize you're no longer in control of where you're about to go. It's a moment in which panic thrums in your chest like a drum.

Indira's sentence was devoured by a bright flash. Her teeth rattled. Her vision of the world—and the panicked faces of her team—all spun into a vortex of bright colors. Indira gritted her teeth as the B33 device sent them spiraling through space and time.

6

Off Course

Indira was in a tree.

An *actual* tree.

She blinked against the light that cut through the branches and leaves overhead. It felt as if several hours had passed, rather than just a few seconds. She tried to sit up, and the movement almost sent her falling to the ground. Her stomach tightened. The drop was about fifty feet, straight down.

"I'm in a tree." She was careful to keep her balance. "Why am I in a tree?"

A flash of memory. They had been inside the group teleport machine. Their destination had been a town called Ordinary, located in the land of Plot. Indira remembered the look on Gadget's face when the girl had realized one of the parts was missing. Clearly, their teleportation hadn't worked as planned.

"Hey! A little help here!"

Indira's eyes followed the voice. In the next tree over, Phoenix was struggling to keep his balance on a branch of his own. The only difference in their situations was that the branches above him were on fire. Indira shouted, "What happened?"

"I saw you and Gadget panicking before we teleported," he called back. "I guess it made *me* panic. And sometimes when I panic . . . fire comes out."

The flames were spreading. Indira glanced down. Gadget was standing well below them, safely on the ground. Allen was lying in a sprawl beside her. Indira cupped her hands to call down. "Gadget! Is he okay?"

Gadget looked up and her eyes widened at the sight of the fire. "Allen's asleep! What happened to—oh no . . . I think . . . Let me see what I can do. . . ."

The girl scrambled around the base of the tree, searching for ways to be helpful. Indira's eyes were drawn back up. The branches directly beneath Phoenix looked too small for climbing down. He needed to go back to the main trunk, wrap around the other side, and go down that way. There was just one problem with that plan, though.

"The fire is cutting me off!" Phoenix shouted. "What do I do?"

Carefully, Indira stood. She waited a few seconds, fighting for balance, and called back. "Sit on your branch.

I'm going to throw my hammer. When I catch it, you're going to catch me. Got it?"

He sat down, straddling the limb. "Are you sure about this?"

Indira didn't answer. A glance down showed Gadget circling helplessly. They were too high up for the girl to help them. There weren't any other options. Indira took aim. Her hammer's path would have to take her right between Phoenix's branch and the limb above him. Her eyes narrowed. She took a deep and steadying breath. Before doubts could form in her mind, she flung the hammer through the air. Her entire body whipped forward as she teleported.

And landed unsteadily on the branch next to Phoenix.

There was a glint of silver in the air. She reached up on tiptoes and caught the spinning hammer. Phoenix barely managed to grab her. He held on tight as she lowered herself back down onto the branch with him. The first thing she noticed was the warmth.

It was *really* hot now.

Overhead, flames chased across branches, browning the leaves. Phoenix stared at her, clearly still panicking. "But now you're stuck over here too! What was the point of that?"

Indira couldn't help grinning. "Do you trust me?"

Fire was licking across the limb overhead. "It's never a good thing when you ask that."

"Come on," Indira replied. "Stand up."

It was hard to do more than crouch as the flames lashed overhead, but both of them got to their feet. Indira held out her hand until Phoenix grabbed hold of her.

"I'm going to need you to stand very still."

He resettled his grip on her hand and nodded. Indira leaned out over the branches as far as she dared. The fire was *really* pressing around them now. She needed to work quickly. Pinching her hammer's grip between two fingers, she held it out like a pin. It was a huge drop. She knew she'd only have one chance at this.

Breath held, she released the hammer.

Her grip tightened on Phoenix's hand. The familiar tug came as she teleported through the air, but she'd never tried to take someone else with her. It took all her focus to drag Phoenix out of the tree and down to the ground, where her hammer was about to land. Both of them blinked back to life on the forest floor. Allen was still lying just fifteen feet away. Indira could even hear him snoring. Gadget circled around in front of them, eyes wide.

"Whoa! What? You were just . . . that's not possible . . . how did you . . ."

Indira ignored the girl. Her eyes darted up. And her stomach gave a sickening turn. There was one branch dangling above. Directly in the path of her hammer. The weapon nicked the limb as it passed. Instead of falling straight down, it bounced awkwardly out to the right.

Indira held tight to Phoenix's hand and pulled him into a run.

"Phoenix! We have to catch the hammer to teleport. Jump!"

As one, they took three giant strides and leaped through the air. Indira reached out to catch her hammer . . .

. . . and missed. The weapon bounced out of reach. The magic that would have safely teleported them away undid itself. Indira stared in shock as the heat came roaring back to life all around them. They were back on the branch, surrounded by flames.

"No, no, no . . . I missed it! What do we do now?"

The hammer had been her only plan. Phoenix drew her lower against the branch. He unfastened his wizard's robe and pulled it over both of them.

"Try not to breathe in the smoke. There's got to be something. . . ."

Indira squinted down. "Maybe Gadget can throw my hammer back up?"

But Indira saw that that was impossible. She could make out the girl's shape through the smoke, but they were far too high. A massive snap sounded overhead. Indira and Phoenix ducked closer together as a flaming limb crashed down to their right, barely missing them as it fell to the ground. Indira was still scrambling for a solution when a softer sound filled the air.

A light pitter-patter. It was coming from above.

"Rain," she whispered. "It's raining."

The sky had been completely clear a few seconds before. A typical afternoon blue. Now it was full of dark grays. Indira listened as the sprinkling rain turned into a downpour. It took a few minutes, but the fires overhead couldn't fight the sudden drenching. One by one, each of the flames died away. Phoenix and Indira were still huddled together when he pointed down to the forest floor and let out a whoop.

"Nice work, Squalls!"

Indira saw it now too. Allen was no longer sleeping. His hands were both raised and his eyes glinted with light. She wasn't a trained wizard, but it was pretty clear that he was performing a spell. She couldn't believe it. He'd summoned an actual storm to life.

"Squalls. I get it now." She grinned. "So, I guess our crew has two wizards?"

Together, she and Phoenix navigated their way to the ground. It took time to carefully test each branch, but eventually they set their feet back on solid earth. Allen Squalls was standing there, blinking around in confusion. He finally noticed their approach.

"Sorry. Blanked there for a second. What just happened?"

Phoenix grinned at him. "You saved us with a storm."

Allen blinked again. "I did what now?"

"You really don't remember?" Indira asked. "You just summoned a storm!"

He shook his head. "We were teleporting. Gadget said she was going to cut us up into a million pieces . . . and then I was standing here. In the forest. Right now."

Very interesting. Indira wondered what the connection was between sleep and Allen's magic. They'd have to figure that out as they went along, she guessed. Phoenix clapped Squalls on the shoulder, thanking him again, as Gadget joined the group, looking properly embarrassed.

"Guys, I'm *so* sorry. I should have triple-checked everything. That missing sensor was clearly why we were off course. At least, I'm pretty sure the teleport wasn't designed so that we'd land in a tree. I'm just hoping now that our location isn't too far off. I installed all the other guidance sensors besides that one. Which means we should only be a *little* bit off course."

"All good," Indira replied. "Let's get our bearings. Where'd we land?"

An answer came—not from the group but from somewhere deeper in the forest.

All of them flinched at the sound of a loud and echoing howl.

7

The Hero's Journey

The howls were followed by footsteps and snapping branches. Indira turned in that direction, hammer out and ready. The rest of the crew circled to stand with her. A shadowy figure was pressing through the trees and closing in on their location.

"Wolves," Squalls muttered. "No one said anything about wolves. . . ."

But it was most definitely *not* a wolf.

Indira squinted as one figure became three. It almost felt like she was looking into a fun-house mirror. Three women approached, their faces identical. Indira could not tell if they were sisters or clones or something more magical. Only their clothing and age didn't match. The first girl could not have been older than ten. She wore a delightful sundress and an excited smile to match it.

The second girl looked like a teenager. The sleeves of her more practical dress were muddy, and her hair had been thrown into a quick ponytail. Indira saw she was gritting her teeth, as if braced at any moment for an attack. And the final sister was nearly an adult. She wore majestic armor and—if Indira wasn't mistaken—a matching crown.

"Welcome to the land of Plot," the youngest said. "We are the rulers of this region, and your official welcoming party. You may call me Beginning."

The teenager with the dirtied sleeves nodded. "I am Middle."

"And I am End," the queen said crisply. "We were worried when you didn't arrive at your scheduled time, or at your scheduled location. It was a wonderful idea to send up flares! We saw the fire and headed straight here to welcome you."

Phoenix glanced over at Indira before shrugging at them.

"Er. Yeah. Flares. Those were flares."

Indira had to hide a laugh. Gadget, meanwhile, was studying the three of them like a science exhibit. "You're the same person, aren't you?"

"No," End answered with a sly smile. "And yes."

Beginning looked like she might burst from all the excitement. "Is anyone the *same* person they were at the start of the story? So much can happen! So much can change! I am the same as them, and at the same time I am who I am *now*. The three of us have ruled Plot for centuries. You'll start your adventure in my neck of the woods, obviously."

"And then you'll pay me a visit," Middle added. "Don't expect it to be fun."

End smiled. "And I am the final chapter of your story. We will not know how your journey ends until the very last page. Exciting, is it not?"

Beginning lugged a briefcase forward and set it down on the ground in front of them.

"No time to waste!" she exclaimed. "I want you in place by nightfall. You're here for the Hero's Journey tutorial. Every story has a Beginning, Middle, and End. But we've developed some more specific strategies for storytelling in Plot over the last century. The Hero's Journey is our most popular method. We've got some top-of-the-line tech for teaching the method."

Indira and the rest of the crew crowded forward to get a look. All except for Squalls, who was still nervously eyeing the woods behind them for any sign of approaching wolves. The interior of Beginning's briefcase had a black velvet surface. Six dime-size devices were set into the padded material like precious jewels. Gadget let out a gasp at the sight.

"No *way*," she exclaimed. "We get to use tutor devices?"

Indira had never heard the term before, and she was thankful when Middle explained what Gadget already seemed to know. "*Tutor* is short for *tutorial*," she said in that steady voice of hers. "These devices are teaching instruments that will walk you through each step in the Hero's Journey."

Gadget was nodding excitedly. "They record everything, too. So we can analyze the data later. And tutors provide graphics as we go through the quest. It's like a video game. So cool."

Beginning smiled. "I have a device for each of you. The tutor will begin with a description of your role in the upcoming story. Most of the time you're just following your instincts and playing out the scenario you've been given. If you start to get away from the classic Hero's Journey story line, these devices will help you get back on track. It's like one giant training session."

Indira nodded. "That's actually pretty cool."

Beginning carefully lifted out the first device. It was just big enough to cover the tip of her finger and—to Indira's untrained eye—looked a lot like a contact lens.

"Let's start with you, Gadget, since you're obviously the most excited."

Excited was an understatement. Gadget was gripping the young emissary's elbow and actually leaping up and down like a little kid. She didn't even need instructions on how to use the device. She simply pulled down one eyelid and slid the lens inside.

After a few rapid blinks, she let out a delighted squeal. "Wicked! I've been dying to get my hands on tech like this!"

Beginning turned to Phoenix, offering a device. "Naturally, we designed yours to be fire-resistant."

Allen Squalls was next. The emissary handed his over, and he promptly fumbled it. Indira watched as he snatched it out of the dirt. He did his best to wipe the device clean on his shirt, even blowing on its surface. And then, lifting it up, he fumbled the device a second time.

"Slippery little suckers!" he complained.

Indira couldn't help smiling. Allen was a little bumbling, but at least he would add some humor to the trip. The emissary approached Indira next.

"You're the leader," she explained. "All the devices will calibrate to yours. So if you change the direction of the story, the advice the others receive will adapt to what you're doing."

Indira nodded. "Makes sense."

Middle had marched over and was attempting to roughly jam the device into Allen's eye. Indira pulled down an eyelid. It was horribly uncomfortable to try to touch her own eyeball. She flinched and blinked and grew annoyed before finally opening her eye and sliding the device inside. She'd never worn contacts before, and the feeling was incredibly invasive. It took her several blinks and a few tears to situate the lens properly. Glancing up, she was disappointed to find that the surrounding forest looked exactly the same as it had a moment before.

"How does it—"

Indira fell silent. Words and objects were appearing in thin air. The curtain of trees was still there, but now little icons were imposed over her view of them.

"Wow!" she said. "It really is like a video game."

At the bottom center of her vision, Indira saw her own name floating in the air. The number zero glowed beside it. In the left corner, there was a neatly formatted list running down in an organized column. Indira read the first few items curiously:

THE ORDINARY WORLD

THE CALL TO ADVENTURE

REFUSAL OF THE CALL

SUPERNATURAL AID

Indira noticed that the first line was glowing and bold. The other items in the list appeared to be slightly faded. She was half listening as Beginning started giving instructions.

". . . go ahead and read your introductory paragraphs," she was saying. "I'll escort you into town when you finish the orientation process."

At the very center of her vision, Indira saw a slightly faded paragraph of text. She squinted, trying to bring it into focus. The response was immediate. The words glowed bright enough to read. Gadget wasn't kidding. These devices were wicked cool.

Indira read:

Welcome to the Hero's Journey tutorial! The concept of a Hero's Journey was first made popular in the Real World by Joseph Campbell. His theory was that nearly every great story in the world followed the same predictable pattern. *The Wizard of Oz*? *The Hobbit*? *Star Wars*? *The Lion King*? All those stories—and so many others—follow a standard plot pattern that he called the Hero's Journey. We believe that taking this tutorial will sharpen your instincts and give you a natural sense of where an Author is heading in any story. <u>Ready to begin?</u>

Indira saw that the last sentence was underlined. She stared at those words, and the device seemed to read her mind. That paragraph vanished, replaced with a new set of instructions:

Head to the town of ORDINARY. You live in the brick house with the frog statues on the front porch. Open the door and head up to your room on the second floor. The scenario will begin in the morning after you get a good night's sleep.

The device must have sensed she was done—because the second she finished reading, the text vanished from sight. Her actual vision shifted back into focus and her eyes found Phoenix's.

He grinned at her. "I'm a farm boy."

"Flames and hay." Indira winked. "That's a dangerous combo."

Squalls was still blinking at his own instructions. Gadget actually groaned.

"I'm apparently the town outcast?" she said.

"And I live in the frog house," Indira said with a smile. "Let's get started."

Beginning let out a little squeal at those words. The emissary led them excitedly out of the forest. Rolling hills waited in the distance. The countryside was dotted with rather average-looking farmhouses. Beyond those stood the town of Ordinary. A single stone wall circled fifty or so buildings. The gates of the little town stood open in welcome.

"Ordinary," Gadget pronounced. "Pretty fitting name choice."

She wasn't wrong. The place looked plain as sand.

"That's how it should be," Phoenix replied. "Look at the status in the left corner of the tutor device. We're on the Ordinary World step. Isn't that how most of the stories start? Heroes are always living such normal lives in the beginning."

Beginning nodded her approval. "Ten points to you! As you advance through the tutorial, you'll notice that the bolded step will change to indicate where you are in the Hero's Journey."

Indira was still thinking about the Ordinary World step. She knew that was how the story she'd been chosen for had begun. Everything had been pretty plain. It had taken several scenes to get to the cool stuff. As the crew approached the town, it was hard not to notice just how empty it was. Not a soul could be seen. Farm tools were scattered at random. The lone guard post had been abandoned.

Her mind started racing through clues. Was this the start of their practice journey?

"So the townspeople went missing," she guessed. "And it's up to us to figure out what happened to all of them?"

A little red −10 appeared in Indira's vision. She frowned.

Beginning explained. "Not exactly! The Hero's Journey starts in the morning. When you wake up, the town will be full of people. All of you will have temporary families. Most of the actors are unfinished characters. Some very talented characters in the bunch. Just remember that everyone in the scenario with you is playing a role. Your job is to trust your instincts and practice.

"Which brings me to the point system. Right now Indira is in the negative. Phoenix is in the positive. This is just practice, though. The points will wipe clean at the start of the scenario. You'll find as you move through the Hero's Journey that good story instincts earn you more points. Every time you do something well, you'll be rewarded. Going off track or slipping out of character will be scored negatively. Your brainstorms will use those scores to assess your performance at the end."

End offered a queenly wave.

Indira found herself nodding, grateful that her negative score would be reset. She was very familiar with practice roles. It was kind of like living with the Penningtons. They'd started out pretending to be family, and after a time, she'd fallen into character and become their *actual* family.

"This is where we part ways," Middle said quietly. "But do not fear, it will not be long."

End smiled. "Longer for some than for others! See you at the close! No spoilers!"

"I'll be around if you need me," Beginning said. "Any final questions?"

Allen's hand shot into the air. "I'm pretty sure my device is broken. It says that I'm Phoenix's guardian. Which is fine, I guess. I'm not sure if I'm really cut out for *guard* duty. But then there's this footnote. . . ." He squinted to read text the rest of them couldn't see. "It says I have a seventy-five percent chance of dying to protect him during the tutorial! That's like . . . a lot of percent. Isn't it? That's more than half! I'd have a better chance of surviving a coin flip! I guess I'm just wondering if it makes sense for me to trade for a different role? Maybe I'm the kid at the start of the story who makes a joke and you never see him again?"

Beginning smiled. "You have a role to play. We all do. And keep in mind that the story will change as you go along. There's always that twenty-five percent chance you survive! Trust the tutor device to guide you. I promise that it will explain everything. Any other questions?"

Squalls was still muttering to himself. ". . . seventy-five percent. That's like really close to one hundred percent. . . ."

When no one else spoke, Beginning dipped into a gracious bow. The three sisters walked arm in arm toward the woods. Indira watched and thought she saw them become one person again as they reached the edge of the woods. Turning back, she found the others waiting for her.

Right, she thought. *I'm supposed to lead.*

"Any other special instructions?" she asked. "Mine just says to go to bed."

Gadget grinned. "Mine says I get to tinker with some inventions tonight. Sweet!"

"I'm apparently not allowed to use fire," Phoenix said.

Indira frowned at that. "Weird. That's kind of what you do."

"It actually says fire is *forbidden,*" Phoenix corrected himself. "That's the exact wording."

Indira considered that. It felt good to stand on the edge of a fresh new mystery. Last year, her adventure had involved a lot of bad grades and failure and frustration. She had a feeling that this adventure would be a *lot* more fun. Excitement raced through her veins.

"I'm sure it will make sense in the morning," she said. "Let's get some sleep."

Overhead, the light was fading fast.

"I'm up there." Phoenix pointed. "The house on the hill."

"Me too . . . ," Squalls said, his voice full of concern. "There's probably a monster hiding in that barn. Or the house will be haunted by vengeful ghosts. It looks very exposed. A good wind might knock the whole thing over on top of us. We'll have to test every floorboard to make sure it's all structurally sound. . . ."

Phoenix threw an arm around him. "Squalls. It's going to be okay. Come on. We'll go up there together and check everything out."

Allen's steady stream of fears went quiet. Their crew exchanged goodbyes. Indira walked into the center of town with Gadget at her side. It took a few minutes to find their assigned houses. Gadget's home looked like it was located right above a strange workshop.

Before Indira could say good night, Gadget nodded to her.

"What's it like?" she asked.

Indira frowned. "What's what like?"

Gadget stared down at her own feet. "Being in a story? A *real* story?"

It took her a moment to remember Gadget's file. The girl had been in school for years now, and still hadn't found a story of her own. This was one of her last chances to prove she had what it took. Indira waited until the girl looked back up. She smiled, trying her best to sound confident.

"I could tell you," she answered, "but after we crush this tutorial, you'll land your own spot with an Author. And then we can compare notes. How's that sound?"

Gadget didn't look like she believed it, but she nodded. "Sounds good."

Indira wished the girl a good night, found her house, and headed inside. As she walked up the stairs to her bedroom, steps echoing, she felt a change in the air.

Adventure.

She couldn't have been more ready for it.

8

The Ordinary World

Indira woke up to a *very* distinct sound.

"Is that . . ."

Instinct saved her from a sharp peck on the cheek. She thrust the covers up, barely turning the blow away, and retreated to the corner of her bed.

"Why is there a rooster in my room?"

The bird's bright tail twitched as it tried to find a way around Indira's quilt barricade. It pecked once more at the covers before leaping to the floor in a flutter of wings. Indira stared as the rooster darted through a little hand-made opening at the bottom of her closed door.

She almost laughed. "Seriously? Is that a *bird* door?"

It was a little disorienting. She rubbed her eyes and realized she wasn't in the Story House. This wasn't the Penningtons', either. Indira looked around the sparsely decorated room and couldn't remember how she'd gotten there. "Where am I?"

In answer, her vision doubled. She was still looking around the random bedroom, but now video-game graphics were imposed over her vision. Of course! The tutor device. She watched as little glowing arrows appeared, all pointing toward the door. She saw her name printed right where it had been the day before, and a fresh score of zero.

In the right corner of her vision, she saw that the Hero's Journey steps were still waiting in their orderly column. And the current status—**THE ORDINARY WORLD**—appeared in bold.

A paragraph of text flashed into view:

Your story begins in the Deacon household. You are the only daughter of the town's recently elected mayor—Minerva Deacon. You are expected at breakfast shortly. Note: You have a rocky relationship with your mother because of how busy her new role as the mayor has made her. Feel free to show a little annoyance and flash a little sass!

Walk through the door to initiate the scenario. If you struggle with the stages of the journey, you'll be given clues to help you get back on track.

As Indira finished reading, the paragraph faded from sight. Cool. The glowing arrows were still there, though, so Indira took a deep breath and reached for the handle.

"Here we go."

There was a little noise—like a digital *swoosh*—and the tutor's visuals faded to the background. She found herself staring down a rather steep set of stairs, and couldn't help wondering how the chicken had survived the descent.

Noises echoed up the stairs from the kitchen. There were a number of voices darting back and forth in conversation. Indira also heard the telltale squawking of the aggressive chicken that had woken her. It was the scent of smoked meat, however, that lured her down into a rather busy kitchen. Indira took in the most unusual breakfast scene she'd ever encountered.

A woman in a lovely but old-fashioned business jacket sat at the head of a farmhouse table. Assistants were rushing around the room, exchanging papers, arguing with one another. Most of the food sat untouched on the kitchen counter behind them. Indira noted the chicken darting under legs and squawking whenever someone brushed too close to it. She was still taking in the scene when the woman in charge—Minerva Deacon—noticed her.

"Oh! Look who it is!" Minerva smiled. "I sent Peck to wake you up. I knew he'd get the job done. Why don't you grab a plate of food before school, Indira?"

Indira blinked. She hadn't expected the woman to know her name, but that made plenty of sense. Minerva was an actor. She was here to play the role of Indira's mother throughout the tutorial. It took Indira a moment to recover from her surprise and fall into character. She remembered the note the tutor had provided her about their rocky relationship and decided to show a little of the suggested annoyance.

"Sure," she said. "Nothing like a quiet meal to start the day."

Minerva frowned as Indira crossed the room. The assistants didn't break character once. They continued swirling busily around the table. "Ms. Deacon," one was saying. "Here's the speech. Want to look at the final lines before we send it to the typist?"

Indira quietly gathered a plate of food. The rooster—named Peck, apparently—walked proudly over to her and ruffled her leg affectionately. She smiled down before returning to the table, dodging past a few of her mother's assistants, and taking the farthest seat from all the chaos. She couldn't help feeling a little impressed by the performance the group was putting on so far. It had her wondering how many times they'd done this particular quest tutorial.

"Let's take a break," Minerva announced, eyes settling on Indira. "Everyone meet me at the courthouse. We'll resume there. Someone check on Jarva, please. I know he was feeling ill last night."

Indira forked a bit of the eggs as the assistants gathered their things and began filing out of the room. She was starting to understand what Phoenix had been talking about the day before. This was how a lot of stories began. Setting the reader's feet down gently. Offering up a picture of the *ordinary* world.

As the others left, the room fell silent. Her playacting mother caught her eye and offered a forced smile. "So the festival is coming up."

Indira shrugged before taking another bite of food. It felt like an appropriately annoyed-teen gesture. Indira was pleased to see a **+50** appear in her vision. Apparently, the tutor device liked her use of sarcasm and sass. Minerva didn't look like the kind of woman who gave up easily, though.

"You're really going to pretend to not be excited?" she asked. "Come on, Indira. It's your favorite time of the year. All the gamble-games. Those sea-salt taffies you love so much."

Indira meant to respond, but she'd taken a rather large bite of meat that was a little tougher than expected. The resulting silence drew a little frustration into Minerva's expression.

"Honey. I know this hasn't been easy." She gestured to the sprawl of papers. "I promise that it'll get easier. Once I'm settled into the position, I'm going to have more time to spend with you. How about at the festival next week? We'll go together. Just the two of us."

The front door of their house flew open. Both of them looked up as one of the assistants came bustling back into the room. At the same time, Indira's tutor device flashed a little note of advice. Indira eyed the highlighted suggestion as her mother's assistant offered an apologetic look.

"I'm sorry, Ms. Deacon. There's a small emergency at the courthouse. We could use your help with it. I didn't want to interrupt. . . ."

He trailed off. Indira stood angrily. She shoved her plate away with the appropriate amount of annoyance before looking directly at her pretend mother.

"It's fine. You've got more important things to do."

"Indira . . ." Minerva stood, looking concerned. "Wait."

Indira rounded on her and read the glowing line the tutor device had written for her.

"I'm going to be late. Oh, and sea-salt taffies? Those are *your* favorite. Not mine."

She lingered long enough to see that her words had struck true. There was a stung expression on Minerva's face. Indira pushed past the assistant, through the door, and out into the streets of Ordinary. As the door shut, she allowed herself a sigh of relief.

That had been a strong opening scene. She never liked being mean, but she'd learned in her own Story House that there was a time for every emotion. Good characters had range. They could be mean and kind and curious and sad—depending on what the plot called for. She was really impressed with Minerva. It was hard to believe someone so talented was an unfinished character.

She watched as the device funneled points into her

score. Thirty points for the dramatic plate shove. Another hundred points for using realistic mother-and-daughter dialogue. Her score was heading in the right direction. Excitement chased through her.

This was definitely her kind of adventure. Overnight, the town of Ordinary had come to life. Indira noticed that the tutor device was providing more directions. Arrows pointed down the front stoop before swinging left. She followed, enjoying the slight breeze. Neighbors were out and about for morning activities. One man was hanging clothes on a line to dry. Another stood by the mailbox, flipping through letters.

Indira waved at both of them, enjoying all the little details. The tutor's directions led her to the end of the street. Another paved road ran perpendicular to the first, but was lined with businesses instead of homes. She remembered it from the night before. Gadget's "home" had been this way. Sure enough, Indira's route led her past the workshop.

A glance inside showed that the store was already busy with movement. Electric lights glowed in every corner. Little machines whizzed into the air. Customers were walking around, looking delighted. Employees stood in fine navy-blue aprons, waiting to help them with purchases. Indira didn't see Gadget inside.

She looked up and found that the arrows were flashing a little brighter now. Indira guessed she wasn't supposed to stray too far from the plan. She followed the path again, past businesses and vendors. It took a few seconds to realize everyone recognized her.

"Good day to you, Miss Deacon!" One man tipped his cap. "It's a fine morning, isn't it?"

A smiling baker even thrust a croissant into her hand. "On the house, love."

At first she thought they recognized her because of what she'd done in Fable. Maybe news of her encounter with Brainstorm Ketty had reached across the whole continent? It took her a few seconds to piece together that this was all a show. The man had called her Miss Deacon, after all. These were characters acting out an assigned scenario. She was getting free treats because she was the mayor's daughter. Of course.

"Well, if it isn't the empress herself."

Indira looked up in time to see a young boy edging out of an adjacent alleyway. The sensors in her tutor device swiveled like crosshairs, glowed around the approaching character, and gave a slight ping. A message flashed into her vision:

Ledge Woods—Low-Level Antagonist

Indira could have guessed as much. This was clearly one of the bad guys. There was a buried threat in his voice, anger in his open stare. Indira didn't have to look twice to know he was no friend of hers. The boy wore suspenders, a three-button long-sleeved shirt, and a pair of fine leather gloves. Her gaze lingered longest on the gloves, because they truly were far finer than anything else he was wearing. His boots were threadbare, his pants slightly stained. But the gloves looked pristine, threaded through with strands of gold.

Ledge noticed her staring at them.

"Like them?" he asked. "I was finally approved for kingswolf training."

He flexed his fingers and a slash of magic cut through the air. Indira watched as the gloves began to transform. Leather became fur; fingernails became claws. The boy took a threatening step forward and lifted one of the razor-sharp talons until it was a few inches from her face. Indira stood her ground without flinching.

"You know—they say that a kingswolf can smell fear." Ledge grinned spitefully. "They say kingswolves can smell *secrets,* too. You wouldn't happen to have any of those, would you, Empress?"

She gritted her teeth. "Stop calling me that."

There was another slash of magic and Ledge's hands returned to normal. Just gloves again. It was clear he enjoyed taunting her. Indira was trying to think of something clever to say when Ledge put on a falsely apologetic expression and ducked out of her path.

"I'm so sorry!" He made his voice loud enough for all to hear. "Of course! You were waiting for me to *bow* to you before passing. I should have known. Have fun at school, Empress."

As the eyes of the other townspeople were drawn their way, Ledge bowed down before her as if she were an actual queen. Embarrassed, Indira hustled past him.

Her score slowly rose again. Another successful scene. Even though she knew it was just part of the scenario, Indira still hated the helpless feeling in her gut. This was how it always felt to meet one of the antagonists. She remembered the first time she'd felt that way, the painful, sinking sensation as she'd faced off with Peeve Meadows during auditions.

She also couldn't help noticing that Ledge's description had labeled him a "low-level" bad guy. That meant something *worse* was out there. She couldn't imagine what would be worse than a jerk with wolf claws, but she needed to prepare herself for that eventual threat.

Thankfully, the arrows of the tutor device didn't point her toward more danger. Instead she was led around the corner and right to a familiar face. Indira nearly laughed at the sight.

"Are you wearing farm clothes?"

Phoenix flashed a grin. "Traded my wizard robes for them last night. How have your scenes been going so far? Positive score?"

Indira nodded. "I have a pet chicken, a busy mom, and a potential werewolf enemy."

"Ledge?" Phoenix asked. "He was in one of my first scenes too. Kid is a little dramatic."

Indira laughed. She remembered that Beginning had said that many of the actors in the town were unfinished characters. She wondered if Ledge, however, was a student at Antagonist Academy. Maybe he was here for practice too. Before she could ask Phoenix, Allen Squalls came jogging around the corner of another building. He shot Phoenix a scolding look that would have made any grandparent proud.

"Phineas! I told you *not* to leave without me."

Phoenix turned to Indira and rolled his eyes.

Squalls was almost out of breath. "How am I to . . . protect you?"

"Protect him?" Indira blinked. "And did you call him *Phineas*?"

"I have a secret identity," Phoenix whispered. "Apparently, I go by Phineas here."

"And I'm his guardian," Squalls added. "Right now I'm pretty sure that just means I'm going to be eaten by wolves so that he can escape. Or maybe I'll fall into one of those silos we passed. Drowning by molasses! I read that in a story one time. . . . Seventy-five percent chance of death . . . it's like a bad weather report that I can't escape."

Indira could see that Phoenix was trying his best to stay positive. Allen was kind of like his doom-and-gloom companion. She had to remind herself why Squalls was here in the first place. Brainstorm Ketty had targeted him. Whatever confidence he'd had when he'd arrived at Protagonist Preparatory had been shattered by her scheming. This tutorial was his chance to recover. She wanted to do her best to stay encouraging.

"Remember, it's all practice," Indira said. "You're playing a role. And based on what you did the other day with that storm, I'm pretty sure you're off to a good start as a guardian."

Squalls smiled nervously, looking a little surprised by the compliment. She thought he was going to latch on to that confidence, but a moment later, she heard him muttering.

"Storms have lightning. And floods . . . that's another possibility. . . ."

Before Indira could answer, a scream sounded from within the schoolhouse.

Indira and Phoenix locked eyes.

Together, they sprinted inside.

9

Backstory

Indira led the way, hammer in hand. She followed the only hallway into the only classroom. It wasn't the nightmare she'd been expecting. Rows of desks led to a stage in the front. Other students had gathered there to watch the spectacle. Their schoolteacher was cowering against the blackboard as three metallic bees—each about the size of an apple—swirled threateningly overhead. It took a second to figure out that the scream had come from him. A familiar student stood apart from the others: Gadget.

Their crewmate was positioned at the edge of the stage with a remote control in hand. As Indira crossed the room, eyeing the scene, she realized Gadget was actually controlling the robotic insects.

"Gadget!" the teacher shouted. "This isn't funny! Please recall them!"

She nodded. "I'm *trying* to do that, Mr. Finch, but they keep overriding my control. There must be something . . ." Her eyes flicked down to their teacher. "Of course! It's the sweater! Your sweater! It's too bright, Mr. Finch. They think you're a flower. All that color must be kicking their pollination mechanism into overdrive."

Indira had reached the end of the row. She noticed that Gadget was right. Their professor's sweater was an aggressively bright shade of yellow. He'd started tugging at the too-tight sleeves, working the fabric overhead, but Indira saw that one of the bees was preparing to strike.

"Watch out!" she called.

She shoved Gadget out of the way, tracing the bee's flight, and brought her hammer forward in an arc. Right as the bee darted down toward the helpless professor, the flat end of her weapon came sweeping across its path. There was a sharp collision of metal against metal and the little bee shattered into hundreds of pieces. Indira planted herself in front of the professor, eyes scanning upward for the next potential threat.

"Hey!" Gadget shouted. "I was fixing them! It was fine. Why'd you do that?"

Both of the remaining bees buzzed back down, landing softly on Gadget's shoulder. She pushed past Indira to get to the third, fallen bee. It was making strangled noises, clearly no longer functional. Gadget shot a look back at her. "Seriously? This thing was expensive!"

Indira gestured back to their teacher, who was still

trying to regain his composure. She was surprised when Gadget's annoyance was echoed in the tutor device. Text appeared in her vision, briefly reading:

–500 points! Your tutorial has been designed to encourage teamwork and thoughtful engagement with other characters. In the future, focus on solving the problem without immediately resorting to your own abilities.

The message vanished almost as quickly as it appeared.

Indira couldn't help frowning. "But he was in danger. . . ."

There was a final sputter as the electronic bee died.

"Great," Gadget complained. "All of this is useless now. These were supposed to pollinate the whole village. Now I'm going to have to reprogram the entire sequence."

Indira glanced back at the teacher, hoping at least she'd have his thanks for taking action.

"While your heroics are appreciated, Indira, I do think you should stop and think it through next time before taking action." He gave her a measured look. "You know how valuable these tech resources are in our town. The last thing we can afford is wasted materials." Mr. Finch let that sink in before rounding on Gadget. "And, Gadget, please make sure you calibrate and test out your devices before bringing them into the classroom. Understood?"

Gadget had scooped up as many of the pieces of the fallen bee as she could.

"Understood."

Mr. Finch clapped his hands. "Well, let's take our seats and begin class."

Frustrated, Indira took a deep breath and followed the arrows of her tutor device. It led her to a seat near the front right side of the classroom. She couldn't help feeling even more annoyed. Of course the mayor's daughter sat at the front of the room. Other students were filing in from the back, eyeing the mess she'd created. There were whispers, too, and Indira could hear words like *waste* and *rich kid*, words that echoed what Ledge Woods had implied with her nickname.

Empress.

Indira knew it was just the scenario. Nothing personal. She was the mayor's daughter, so clearly other kids didn't like her a lot. It made her all the more thankful when Phoenix plunked down in the seat next to her and offered a grin. He whispered, low enough that only she could hear, "Solid form on that hammer strike."

She grinned back—her stomach fluttering—as class began.

It was hard at first to focus on the teacher's lecture, but Indira remembered that this was how stories worked. All the little details one learned at the beginning would echo through the rest of the plot. This was the Ordinary World. She decided to pay attention closely, because the better she knew how things worked, the more effective her character would be.

Apparently, a new king had just taken over the throne. He was the third generation of the Howling Kings. Indira listened to the story of how the first ruling family had been the Dragos. Like any good historian, Mr. Finch grew more and more excited as he lectured.

"Most of you know what happened next," he was saying. "When the Drago family fell out of power, the first Howling King removed fire from the land. And now fire is only permitted in the most basic cooking. Never more than that. Every member of the Drago family was hunted down. Exiled or worse! And the first of the Howling Kings established his regal order of kingswolves all over the realm."

Indira almost jumped when the rest of the class responded in one voice.

"Fire is forbidden. Dragons are cruel. Long live the king."

She shot Phoenix a meaningful look. Now it made sense why he couldn't use fire. The scenario they were in — and the backstory — clearly forbade it. Indira couldn't help frowning. How was Phoenix supposed to get in any good training if he couldn't use his main strength?

Her thoughts were interrupted by a loud crash outside the building.

Mr. Finch shot a look at Gadget. "Is this another one of your devices?"

She held both hands up innocently. "No! I locked all the bigger stuff away!"

Raised voices followed. Indira couldn't resist. Neither could the rest of the class. Mr. Finch forged a path to the back of the room, bravely leading them out to see what the commotion was. Everyone crowded forward, and Indira found her shoulder pressed tight to Phoenix's. She didn't mind their shoulders touching, not one bit. Allen Squalls offered a strangled complaint, lost somewhere in the back of the crowd. Outside, the cause of all the commotion was easy enough to locate.

Indira stared at a huge, horseless carriage. It didn't quite look like a car, but Indira had the feeling it was motorized in some way. The driver was down on the ground, surrounded by a few townsfolk, nursing a cut on her forehead. Citizens who weren't helping stood off to the side, and all of them were staring at the reason why the vehicle had crashed.

In the very middle of the street stood a *massive* wolf.

10

The Call to Adventure

Well, it wasn't that massive. Indira realized the wolf looked larger than normal because it was standing upright. And it had scales? Or armor of some kind? She squinted. It was hard to tell from this distance. Their class joined the gathered crowd, but it was clear that everyone was being careful to keep their distance from the creature.

Was this the next step in the journey? Instinct told Indira to protect everyone from the wolf. She wanted to grab her hammer and march forward into the fight. But now the tutor's message was replaying in her mind. She'd already made the mistake of jumping in and trying to fix things her own way. Brainstorm Underglass had designed this tutorial to force her to work with a team. Which was what she decided to do.

She took a deep breath and calmly let the scene unfold.

It took a few seconds to piece together some of the clues she'd already been given. This wasn't some random wolf in the streets of town. It was a kingswolf.

Ledge had sported the same shape-shifting gloves. Indira guessed that—since he was just starting training?—he had a limited amount of magic. The creature standing in the center of the clearing was obviously a full kingswolf. But that didn't explain *why* it was here. . . .

"What's the meaning of this?"

A voice cut across all the swirling whispers. Indira felt unexpected pride as her pretend mother strode boldly forward. Her steps didn't slow. She walked right up to the creature and put both hands on her hips, like she'd had quite enough.

"Are you lost or something?" she asked.

The creature's lips pulled back in a snarl that looked almost like a smile. Indira and the rest of the crowd watched as the wolf transformed. There was a burst of magic that caused Minerva Deacon's cloak to billow. Blink and gone.

A man now stood before them, although Indira couldn't help thinking he still looked like a wolf. His facial features were all narrow and sharp. He had an untamed beard and wild hair that fell down to his shoulders. He circled Minerva like an animal stalking prey through the forest.

"There was a fire to the north," he growled. "Up in the hills. Just outside your town's established boundaries. I've investigated the location. Several trees burned down.

It wasn't an accidental cooking fire that got out of control. Someone's been playing with a dragon."

The townspeople gasped, as if the words *fire* and *dragon* were dark curses. It took a great deal of effort for Indira to not look at Phoenix. Her neck prickled uncomfortably. She was dead certain that they had been the ones who'd started the fire the kingswolf was talking about.

Minerva stood her ground. "All of our fire use is legal. We follow the codes."

"Is that so?" The kingswolf's eyes scanned the crowd hungrily. "Then you wouldn't mind me looking around. Asking questions. In the name of the king, of course."

The crowd looked concerned, but Indira's mother didn't so much as flinch.

"I'd love for you to inspect our engineer shops. I'd love for you to see the production lines in our factories. I'd love for you to witness the innovations we've made to our cooking equipment and the measures we've taken to make sure campfires never spread . . ."

The kingswolf leaned forward hungrily, expecting permission.

". . . as long as you produce a rite of passage to enter Ordinary."

"A 'rite of passage'?" the kingswolf echoed. "I am not sure what you mean."

"Ah. You don't know the recent laws." Minerva circled, and now the wolf looked like it was her prey. "It was recently discovered that certain kingswolves were disrupting local economies. Pretending to search for Drago families but feasting on a town's resources instead. Interrupting the local businesses. That naturally impacts the amount of money the king receives from taxes."

The kingswolf started to object, but Minerva pressed on.

"So while we would love to host you, I'll need you to return with the correct documentation. Surely you understand. I would not risk upsetting the king because of some faint suspicion from one of his underlings."

Indira briefly forgot she was in a scene. It all felt so real. She loved how strong and bold Minerva Deacon's character acted. And the kingswolf was a really creepy antagonist. She'd been so immersed in the scene, in fact, that she hadn't noticed the update in her tutor's graphics.

In the corner of her vision, the steps of the Hero's Journey rotated. She watched as the bold highlight moved down the list and settled on the next step. As **THE ORDINARY WORLD** faded, it was replaced with bold letters that read: **THE CALL TO ADVENTURE.**

Indira frowned. How had they reached the next step in the Hero's Journey while standing still? That didn't make any sense.

A growl drew her attention back to the kingswolf. He was grinning at Minerva.

"Very clever, but I do hope you realize you've made a mistake." He raised his voice now so that the entire crowd could hear. "There's Drago blood in this town. The fire was our first hint. Your mayor's decision is the second. One of the dragons is hiding here. Someone with fire in their veins. Don't worry. I'll return with a rite of passage, but I won't come alone next time. I'll bring other wolves with me. And if the king allows, I'll bring one of the Stained, too."

That single word produced even more panicked whispers in the crowd. Indira had never heard the term before, but she guessed the Stained were worse than the kingswolves? Her stomach turned. She had a feeling that would be the big bad guy waiting for them at the end of the tutorial. Just wonderful.

"We'll turn this town upside down," the kingswolf threatened. "It would be better for all of you if whoever you're hiding is found. Give them up and it'll be painless. But if you hide them?" He grinned again. "Well, I'll leave punishment to the Stained."

Another slash of magic. Indira watched the wolf form return. The creature let out an unearthly howl. Indira shivered as other howls answered in the distant hills. She didn't know what they were saying, but clearly other kingswolves had been waiting for word from this one. She wondered how long it would take for them to return with the document Minerva had mentioned.

The kingswolf lowered onto all fours, sprinted toward the nearest gate, and vanished from sight. Indira felt a little chill run down her spine. She glanced to the right and found Ledge Woods watching her. His suspicion was obvious. He thought she was connected to all of this.

Which, technically, she was.

A second glance showed Gadget sitting off to the side, fiddling with her mechanical bees. The girl didn't even look like she was paying attention. Indira made a mental note to talk to her about staying focused on the story as the rest of the gathering turned into a panicked mob. Complaints from some. Concerns from others. Indira watched Minerva do her best to quiet them.

"Calm down," she said. "I dealt with kingswolves nearly every day in the capital. They're all talk. Especially the wilder ones. A wolf like that will never get a rite of passage based on one forest fire outside our town limits. That's not how things work."

Some of the voices fell silent. Others grew louder and angrier.

"But what if they *do* come back?"

"If someone is sheltering a Drago, we deserve to know."

"Get them out!"

Minerva patiently held up her hand until the cries fell silent. "This is what they want! Kingswolves spread fear. He doesn't *actually* believe there's Drago blood in a village like this one."

"'A village like this one,'" someone echoed. "What's *that* supposed to mean?"

Minerva looked impatient as the crowd grew loud

again. One voice rose above the rest, and this time it wasn't Indira's pretend mother. A heavyset man strode forward. His apron was covered in splashes of dried blood. Indira's eyes widened. Every single feature was an older but mirrored image of Ledge Woods.

"You're not really from here," the man said loudly. "Didn't grow up here. I thought it was a mistake when we elected you. Maybe you meant well today, but the truth is, most of us don't have anything to hide. We're not harboring Drago fugitives. The kingswolf would have performed the standard sweep and moved on. But now? After the stunt you pulled? The kingswolves will come back in force."

Indira heard the word *Stained* in the whispers all around her. She felt the same tide of anger listening to Mr. Woods that she had felt earlier with Ledge. The apple apparently hadn't fallen far from the tree. Minerva looked as annoyed as Indira felt.

"I'm asking you to trust me," she answered, loud enough for all to hear. "We can respect the king without being taken advantage of by his henchmen. That's why this town elected me, Mr. Woods. I promised to protect and serve by using all the knowledge I learned in the capital. I know you think I'm a stranger, but my parents lived here. It was home for me once."

"Once," Mr. Woods echoed. "You all can do what you want, but I'm not going to just sit back and wait for them to rip our town apart with their searches. If there's even a whiff of smoke in the air, I'm turning in the person responsible. All of you better watch your backs."

With a final look, he stalked off. Indira watched Ledge follow. Minerva was trying to regain momentum, answering questions with calm statements. Indira didn't hear any of it, though. There was a slight tug at her elbow. She turned and found Phoenix standing awkwardly close to her. A spark of heat flared in the air between them. Indira was briefly excited and afraid and nervous that he was about to kiss her. Instead, he whispered under his breath.

"We need to talk. Now."

11

Refusal of the Call

As the rest of the townspeople dispersed, Indira followed Phoenix and Squalls through back alleys, out one of the smaller town gates, and toward a farm set on a distant hill. She wasn't exactly sure what was happening, but the arrows of the tutor device were all pointing in his direction.

The phrase **THE CALL TO ADVENTURE** continued to glow in her vision. She found herself tracing back through the scene with the kingswolf. The next step in their journey had clicked into place during his speech. It wasn't too hard to figure out that their quest would be connected to the kingswolf, and to the threat he had made to return and search the town.

Indira found herself smiling. She'd been picturing

some kind of study hall where they learned new vocabulary words. This tutorial was way more fun than that.

"Where are we going?" she asked.

"Just follow me," Phoenix answered.

Squalls spoke in a low voice. "I don't think this is a good idea, Phineas."

Indira almost rolled her eyes at the fake name.

"You said we need help," Phoenix answered. "She's the one I trust the most."

Indira started blushing before realization struck. Allen wasn't nervously complaining about all the ways he might potentially die. This wasn't normal conversation at all. The two of them were reading lines from a script! She hadn't even realized they'd moved into a new scene in the scenario. Her own tutor device was floating directions into her vision. She squinted at the line she was being given.

"Uhh . . . Shouldn't we get back to school?"

"I need your help," Phoenix replied. "It's important."

Squalls made a frustrated noise. Instead of heading to the farmhouse, Phoenix directed them toward a barn on the far end of the property. Indira had that nervous and excited feeling pulsing in her chest. She felt like she was about to discover something really cool.

Phoenix paused in front of a pair of padlocked doors. Indira was surprised to see there were combination locks on them. He whirled through the numbers as if he'd gone in and out of this barn a thousand times. "It's in here," he said. "Come on."

The doors groaned open. Phoenix tugged a hanging switch and the overhead lamps fluttered on, filling the room with gentle light. The barn wasn't what she'd been expecting. There were no bales of hay, no wooden stalls, no animals. In fact, the whole room was empty. And walls that had appeared wooden from the outside were actually constructed of a shining, metallic material.

"What is this?" she asked. "Why do the walls look so weird?"

Phoenix didn't answer. He crossed to the center of the room before turning to face her.

"I need to show you something."

He held out his right hand. A snap of his fingers summoned fire. It was always so beautiful, the way the flames tossed back and forth in his open palm. Indira frowned.

"Fire," she said, a little confused. "I know. You've always had fire."

"It's more than just fire."

Phoenix's fingers flexed wide. Indira almost cried out as the flames raced across his entire body in a bright flash. A burst of heat filled the room and forced her to look away. Her heart was hammering in panic until she squinted into the light. The flames were . . . growing.

"Phoenix?"

Taller and wider. Phoenix's outline in the flames blurred. There was a snatch of powerful magic—like a clap of thunder—and the fire extinguished. Indira's eyes widened. She couldn't believe what she was seeing. It wasn't possible. A creature stood at the center of the room that was a little larger than a tractor. Phoenix was gone. In his place, there stood a dragon.

An actual dragon.

Indira was certain, too, that it was Phoenix looking down at her. Even in another form, there was no mistaking that look on his face. The look he often gave her with that one eyebrow raised in question, though now that eyebrow was replaced by scales the color of burnished clay. He looked like he was grinning too, except his teeth had transformed into rows of fangs.

It was impossible for Indira to stay focused on their pretend scene.

"Are you serious? This is *awesome.*"

Her tutor subtracted fifty points from her score for breaking character, but she didn't care. This was one of the coolest things she'd ever seen. Phoenix made a snorting noise she knew was laughter. Smoke curled out of both nostrils as Indira rushed forward, curiously inspecting him. He extended a scaled arm and showed off charcoal talons. She admired the lovely color of each scale as light chased across his armored body.

"You're a dragon," she said, running her hand along his forearm. "This is the coolest!"

Squalls looked a little nervous. "Er. Remember the scenario, Indira. We're still in the scene . . . and this is *really* dangerous. Didn't you hear the speech that kingswolf just gave? Phoenix caused that fire. He's clearly one of the Drago they're hunting. His father and mother hid him in this town when he was born, but his powers have grown. If the kingswolves return, they're going to trace all of this back to him."

Phoenix let out a sharp rumble that Indira thought must have been a growl. She didn't like the idea of anyone trying to hunt her friend.

"But you're *huge*. And you can breathe fire, right?"

She watched as he leaned back on his haunches, arching his neck. Snout raised to the ceiling, he blew a few fiery sparks into the air. Indira grinned.

"See? You can just fight them off!"

But Squalls quickly rained on that parade. She could tell he was squinting at the information provided by his tutor device. "It's . . . not that simple. Dragons are powerful, but there's a reason the Howling King was able to defeat them: the Spain!"

Phoenix snorted loudly. Indira saw Squalls frowning.

"Pretty sure you mean the Stained," she whispered.

Squalls nodded. "Right. Yeah. The Stained. A group of . . . elite soldiers that are loyal to the throne. It was their dark magic that defeated the dragons in the first place. . . ."

He was still squinting. Indira waited, wondering if he had more to read, but after a long and awkward pause he looked back at her. "Pretty sure that's all I have to read."

Indira eyed the highlighted step of the Hero's Journey.

"So this is the Call to Adventure," she said, thinking

out loud. "It all makes sense now. The kingswolves are coming back, and when they do, they'll find Phoenix. So we have to leave if we're going to keep him—and the town—safe."

And that was the beginning of their adventure. Indira was smiling as her tutor device whirled to life again. She hadn't bothered to read the next step in the Hero's Journey. As the highlight rotated, scrolling down, she read: **REFUSAL OF THE CALL.**

Directions appeared at the center of her screen. She tapped the paragraph and the text went bold:

As the mayor's daughter—and someone known for following the rules—you're going to reject their offer to go on the adventure. Good luck!

Indira sighed as the text vanished. She didn't *want* to reject their offer. The adventure sounded awesome, but she supposed this was the whole point of the practice tutorial? She needed to get some training on concepts she wasn't as familiar with. . . .

"Indira?" Squalls interrupted her thoughts. "Did you hear me?"

She shook herself. "Oh. Yeah. Sorry! What'd you say?"

"We need your help." He gestured toward Phoenix. "It won't be easy to get Phoenix—I mean, Phineas—out of town. We'll need your mother's motorized carriage. I've got food and supplies. There will be kingswolves in the area, keeping an eye on the town. We'll have to make it look like a market delivery. I think we can get to the foot-hills before dawn if we leave soon. . . ."

Indira took a deep breath and fell back into character. She backpedaled. "Look . . . this . . . I'm sorry."

Squalls blinked. "You're sorry?"

"I can't do this! I can't go with you!" She was trying to channel the rules-following daughter of a mayor. "I won't tell anyone about him. I promise. But there's no way I can go with you. The foothills? Do you know how far away that is? I can't just leave my mom behind. . . ."

Squalls was supposed to be convincing her otherwise, but for a moment he looked ready to agree with her instead. She guessed there was less chance of him dying if he just stayed put in town. Phoenix looked disappointed by the exchange. Indira was wondering how long the hero was supposed to refuse the call to adventure when a little *buzz* sounded.

All three of them fell silent.

The buzzing sharpened. Indira thought it almost sounded like drilling. She looked around the room until her eyes located the source of the noise. A little hole was forming in the exterior wall of the barn. Indira asked, "What on earth is that?"

Squalls turned to Phoenix. "How fast can you transform back?"

It was too late. A silver head poked through. Little

claws dug rapidly, carving a wider entry, and the metallic insect plunged into the air. The wings spread. Indira finally recognized it.

"That's Gadget's bee!"

The device hovered in the air above them. Squalls darted toward the barn's entrance. He was outside in less than a breath. She'd never seen him move so confidently. Indira's eyes followed the bee's buzzing progress. Phoenix crouched in perfect stillness at the center of the room. She couldn't tell if he was trying to transform back or just trying to not be noticed by the hovering insect.

"Hey! Come on! Let go of me!"

Gadget's voice. The barn door swung open and Gadget stumbled roughly inside. Squalls followed her nervously into the room. "I found her outside. Spying on us."

"*Spying?*" Gadget shot back. "I was just trying to track my bee! I wasn't trying to—" And then she finally saw Phoenix. "Is that a *dragon*? Where did you get a dragon?"

Squalls closed the barn door. "It's not a dragon. It's Phineas."

Gadget frowned. "Who?"

"Phoenix," Indira answered. "He's a dragon. Kind of awesome, right?"

The girl fell silent as her eyes unfocused. It was clear Gadget was reading her own instructions for their current scene. The others waited patiently for her attention to return.

"Is anyone else struggling with these scenes?" she asked. "I'm at like minus two thousand. . . ."

Squalls sighed. "Focus!"

Gadget shook herself. "Right, yeah, sorry! But if he's a dragon, we'll get in a lot of trouble!"

"Your bee," Squalls said, stifling an unexpected yawn. "Does it record what it sees?"

"No," she answered. "There aren't any visuals. The bee focuses on auditory and olfactory recordings—scents and sounds, mostly."

He shook his head. "Great. So it will pick up the conversation we just had using the word *dragon* over and over? That kind of evidence can get us in trouble. We have to destroy them."

"Wait!" Gadget held out her hands. "That's not how it works. The information feeds back to a storage device at the workshop. Destroying the bee won't do anything."

Indira stood there, waiting for Squalls to answer, when she realized he had fallen asleep. His chin nodded down toward his chest. As she watched and waited, a little snore sounded. Gadget's jaw dropped. "Really? I've been accused of being boring and overly technical before, but I've never had someone actually fall asleep on me in the middle of a conversation. . . ."

Before Indira could say anything, another sound caught her attention. She whipped around. The walls had given a telltale groan. There. Right where the bee had carved a path through the barn was a hole. And in that hole there was a face.

A very *familiar* face.

Ledge Woods.

Indira shot toward the barn door. Gadget shouted something. Phoenix's great dragon body unfolded with movement, too. She ignored them both, throwing off the locks and pulling the heavy barn doors open. She was too late, though. Ledge Woods was sprinting down the hill, already halfway to town. Gadget shouldered into the entrance beside her to watch.

"He saw Phoenix," Indira whispered.

"And all of us with him," Gadget added. "He'll think we're in on the conspiracy."

Indira's vision blurred slightly as the Hero's Journey rotated to the next step. Her eyes focused on the new phrase. She wasn't exactly sure what was going to happen, but she knew it was the one thing that might save them from the trouble Ledge was about to stir up in town.

Just two glowing words that hinted at something powerful: **SUPERNATURAL AID.**

12

Supernatural Aid

An argument broke out.

Indira suggested returning to town and getting help from her mother. It was their word against Ledge's word, after all. Gadget pointed out that Ledge had likely heard what she'd said about the recording being stored in the workshop. If he got down there before them, he could make sure that they never reached the device to erase the evidence. Phoenix had transformed back into his normal form. He suggested running, but it was clear that they wouldn't get far on foot. Not with kingswolves roaming the countryside.

All of them fell silent when Squalls walked through the entrance. His eyes were still closed. His arms were at his side, and his palms were to the sky. Indira stared at him.

"Is he sleepwalking?"

Gadget was the first one to notice the sky. "Those cumulonimbus clouds are forming at an impossibly fast rate. What is happening . . . ?"

A massive storm rolled over the plains. The thunderheads gathered above the town in less than thirty seconds. It started raining instantly. Only when the entire sky was black did Squalls blink to life again. He glanced over and noticed them all staring.

"Sorry. Blanked again. Is it my turn to say something?"

Phoenix let out a laugh. "We're going to have to talk about your magic, Allen. Something weird keeps happening. But for now, that storm you just summoned will give us cover to sneak back into town. We need to steal a motorized cart."

An initial trickle quickly transformed into a downpour. Indira followed Phoenix and Squalls down the hill until she realized Gadget hadn't moved. Her tutor device fixed on the girl and pinged a message into the air:

Prepare for the classic stubborn-friend sequence.

"Gadget," Indira called. "Let's get moving. There's no time to waste."

She shook her head. "If I stay with you, we have a seventeen percent chance of making it out."

Indira was prepared to make a speech but was surprised when Phoenix turned around, his expression fierce.

"Ledge will accuse all of us, Gadget. He'll claim that you helped hide me. If you think the kingswolves care about explanations, or that they'll forgive you, you're wrong." His jaw clenched. "It must be nice to go home, safe and sound. Do you have any idea what they'll do to me if they catch us? I'll have a *zero* percent chance of surviving. Hope you can live with that."

With a final glare, Phoenix turned and started marching toward town. Indira fell in step with him. He offered her a little smile. "I've been practicing my monologues," he whispered.

"I can totally tell. Great job."

Back when they'd first met, he'd never have been able to pull off a speech like that one. Squalls jogged to keep up with them, but Gadget hadn't budged. Indira knew the girl was following the tutor device's instructions. It was strange they'd split up this early in the story, but there was nothing they could do about it now.

Indira directed them toward a different entrance from the one Ledge had likely used. There was no telling what the fool had said to the guards.

The heavy rain helped hide their approach. Normally there'd be soldiers stationed there, but Indira saw that the post had been abandoned. They slipped into the town unnoticed. Market stalls in the town center were being hastily packed up as the rain continued to drive down from above. The tutor device's arrows pointed Indira to an alley on their right.

"This way," she said. "I know where my mom keeps her carriage."

Down side streets and under awnings. Indira knew there was no way they'd have gone unnoticed without the storm Squalls had summoned. She turned a final corner and found the carriage waiting beside an official government building. Indira assumed it was the courthouse.

"There!"

She pointed. The carriage had four thin wheels that looked more like bicycle tires. The body of the carriage was raised in the air, and the seats were protected by a thin overhead covering. The three of them crossed the street and climbed inside quickly.

"We're supposed to go west," Squalls recited. He was still a little unnatural anytime he read his lines. Indira made a note to practice with him later. "Head for the foothills. There's a mountain that looks like . . . a smile? We'll head there. The rebellion awaits its king."

After he finished, she heard him mutter under his breath.

"Mountains have snow. And avalanches. And cliffs to fall off. Just great . . ."

Indira tried to keep them focused. "Let's get this thing moving."

Her tutor device pointed to a central console. She stared down in confusion, though, because there was a blank space where the tutor was pointing. What was she supposed to do?

"Looking for this?" a voice called. Across the street, Ledge Woods stood in triumph. He held up a small wooden block with several attached levers. "There's no escaping now."

Indira looked around helplessly. Ledge had disabled their getaway vehicle. His father was walking down the street behind him with a small crowd of other towns-folk. The approaching mob looked angry. They'd come for Phoenix, and Indira knew they wouldn't leave without him.

She was trying to come up with a plan when a second voice cut through the rain.

"What is the meaning of this?"

Minerva Deacon led a second crowd, mostly made up of her assistants, down the courthouse steps. The determined look on her face faltered slightly at the sight of Indira in the driver's seat of their family carriage.

"We caught them!" Ledge called. "Phineas is a full-blooded Drago."

Mr. Woods threw a hand around his son's shoulder. "My boy saw him in dragon form. And your girl? She's been helping keep him hidden. So has the engineer's daughter. All of them are guilty. Harboring fugitives right under the king's nose!"

Minerva's eyes locked on Indira. "Is that true, Indira? Is he really one of the Drago?"

The look on Indira's face must have said everything. Indira saw the trap closing in around them. Both crowds clogged the streets, but both crowds had also paused. Indira realized that Phoenix was standing in the carriage behind her now.

Anger was written on his face and fire was etched in his eyes.

They were afraid of what he might do.

"We have plenty of evidence," Ledge shouted. "They're guilty!"

Indira looked back to Minerva. She was hoping her mother would know exactly what to say to get them out of this, but the woman just looked crestfallen.

"The two of you should come with us," she suggested. "A temporary arrest. Come down from the carriage and we'll talk. Just some interviews to get to the bottom of this. There's no reason to be scared, understand? Let's just take a deep breath and figure all of this out."

Indira shook her head. Surely her mother saw the truth. If Phoenix turned himself in, he'd be handed over to the kingswolves. She would not allow harm to come to him.

As she reached for her hammer, several things happened at once. Ledge and his father lurched forward threateningly. Phoenix summoned fire into one palm. And Minerva's crowd scattered as a second carriage came whipping down the street.

Time stretched as Gadget's vehicle slammed to a stop right beside theirs.

"We had a seventeen percent chance of survival if I stayed with you," Gadget shouted, half grinning, "but a fifty-two percent chance of survival when we split up. Never hurts to have a backup plan. What are you waiting for? Jump!"

Indira leaped into the back of Gadget's carriage without thinking. She landed hard, braced herself, and turned to help the others. Phoenix thrust his fire bolt in the crowd's direction, briefly scaring Ledge and his father back several steps. It bought them both time. Squalls leaped, tripping as he did, and Indira barely managed to reach out and save him from face-planting. She yanked him by the collar into the back of the carriage just before Phoenix leaped across.

Gadget punched the accelerator and their carriage shot forward.

Indira saw Ledge Woods lunging for them, his activated kingswolf claws stretching. They caught the very edge of the carriage—causing the whole thing to shudder—but before he could dig down into the wood, Indira brought her hammer slamming down against his knuckles. He let out a scream as their cart whipped around the corner.

Mud spewed in every direction. Gadget punched the accelerator again. Voices echoed after them. Calls sounded for the gates to be closed, but Gadget drove faster than Indira could have ever hoped. They took a final corner and punched through the closing gates, out into the open countryside. Indira looked back as the posted guards fired arrows from the ramparts, but each of them fell well short.

Relief thundered through her. They were safe. They had escaped. But as the carriage flew down the stretching, dirt-packed roads, another sound echoed in the distance: howling.

13

Crossing the Threshold

Have you ever rolled down the window, out on the open road, and set your hand against the wind, dear reader? You have to angle your hand just right, or the wind will keep catching it and throwing it backward. There's a point, however, when you find the right rhythm, and your hand glides like a surfer on invisible waves. That's how Indira started their journey into the unknown. Her hair tossing from her shoulders, hand outstretched, watching the countryside whip past.

Gadget turned out to be an excellent driver.

As the sun began to set, she kept them moving at high speeds across the winding countryside of Plot. Towns would appear, only to vanish just as quickly behind them. The howls chased them for a while, but eventually even they grew distant. Allen Squalls was calculating all the new threats that awaited them now that they'd left the safety of Ordinary. These included wolves, bears, and a mythical combination of the two that he'd creatively named were-bears. Squalls sat up front with Gadget and was discussing the genetic impossibilities of such a creature as their carriage followed the western road toward the mountains.

Indira finally had a moment alone with Phoenix.

"So," she said. "You're a dragon?"

He grinned. "I wasn't allowed to tell anyone. It's in my Words."

A knot tightened in her stomach. His Words. She knew from experience that a character's First Words were a promise and a warning. They'd hear those Words one day, but only if they actually made it into a story. Did Phoenix know how important this tutorial was for him?

Underglass had mentioned that this was an opportunity for Phoenix to prove that his connection with Indira was strong enough to work in their eventual story. Indira guessed that Phoenix had no clue about the other possible romantic lead—or the fact that he'd be unfinished if this didn't work out. She forced herself to nod.

"It's pretty cool," Indira said. "This scenario's actually kind of fun."

"I thought we were going to be in a classroom! The word *tutorial* had me picturing a professor going over theories or something. This is *way* better." He hesitated before lowering his voice. "Besides, it doesn't hurt that we get to do it together, either."

Indira smiled at him. "No, that doesn't hurt at all."

Fire kicked to life in his eyes, ringing his pupils with golden light. Indira thought about telling him how nice they looked, but at that exact moment, Gadget slammed the brakes. There was a stretching second where the world seemed as if it had hit the pause button. And then momentum threw Indira into the side of the carriage. Phoenix was flung into her. She caught an elbow in the stomach and their foreheads collided painfully.

Groaning, Indira pushed to her feet. Phoenix awkwardly untangled himself, his cheeks blooming a brighter red. The two of them crossed to the front of the carriage to see what had happened. Allen Squalls was huddled in one corner, checking himself for wounds.

"I could have been thrown from the vehicle!" he said.

"But you weren't," Phoenix pointed out. "Twenty-five percent is looking pretty good."

The nervous boy had no response to that. Gadget stood in the driver's seat, framed by an eerie glowing light. Indira wondered if the Stained had come for them. Her hand glided down to the grip of her hammer. She glanced at the Hero's Journey tutorial for confirmation, but it showed they were still on the same step they'd been on since bursting through the gates of Ordinary. It

was the one step that Indira hadn't immediately understood:

CROSSING THE THRESHOLD

"Whoa," Gadget said. "You guys have to check this
out. . . ."

"Are there aliens?" Squalls called. "Because if it's
aliens, I'm a hard pass. . . ."

Gadget didn't answer. Instead, she leaped down from
the carriage.

Indira finally saw the source of the light. Digital
stations—each one about her height—circled a massive
stone memorial. It had been built like a sprawling tabletop, the kind a general might use to make a plan of attack
before battle.

As Indira climbed down from the carriage, she
couldn't help marveling at the details. The tabletop had
been carved to match the surrounding countryside. There
were little stone farmhouses and quiet villages and slant-
ing rivers.

At the very center of the table, however, a straight
line ran across. The canyon separated those familiar villages from a dark beyond. Indira noticed that end of the
table was carved to mimic a swirl of shadows and waiting
threats, all on the verge of taking shape.

Indira knew Gadget couldn't resist playing with tech.
She watched as the girl tapped the nearest interface. The

display glowed brighter. There was a flash of light, and then the image of a girl projected out onto the road they were standing on. She wore a checkered blue-and-white dress, had brown pigtails, and clutched a little dog tightly to her chest.

Her eyes grew wide as she said, "Toto, we're not in Kansas anymore. . . ."

The image shimmered brightly before flickering out.

"That was Dorothy," Squalls whispered. "From the *Wizard of Oz.*"

Another console activated. Another character—and Indira felt certain this was also a famous character—flashed out onto the road. This one was a young boy with a straw hat, dirty overalls, and bare feet. He grinned at them like they were all old friends.

"It's the little things that smooths people's roads the most. . . ."

He winked before vanishing like the first image.

"That was Huckleberry Finn!" Phoenix whispered in awe. "Remember, Indira? We studied him in Sympathetic Characters class with Threepwood."

Indira nodded, though she didn't remember that. As they stood there, other characters appeared. Old lines written by ancient Authors were recited. It felt sacred to sit there and listen to little snatches from their stories. Indira also noticed that most of the lines had to do with moving forward into the unknown.

The final console cast the image of a young knight. He

surprised Indira by climbing right up onto the table. A glowing sword appeared, half plunged into the stone. He gripped the hilt, set his feet, and pulled with all his might. There was a sharp sound as the sword came free in a brilliant flash. Indira knew this story. Almost every character did.

"Good evening. I am King Arthur." The young knight strode to the edge of the table and looked at them. "This was my moment of Crossing the Threshold. You have come to *your* moment in the Hero's Journey tutorial where you will do the same. When I pulled the sword from the stone, everything about my life changed. It was the day that I left *ordinary* behind.

"The way forward will not be easy. You will find a Road of Trials awaiting you. Strange conflicts. Difficult quests. But the truth—for every brave character—is that your journey cannot begin without crossing out of what you know and into what you do not. It is our greatest calling. Whether it means entering the land of Oz or claiming our rightful title as king, this is the moment that marks your first step into something more."

He leaped down from the edge of the tabletop. They all watched as the digital king dragged the tip of his sword across the very real road. An actual line formed in the dirt and began to glow with light. Indira found herself mesmerized by it. "Cross this line," Arthur commanded. "Begin your journey. Become the heroes you were born to be."

The image vanished.

Indira looked around at the others. Everyone stood a few inches taller. Allen Squalls was the first to speak, and the nervous edge in his voice was barely noticeable now.

"I hope—I hope one day I have a line in my story that everyone remembers. Or a cool moment that echoes through the worlds forever! It'd be amazing to have that."

Gadget was quieter. "I just want to be chosen for a story. That would be enough for me."

"Same here," Phoenix said. "But that's how each of them started. I don't think they knew they'd become legends, or that their words would be programmed into memorials. I'd bet each one of them started out like us. Just a character hoping to find a role in a story."

"What a fine speech!" a voice behind them called. "Fifty more points for you!"

The crew turned to find Beginning strolling up the road. She still had that wide grin on her face. "That was a truly wonderful start to your scenario! One of the smoothest we've seen. There were secrets and daring escapes and unexpected friendships! Oh, I knew you all would be up to something good. It's time now to hand you off to my sister."

She gestured down the road. Indira looked. The teenage version approached from that direction. Middle was unsmiling. She wore a determined look that matched her tougher appearance. Indira finally understood why she looked the way she did. The middle of the book was where all the true tests waited. In the beginning, things were bright and exciting, the way the youngest sister appeared. What came next would be a true measure of their team's strength.

It was almost as if Middle read her thoughts, because the girl called out from where she stood. "Come enter my realm. Let's see what you can *really* do."

In the silence that followed, all three of Indira's crew members looked to her. She thought about all the dreams and hopes they'd just shared. Truths that had nestled deep in each of their hearts. It wasn't lost on Indira that she had already achieved the dream each of them was still reaching for. She'd been viewing the tutorial as a game, a chance to brush up on her skills.

It was so much more than that for the others. This was their chance to prove their worth. This was an opportunity to cross their own thresholds and find a story that would last forever. Indira looked each one of her crew in the eye. "From what I've seen so far, all of you have a story waiting out there. Let's keep practicing. Let's finish this quest. Let's score the highest marks any tutorial has ever seen. Who's with me?"

The crew responded with a cheer. Phoenix flashed her a smile as they walked back over to the carriage. Indira saw Beginning skipping back down the road toward Ordinary. Middle knelt on a nearby hill, ready to witness the very moment they entered her territory in the land of Plot.

Nothing happened when they crossed the glowing

line in the road. There was no special flash of light. None of them grew wings or discovered special superpowers. But Indira could tell that each one of them was sitting up straighter, holding their head higher, their eyes searching the dark horizon for whatever came next.

14

Down the Road of Trials

Their crew made good time—taking shifts driving or sleeping—and Indira found herself enjoying the adventure. Phoenix was right. The company of her crew made all the difference in the world. She liked some of them even more than she'd liked the characters in her own story.

Dawn arrived, and it brought a glimpse of looming mountains with it. The group gathered around the front of the carriage to watch as sunrise painted the horizon with bright colors. Phoenix and Squalls were sitting up front, talking quietly as Phoenix drove. Indira decided it was a good chance to learn a little more about Gadget. The girl was in the middle of polishing a set of wrenches when Indira plunked down in the seat beside her.

"So, how's it going so far, Gadget?"

She shrugged. "My score isn't great. I missed a scene

yesterday morning because I got distracted working on the bees. But I did get a lot of positive points for the driving scene. I'm having a hard time understanding the point system. In both cases, I was doing what I love to do—I was playing with tech. I'm not sure why one gained me points and the other lost me points. . . ."

Indira nodded. "Well, you drove that piece of tech into the middle of our scene, provided our escape route, and saved us from an angry mob. It seems like you got more points when you focused on using the tech to help people. Does that make sense?"

Gadget shrugged again. "I guess so. I'm just not . . . like you."

"Like me?"

She nodded. "You and that hammer . . . you're all instinct. You just jump right in and start swinging. It's pretty cool. That's not how my brain works, though. I like having a plan. I do a *lot* of research. But it seems like by the time I've figured out the answer, the scene has already passed me by."

Indira thought she understood now. "Well, my way of doing things doesn't always work either. That's kind of why I'm here. I'm supposed to learn how to work with a team. I've always done things on instinct, but Brainstorm Underglass wants me to learn a new way. Maybe that's why she paired us together. I can teach you instincts. You can teach me how to look at the bigger picture. Sound like a plan?"

Gadget smiled. "Affirmative. Pretty cool that you're still learning, even after getting in a story. Didn't expect that. My hypothesis was that you were joining us on this mission to confirm your affections for Phoenix."

Indira nearly choked in surprise. Her voice caught and she hacked an awkward cough. Her eyes darted up front, but thankfully Phoenix was laughing loudly at something Squalls had just said and hadn't heard them. She shook her head at Gadget's curious inspection.

"I'm not . . . what . . . are you . . ."

Gadget raised an eyebrow. "Was that assumption incorrect?"

Indira shrugged. "It's . . . no . . . we're just friends."

Gadget surprised her with a laugh. "Right. I'm no expert on crushes. I've never enjoyed subjects that ignore scientific theory. But every time he looks at you, his eyes literally light up with *flames*. You know what happens when he looks at me? No flames. I don't have any scientific degrees, but I'm pretty sure the flames mean something more than 'we're just good friends.'"

Indira could feel the heat rising in her cheeks. Gadget noticed.

"Didn't mean to embarrass you," she said. "Sorry about that. I'm not the best at this whole talking thing. Machines are easier for me. More predictable. Don't worry. I won't tell him how much you like him. . . ."

Indira was grateful when the girl returned to polishing her tools. Her eyes roamed back to the front of the carriage, where Phoenix was sitting. She wasn't sure how to make her Author choose Phoenix, but she knew Gadget was right. There was more between them than she wanted to admit. For a long time, she sat there, watching the road go past, trying to come up with a solution. But there were no answers written in the morning sky.

During the night, all their tutor devices had rotated. The words of King Arthur's speech echoed, and their newest step in the Hero's Journey was highlighted with dark warning:

THE ROAD OF TRIALS

Indira didn't need anyone to explain this step to her. Her first year at Protagonist Preparatory had basically been one long road of trials. It was the step she felt most ready for.

And the first trial came early that morning.

Their motorized carriage started to fade. The engine shorted out a few times before kicking back to life. Indira heard Gadget messing around with levers, muttering under her breath, but about five minutes later the car died completely. Their crew sputtered to a stop on the side of the road.

"Road of Trials." Indira rolled her eyes. "Guess it's a literal road here."

Allen Squalls climbed out, glancing up and down the road. "I've got a bad feeling about this. I can already see how it's going to happen. Our car breaks down. Another car passes us. It loses control. I leap forward and save Phoenix, but in the process I slip down the hill. There's *quicksand* at the bottom of the hill. . . . I start to sink. . . ."

Phoenix frowned. "Why would there be quicksand? There's never actually quicksand."

Gadget waved them both off. "It's just a little car trouble. Let me take a look at the engine real quick. Just give me a few seconds to see if it's something I can fix."

Indira didn't point out that the last time the girl had inspected the parts of a vehicle, she'd nearly sent them spinning off into some other dimension. The rest of the crew carefully removed their knapsacks from the back of the carriage as Gadget slid underneath. They heard her banging around for a few minutes. All the noise hid the approaching sound of wheels until someone was right on top of them.

"We have company," Squalls said, clearly reading lines again. "Everyone act natural. Let's pretend we're taking a . . . sunny delivery to a town nearby."

"What's a *sunny* delivery?" Gadget asked.

"Supply delivery," Allen muttered. "Sorry. It's hard to read the text!"

Indira eyed the approaching carriage. The man riding up front looked like the most average farmer she'd ever seen. He had a fine mustache and was whistling a little tune. When he caught sight of their carriage, he made a quick adjustment, slowing the speed of his own vehicle until he came to a stop just to their left.

"Ho there, neighbors!" he called. "What seems to be the trouble?"

"Engine gave out," Indira replied, settling into her character. "We're escorting some goods down into the valley. You wouldn't happen to have an extra charge, would you?"

Her tutor rewarded her fifty points for the response.

The man frowned. "Afraid not. And my cargo hold is mostly full."

Gadget slid out from under the carriage. "We'll just have to buy a new one."

Something about her appearance drew a distinct re-action from the stranger. Indira noted the slight rise in his throat as he swallowed. The way his hands tightened slightly on the forward levers of his carriage. She wasn't sure why Gadget of all people would bring out that kind of reaction.

"Well, I could take one of you into town," the man of-fered, his voice a little shaky. "No room in the hold, but I could have one of you ride with me. . . ." He scanned their group, swallowed again, and pointed. "How about you, young lad?"

A little chill ran down Indira's spine. The man was pointing directly at Phoenix. Indira remembered he was the one people were after. A thunderous desire to protect him roared to life in her chest. It took effort to keep her voice calm as she answered the man.

"We'd rather not split up. This is the first time our parents have trusted us to take a delivery this far. The only rule they gave was that none of us were to go off alone. Surely you understand."

The man's eyes darted to Phoenix before fixing back on Indira.

"Sure, yes, of course. That's more than sensible," he said. "Why don't you wait here? I'll head into town and let the engineers know that you're in need of a recharge. Someone should be up in the next hour or so. Just make sure you stay right here!"

Indira watched the man hastily restart his carriage. She couldn't help noticing the layer of sweat that had gathered above his mustache, even though it was quite chilly out still, the sun barely risen. She put on her best smile, thanked the man, and kept waving until he rounded the bend.

"Time to move," she whispered. "Get your things."

Gadget frowned. "But he's coming back—"

"He's going to report us," Phoenix cut in. "He was awfully nervous for a farmer helping out a few stranded kids. You heard the kingswolves howling. Word can spread quickly that way. I'd guess there's a search warrant out for us."

Indira nodded. The reason for the man's reaction to Gadget clicked into place.

"He saw three of us and stopped," she said. "But when Gadget appeared, that made us a group of four. I'd bet anything that the description was of four runaways. And that's why he wanted you to go with him, Phoenix. You're probably worth the biggest reward."

The others all nodded now. It was a shame to abandon the carriage, but Indira saw no other option. They started through the hills, skirting farmland and favoring the sparse forests that curtained everything. Squalls kept muttering about hiding places for wolves as they went.

It hadn't taken long for the Road of Trials to start proving its name.

And it was far from finished.

15

The Foreshadow Forest

First the carriage had broken down. Then the man had arrived to report them. Other issues began rearing up like ugly, coiling snakes. They realized around lunchtime that they had far too little food to survive the long journey. Gadget calculated all the distances and confirmed it would be at least four days of travel to the mysterious destination Allen's directions were leading them to. At some point, they'd have to steal food or risk making purchases from a smaller outpost.

Allen was the first to complain about his footwear. "Can you die from blisters?"

Indira was trying to set a good example by not voicing her own complaints, but even she could feel the skin on the back of her heels being rubbed raw.

The general attitude of the group slowly shifted. At the

memorial, they'd been locked into the quest, ready for the adventure of a lifetime. Now there was mostly silence as they pressed on through one forest after another. And the distant howls sounded closer than ever. Indira guessed the farmer had reported them. It wouldn't be long before the kingswolves found their abandoned carriage. Even if they were making plenty of progress, all of it was on foot at this point. The kingswolves would eventually start gaining on them.

Squalls stopped walking, very nearly tripping the rest of them. "This forest has a sign?"

Indira saw he was right. The curtain of trees ahead of them was thicker than some of the scraggly woodland they'd passed through so far. And there was a signpost in front of it.

"The Foreshadow Forest."

The voice nearly made Indira jump out of her skin. Middle was standing behind their group. Indira hadn't even heard her approach. She marched around them to stand at the edge of the waiting forest. "It's a rather common tool here in the land of Plot," Middle explained. "Authors like to give little hints about what is to come. Perhaps the Author will mention two moons. Over and over they'll mention them, until at the very end, the two moons collide! Every mention and hint was a foreshadowing."

Indira thought she saw shadows moving deeper in the forest.

"Do we have to go through it?" she asked.

"Yes," Middle replied. "It is required."

Squalls spoke in a quiet voice. "Are there wolves?"

Middle shook her head. "Wolves? No, only the future. And its teeth are sharper."

Their group bunched together, shoulders touching. Indira kept her chin high, but she didn't like the sound of this forest. Even magical hammers were powerless against the future.

"A final warning," Middle said. "These glimpses are important, but they're also easy to forget when you're surrounded by whispers and voices and more. . . . Do your best to remember."

The emissary retreated. Indira exchanged glances with the others before steeling herself. She walked forward as confidently as she could. "Everyone stay close."

Leaves crunched underfoot. As soon as they passed the first layer of trees, Indira felt a chill. The sunlight was having trouble fighting through the thick branches above. Indira noted there were hundreds of paths to take. The trails ran off in all directions, twisting and turning and overlapping. Indira picked one and led the crew forward.

At first, the forest did not seem different from any other forest. There were shadows, certainly. And the wind sounded full of whispers. But other than that, it was just a bunch of trees that had decided to make themselves into a neighborhood. It felt normal.

Until the first foreshadowing.

Indira set a hand against a trunk to keep her balance as

they turned a corner in the path. She nearly shouted when the bark of that tree shifted under her hand. It twisted and reshaped itself like a living thing. Indira's eyes widened as she watched the bark form into the shape of a face. Not just any face, either. It was her face.

Indira held in a scream as she stumbled back into Phoenix. The engraved image of her own face grinned at her before speaking. "Sometimes you have to lose if you want to win." The voice laughed. "Isn't that right?"

The question echoed until the bark re-formed into the ordinary surface of a tree. Indira had to shake herself before she could start walking again. The group continued along the path, but a shiver ran down her spine and her arms. What did that mean? That she would lose? And then win? Or that she couldn't win *unless* she lost? Indira frowned at all the possibilities.

That first foreshadowing spooked the others. They did their best to avoid making contact with the surrounding trees, but as the path twisted and tightened, it became unavoidable.

Phoenix accidentally rustled against a stray branch. All its leaves burst suddenly to life, separating from the wood. Invisible hands folded them into new shapes. Squinting, Indira saw they were little green dragons. One by one, the leaves launched from the branch and dove toward the ground. Their voices all whispered the same warning.

"The danger with any powerful thing is that it might fall into the wrong hands."

Indira did not like the sound of that. She did her best to keep the crew moving. Gadget's glimpse came next. She tripped over a hollowed log, which immediately sprouted arms. It pushed up to its feet and glared at her with tiny, ringed eyes.

"You can't tell me what to do!"

The log stuck out a wooden tongue before marching off into the forest.

Gadget stared. "This is the least scientific place I've ever been. I do not like it here."

Indira saw the end of the forest ahead. "We're almost through."

There was more light ahead. Indira pressed on, but a little squeak from Squalls stopped them. He had walked right into a spiderweb the others had ducked below. He struggled awkwardly, trying to remove the little threads, and the web re-formed behind him.

It spelled out a single word: PIRATE.

Squalls looked terrified. "I've been mentally preparing for wolves and bears, and now I have to deal with *pirates*, too? There's no way I'm going to survive. . . ."

Indira was thankful when Phoenix threw an arm around Allen's shoulders and whispered for him to keep walking. Sunlight fought through the branches ahead. She stumbled through the largest gap she could find and burst out into the light, releasing a breath she hadn't realized she was holding.

Turning back, Indira saw the Foreshadow Forest

looming behind, its branches pointing them onward. She stared in confusion, though, because her mind had gone strangely blank.

"What just happened?"

Phoenix shrugged. "Did one of you say something? It's the weirdest thing."

But the others shook their heads, clearly confused as well. Indira felt like there was something floating at the very edges of her memory. Have you ever felt the same, dear reader? That feeling that there is something you're supposed to know. The name of a movie. The lyrics to a song. Our brains can only hold so much, however, and the whispers of the Foreshadow Forest are particularly slippery. Gadget was the first to break the silence.

"There's an abandoned outpost over the next hill. Let's keep moving."

Indira couldn't help feeling they were forgetting something very important, but there was nothing they could do about that now. Her mind chased forgotten whispers as they followed directions and marched on to face their next trial.

16

Out of Place

The group had paused at the edge of a raised hillside.

Below, there was a road that had fallen into disrepair. It was clear no one traveled this route, at least not often. A pair of towers—although the word *tower* felt a little generous—flanked both sides of the road.

"It's pretty narrow," Indira noted. "Good place for an ambush."

Squalls recited to them, "It's the only way into the mountain passes. It was abandoned after the Howling King destroyed all the cities there, because they were loyal to the Drago. No reason to maintain trade routes with a kingdom that no longer exists. We should be fine."

As the group's "supernatural aid," Allen had apparently been given a lot more of the backstory than the rest of them. After brief consideration, they started forward cautiously. Indira's senses told her to stay on her guard. She pulled out her hammer. Phoenix noted that and straightened, ready to summon his fire at a moment's notice. Gadget was distractedly fiddling with a handheld device.

Indira whispered to her, "Gadget. Focus. Maybe pull out a weapon or something?"

The girl looked up in surprise. She frowned once before trading the strange device for one of the larger wrenches on her tool belt. She hefted it into the air for Indira's inspection.

"Guess that'll have to do," Indira said.

The towers appeared empty. Bricks had fallen out of place, leaving sad gaps in the framework. The doors had all been torn off their hinges, and the wild growth of ivy had started splitting the rest of what was left of both buildings. The hairs on the back of Indira's neck stood on end. Footsteps sounded.

"Anyone else hear that?"

Instinctively, their crew circled up at the center of the road. Indira *knew* this place looked like an ambush waiting to happen. She resisted telling Squalls *told you so* as they heard more footsteps. The sound was coming from both towers. Indira realized it didn't sound like human footsteps. There was the gentle scrape of claws on stone: kingswolves.

Her whole body was poised, every muscle flexed and ready, when the enemy finally came flooding out of both towers at once. The sight was more shocking than she'd expected.

Phoenix burst out laughing. "What. Are. Those?"

Not kingswolves. Indira was certain of that much. She started laughing too as a group of puppies surrounded them. There might have been six or seven, though it was hard to tell as the golden balls of fur darted in and around each other. One barreled into Phoenix. Another duo tried to leap on Squalls, but their little legs failed them, and both went spinning adorably into the dusty street.

"Puppies!" Squalls said with relief. "Finally! Something that can't kill me!"

Indira wanted to keep her guard up—thinking maybe this was all a trap—but she couldn't resist. She leaned down and scooped one up. It licked her face twice, huffing pleasantly.

Only Gadget didn't join in. "This is . . . illogical. How does this connect to the scenario?"

"Who cares?" Phoenix called back. He was down on the ground, surrounded by "attackers," laughing as they did their best to wrestle a cloth handkerchief from his grasp.

Indira was still trying to figure out what was happening when her tutor device pinged a message into her vision. The arrows were pointing at the puppies, swirling to follow their movements, and a single warning flashed over and over.

"Um . . ." Indira frowned again. "Is anyone else seeing this message?"

"It says we should attack," Phoenix confirmed. "I'm confused. Why would the tutor device tell us to attack puppies?"

Gadget frowned. "That message is *also* illogical."

Indira turned in a slow circle, her eyes scanning the hills. Something was wrong. The puppies didn't look like baby kingswolves. In fact, she wasn't sure such a thing existed. How was this supposed to factor into the Road of Trials?

The tutor device was starting to get annoying, too. It made the font in Indira's vision bigger and bolder. It even went as far as subtracting points each time she failed to respond. The same order flashed again:

Defend yourself! You are under attack!

"This is so weird," Indira muttered.

At least the puppies were cute. Most of them had turned their attention to Squalls, who was down on the ground, playfully fending them off and simultaneously scratching their bellies. It was nice to see him laughing for once. Indira was about to give in to the fun when a figure appeared on the lonely road ahead of them. The puppy ambush was strange, but this was stranger.

It was a boy with blond hair several shades lighter

than Allen's. His eyes were ice blue, his lips rose red. The colors stood out to Indira because they looked so much sharper than the rest of the world around him. Indira was reminded briefly of the brainstorms at Protagonist Prep. The first time she'd seen them, there'd been an odd quality to their appearance too.

The approaching figure was even more distinct. The edges of his outline seemed to blur in her vision. Indira found herself feeling dizzy if she stared for too long.

His outfit was equally strange. So far the scenario had offered them a rustic look. Farmers in old-school tunics or fashionable suits from an earlier time. This boy wore a mesh tank top that was navy blue. The number twenty-three was printed on the front. He wore a matching pair of athletic shorts. The only other item in his possession was a lacrosse stick.

"Hey!" he shouted. "Those are my puppies!"

Even his voice was strange. It sounded like he was speaking from very far away, as if each word were lightning striking in a distant sky. Indira's crew turned to face the new challenger. She saw her own confusion echoed on their faces. Clearly, something strange was happening. Even her tutor device was struggling. The device kept trying to home in on the approaching figure, but it would flicker weakly, unable to identify the threat. All the guiding text faded.

Her screen went blank. What was happening?

"I said those are *my* puppies."

The boy lifted his lacrosse stick into the air like it was a magical staff. Their only warning was the way the puppies darted fearfully back toward the tower entrances. A second later, magic sliced through the air. Indira's entire crew stumbled away. The space between them and the boy had been empty. Now a massive pirate ship loomed.

Indira's eyes widened. There wasn't an ocean nearby. There were no rivers. Nothing. All they could do was stare up at the impossible. An actual pirate ship had appeared in the middle of the road. The boy stood at the prow of the boat, looking down at them.

"What's wrong?" he taunted. "Never seen a pirate ship before?"

Squalls was muttering to himself. "Oh no. Pirates. Cannons, sharks, walking the plank . . . that's like a hundred new ways to die. I'm going to just . . ."

Before Phoenix could say something to calm him down, Squalls bolted. Indira stared, jaw open, as he made for the nearest hillside.

"There goes Allen," Phoenix said.

Indira didn't have time to deal with this. Her attention turned back to the unwelcome guest. How did this fit the scenario? She wondered if this was one of the Stained that had been mentioned before. She'd certainly expected someone powerful, but all the details felt like pieces to the wrong puzzle. Nothing about this fit with the rest of the story so far.

She could only think of one logical question. "Who are you?"

The boy shrugged. "My name's Joey."

Phoenix and Indira exchanged a glance. He mouthed the name to her. It wasn't the sort of menacing name most antagonists used. Most bad guys went by something like Spike or Bonesaw. At the risk of losing even more points, Indira decided to break character.

"Excuse me, but are you the assigned antagonist? I'm not sure we're getting this. . . ."

The boy heaved a huge sigh. "Boring! This is *boring*. Time to make things exciting. What's that phrase pirates always use? Oh yeah. 'Fire in the hole!'"

Joey pointed his lacrosse stick. Magic filled the air. All the cannons lining the side of the ship came to life. The black mouths pointed at Indira and her crew. Fire flashed within, sparking fuses, spreading from window to window. Instinct forced Indira to backpedal. "Fire number one!" Joey shouted.

There was a stretching moment where Indira thought they were all doomed. Smoke burst out of the first cannon, but it was a misfire. Something with the powder must have failed, because nothing shot out. Joey leaned over the deck and shouted in frustration.

Indira grabbed Phoenix's collar and pulled him into a run. The two of them bumped into Gadget, and all three nearly toppled as they scrambled away from the road. Up ahead, Allen Squalls had already reached the woods. He'd apparently had the right idea.

Joey's voice echoed again. "Fire! They're getting away! Fire!"

Indira barely kept her footing as they sprinted toward Squalls and the nearby forest. More cannon fire thundered out. Something hissed overhead. The ground shook, but Joey's first shot landed thirty yards to their right.

"He's firing on us with a pirate ship!" Gadget screamed. "This makes zero sense!"

Another round of blasts tore through the air. Two cannonballs missed overhead, but a third struck just to Gadget's left. The explosion lifted her feet briefly off the ground, throwing her into Phoenix. The two of them went down together.

"No!" Indira screamed.

She darted back. Phoenix was climbing to his feet, a little shaken. Gadget wasn't responsive at all. Together they dragged Gadget's unconscious form into an awkward fireman's carry over their shoulders. Indira's ears were still ringing as they stumbled on with the girl held in the air between them.

"Come on!" Squalls shouted from the edge of the tree line. Indira was surprised he hadn't kept running. "We can take cover in the forest! Come on!"

More explosions followed. Indira ducked through the first row of trees, but they didn't stop running until the cannon sounds were well behind them. It was only when they reached a clearing deep in the forest that they stopped to assess the damage.

Chests heaving, they looked around at each other, and it was Allen Squalls who summed up their plight best. "We fell for a puppy trap!"

17

The Real Antagonist

After cleaning and bandaging their wounds, the crew retreated deeper into the forest. There were still some howls sounding in the hills, but Indira found those noises more comforting than what had just happened. A random boy had summoned a pirate ship out of thin air.

And fired on them.

It took almost an hour for Gadget to wake. She couldn't hear too well out of one ear, but at least she didn't appear to have any long-term damage. Indira was relieved that all of them had survived in one piece, but that didn't make their next move any clearer.

"What do your tutor devices say?" she asked.

Phoenix answered. "Mine keeps subtracting points. I'm in the negatives now."

"Same here," Squalls added. "It says we're supposed

to go back to the towers. Where I'll probably be fed to sharks. But if we wait here, I'll probably be attacked in the night by wolves. Can't believe I actually thought puppies were safe!"

Phoenix tried to calm him down. "But you didn't die, Allen. We're still here. You survived the attack. Let's try to focus on what's happening, not what *could* have happened. The directions on my device are really specific now. It says we're supposed to survive a kingswolf attack and escape into the mountains."

Allen muttered, "Which will start a chain of events causing an avalanche. . . ."

Indira ignored him. She caught Phoenix's eye and nodded. Her device said the exact same thing that his did. "We know there weren't kingswolves at the tower," she said. "And that kid . . . I'm not the only one who thinks he was strange, am I?"

"He didn't fit the scenario," Phoenix agreed. "His clothes were out of place."

"Could he be one of the Stained?" Gadget asked quietly. "We haven't met one yet. They're supposed to be superpowerful, aren't they? The only description I could find in my tutor device was that they 'used dark magic to defeat the dragons.' Everything that kid did was totally illogical, but maybe we just weren't prepared for a new type of magic."

Indira frowned. "But was that *dark* magic? The kid was cackling to himself the whole time. And you heard him. There was no mention of the Howling King. Nothing about dragons. Nothing about his noble duty to find Phoenix. There weren't any lines or anything! He just said he was bored. He summoned a pirate ship and fired on us out of *boredom*."

Phoenix stood. "We need to go back."

"Go back?" Squalls looked properly terrified. "Are you serious? No way. I did *not* sign up to get killed by a cannon. Or sharks. Or to be launched by a cannon *into* a pool of sharks —"

"Allen. Pull it together," Phoenix replied. "We're all taking a risk. Besides, even if one of us did get launched by a cannon into a pool of sharks — which is really unlikely, by the way — we'd come back to life. That's the whole reason the Ninth Hearth exists."

The Ninth Hearth was back at Protagonist Preparatory. It was also known as the Nine-Lives Hearth, because it brought characters in their world back to life. Indira unfortunately knew from experience how the hearth worked.

"Coming back to life doesn't make death hurt any less!" Squalls complained. "I just don't see the point of going back to such a dangerous place."

"The devices are telling us to go back," Phoenix replied. "It's like we didn't succeed in our mission. I'm not sure what just happened, but clearly the only way to continue the scenario is to go back. Our scores are tanking. If we fail the tutorial, finding a story will be even harder."

"Plus, we need to investigate what happened," Indira said. She didn't see any other options. "He might have left by now. Phoenix is right. The only way to keep the quest moving is to reach the mountains. If Joey's still there, we can retreat and figure out a plan of attack."

Squalls stared at her. "Plan of attack? You want to plan an attack? He summoned a pirate ship with less than a thought! Our *plan* should be to run. Or hide. Or both."

Phoenix held out a palm and summoned fire. "That ship was made of wood. And wood burns, right? My fire would work. Or how about a full-fledged dragon? I didn't react last time because I wasn't sure what I was supposed to do. The tutor devices were freaking out. So I just froze. It won't happen again."

Indira liked his confidence. She met Phoenix's eyes and gave a nod.

Silence was as close as they'd get to having Squalls agree to come. Indira helped Gadget to her feet, and when she was certain the girl had her legs back under her, she led them all out of the forest again. The towers loomed in the growing dark. The ship was still there too. It appeared Joey had abandoned the area. Indira could hear some rustling from one of the towers, and a quick check inside showed the puppies were huddled there. Cautiously, their crew circled the ship.

There was no sign of Joey.

"It's so strange," Indira said. "I just don't get how this fits—"

Movement cut her sentence off. Someone had slipped out of the distant forest. Indira's heart started beating faster, but she let out a little sigh of relief when a kingswolf came loping toward them. Indira's crew gathered around. Somehow, the creature wasn't frightening to her now. Not after what had happened. She stood her ground and called out to the creature.

"You there! Come here. What's going on?"

The wolf transformed. Indira was surprised to see it was a woman. She wore the same half armor, half robe that the kingswolf who'd visited Ordinary had worn. Her human form was also a little wolfish. She had thick eyebrows and too-sharp teeth.

"Is he gone?" the woman asked.

Indira frowned. "Who? Joey?"

The kingswolf nodded.

"It looks like it," Indira answered. "Is he one of the Stained?"

That drew a laugh from the kingswolf. "The Stained? No. The Stained have very specific powers. I've never met someone like him. We were waiting here for the scheduled attack. It's all in the scenario script we were given."

It took Indira a second to realize the kingswolf was breaking character. This was no longer a part of the scenario. This was a trained character—a hired actor—who looked completely terrified.

"Joey stumbled out of the woods," she continued. "He didn't exactly fit the description we'd been given for you all. But we decided to go with it. The scenario changes sometimes. We've had previous tutorials where the characters completely messed things up. When the brainstorms hired us, we were trained to be flexible in our roles and to do our best to get the story back on track.

"So we ambushed him," the kingswolf explained. "Well, the others did. My job was at the end of the fight. You know the surprise attack that comes at the very last second, when you finally think you've won?" The woman's voice was shaking. "That was my job. But Joey saw the other kingswolves coming and he just laughed at them. I watched him point that stick and . . ."

Indira finally understood. "The puppies."

The kingswolf snapped her fingers. "It was over in less than a second. He transformed them into puppies like it was nothing. Just kept laughing to himself about it too."

And that explained the directions from the tutor devices. The tech wasn't smart enough to figure out what had happened. It was identifying the puppies as kingswolves. No wonder it had been confused. It must have been strange to see Indira and the others playing with their enemies rather than fighting against them. Indira traced those threads to their inevitable conclusion.

"So we were right," she said. "Joey isn't supposed to be in our scenario."

The kingswolf shook her head. "I thought he might be a rogue character. That's happened before. Protagonist Preparatory sometimes sends over a crew and the characters don't all get along. It messes up the whole tutorial quest. But I'm guessing he didn't come with you?"

Indira and the others shook their heads.

"We've never seen him before," Phoenix said.

The kingswolf looked even more worried now.

"Well, there's a protocol. We can report this—"

Her sentence was cut off by distant shouting. Indira's stomach twisted, thinking Joey had returned, but this voice was deeper. Allen Squalls looked ready to bolt until Phoenix put an arm around him, whispering something into his ear. As Indira listened, she realized the person was chanting a word that actually fit their scenario.

"Drago! Drago! Drago!"

Their crew rounded the ship cautiously. A figure was approaching from the opposite side of the road. He yelled the word like a wrestler calling out an opponent before entering the ring. Indira couldn't help laughing. This was so clearly the assigned antagonist for their story. Even her tutor device hummed back to life, fixed on him, and pinged a message into her vision:

High-Level Antagonist

Indira found herself agreeing with that description. He was a colossal statue of a human being. His arms had muscles that she hadn't known arms could have. He wore dark leather armor. Even his haircut, short on the sides, looked like a typical bad-guy haircut. Last but not least, there was a black-ink handprint on the right side of his face.

She rolled her eyes. "I assume you're the Stained?"

He ignored her, fixing his eyes on Phoenix instead.

"I am Cavern. Loyal servant of the Howling Kings. I went into the darkspring for seven years and came out the other side. I am a weapon in the hands of the true conqueror, and I have come in search of—"

"You're also late," Indira interrupted. "We already met the *real* bad guy."

The kingswolf nodded in agreement. "She's right. We should talk."

The massive boy looked surprised, then annoyed. Indira guessed he had rehearsed his speech several times. "Uh . . . I have come in search . . . of the Drago. Fire is forbidden. Dragons are—"

"Yeah, we know," Indira cut in again. "We've got bigger problems, Caveman."

And that finally forced him to break character.

"It's Cavern. My name is Cavern. And you know what? I worked *really* hard on this speech. Could you just let me finish it? We're all here to log some practice hours, you know. It's just like a kid from Protagonist Preparatory to think the story is all about them."

Indira rolled her eyes, then gestured. "Go ahead. Finish up."

The boy took a deep breath and continued. "Dragons are cruel! Long live the king."

There was an awkward silence.

"Is that it?"

He sighed. "That was all of it. You—well, you cut me off right at the end."

"Great," Indira replied. "I think there's been a misunderstanding."

Cavern's eyes narrowed. It took Indira a second to realize that the line she'd spoken sounded a lot like the kind of thing someone might say before a fight scene. Cavern clearly thought she was jumping back into character. He took a step forward and *vanished*.

Before Indira could even react, she caught sight of Cavern standing in Allen's shadow. How had he moved so quickly? The antagonist set an ink-stained hand to Allen's cheek.

"Welcome to my world," Cavern whispered. "Join me, friend."

There was a distant scream. Indira watched in horror as Squalls turned, the dark handprint spreading rapidly over one cheek. A second later, the boy's eyes went lifeless.

Phoenix was conjuring his fire, ready to attack, but Cavern moved with blinding speed. His hand grazed Phoenix's cheek. Her friend went statue still. A spin move brought him around to Gadget next. Indira stared as dark marks spread across each of their cheeks.

He'd left Indira for last, which gave her just enough time to react. She darted to the left of his first lunge. The kingswolf was shouting for Cavern to stop, but Indira saw that the antagonist was locked into the scene. He wasn't going to be reasoned with.

She darted away from a second lunge and brought the butt of her hammer slamming into his back. The shove sent Cavern stumbling off the road.

"Hey!" she shouted at him. "Can you wait just one second? We need to—"

Cavern grinned at her. She watched him set that ink-stained handprint to his own cheek. The dark marks overlapped perfectly. His voice was less than a whisper.

"Serve your master."

All three of Indira's friends turned. Indira's eyes widened as they marched toward her like zombies, hands outstretched. She was so shocked that she dodged a moment too late. Phoenix clutched her tunic. Gadget had her by the elbow. Squalls wrapped around her legs.

The three of them—obeying their new master—worked to pin Indira to the ground. Cavern strode patiently forward and knelt at her side. His smile was a twisted thing.

"Embrace the dark, friend."

His hand grazed her cheek.

Everything went black.

18

An Unlikely Ally

"Indira?"

There were voices in the dark. Indira squinted but couldn't make out anything. She stumbled blindly forward and almost got poked in the eye for her efforts.

"Ouch!" she said. "Sorry. Who's there?"

"We're all here." Phoenix's voice. "What is this place?"

Indira wasn't sure. Her eyes were getting slowly accustomed to the surrounding darkness. It was quite cold wherever they were. The only noise aside from their voices was the howling of an angry wind. She did see a pinpoint of light in the distance, almost like a faded star. It took a moment for her vision to adjust. She was starting to get a feel for the shadows and shapes as she made an effort to pair their outlines with the voices she was hearing.

Squalls groaned. "I told you we were going to die!

Should have guessed it would be a muscular guy in too-tight clothing. It's always a muscular guy in too-tight clothing."

Gadget let out a sudden laugh. "Cavern! I get it now. His name is Cavern."

It was Indira's turn to groan. "And we're in a cave. How very clever of him."

"My powers don't work in here," Phoenix said. "I can't conjure any fire."

Gadget answered, "I'm accessing some of the tutorial files. It took time to get through the firewall on my device, but this says that the Stained use magic that makes the dragons powerless. Which means he's trapped us in here. This place belongs to him. It's his private world. We're cut off from our powers."

"And our real bodies," Indira noted. "You didn't see what happened after he touched each of you. It was like you were his puppet or something. He made all of you attack me."

"Creepy," Gadget replied distractedly. "Anyone else's tutor device working again?"

Indira squinted. The highlighted step in the Hero's Journey was now **TESTS, ALLIES, AND ENEMIES.** The message about the kingswolves had finally faded. For the first time since they'd left town, Indira saw a bright arrow in the center of her vision. It pointed straight toward the distant pinprick of light.

"I think we need to go that way," Indira said. "Come on. Stay close."

It took some maneuvering to make sure everyone was together. Indira felt strange. A little lighter, as if she were more spirit than body in this place. She wasn't sure what kind of magic Cavern had used on them, but she knew they needed to get out of here as soon as possible.

Indira did her best to follow the tutor device's arrow, which had them tripping over jutting stones and nearly walking straight over the edges of unseen cliffs. Cavern's name made more and more sense. A gentle mist floated down from above. The darkness behind them was so terrifyingly complete that Indira shivered at the thought of being trapped here forever.

Almost half an hour later, the pinprick of light solidified. The source grew until they stood in front of four distinct circles, glowing out from the wall of the cave. It was like looking through portholes on a ship. Instead of looking out at an ocean, however, they were seeing . . .

"Look at the angles," Gadget noted. "We're basically looking at our own visions of the world. He's walking us down the road. It's like Indira said. We're puppets."

In each circle, Cavern marched ahead. The four angles provided slightly different views of him. Indira heard a distant and muffled version of the kingswolf's voice too. Indira was trying to think of a plan when Phoenix spoke on her right. "Whoa. Look at us."

She glanced his way. There was enough light being cast from the circles back into the cave that she finally saw what Cavern had done. Phoenix stood there, but he was a ghostly version of himself. He was colorless, a pale outline of the boy she knew so well. Gadget stood a little beyond him and looked just as insubstantial. Indira held her own hand up for inspection. The light from the circles passed through her fingers like fog.

"I told you! We're dead!" Allen complained.

"Not dead," Phoenix corrected. "He captured our spirits. Or maybe our consciousness? Don't you see? Our physical bodies are still out there, following him around. This . . ." He patted his ghostly chest. "This is more like . . . who we are on the inside? There are a lot of spells that focus on the separation of the physical body and the mind. I've just never seen someone who can do a spell this powerful in such a complete way. Pretty cool magic."

Squalls was shaking his head. "Yes. Stealing our souls. Very cool."

Indira looked down at her own body. Everything was insubstantial except for her hammer, which glinted silver in the light. Frowning, she turned back to the shimmering porthole. The surface glittered, and for a moment it reminded her of the length of a mirror.

And that gave her an idea.

"Hey. Gather around. I've got a plan."

It took a minute to get everyone situated. Their ghostly arms were linked, their pale legs braced. Indira had tried this same trick with Phoenix during the fire. It hadn't worked then, but this time would be different. It had to work.

"If I do this the right way, we'll appear back on the road. Try not to make any noise. No gasping. No shouting. Just keep walking straight ahead like a zombie. We can't lose our element of surprise."

She waited for the others to nod before turning back to the circles. She took aim. This time she made sure to throw her hammer at just the right height. She anticipated the heavy tug each of them would have on her as she teleported. The silver hammer spun, colliding with the surface of the nearest porthole view. She was worried it wouldn't work right until the moment the surface trembled, like water disturbed by a stone. Exactly the way the mirror in the Glimpse had worked. Everything blurred.

Indira blinked back to life. She was standing on the road. It was strange to feel the weight of her actual shoulders again. No longer a spirit, but a real person. It took all her concentration to snatch the spinning hammer out of thin air. There was a tug on her limbs as the magic dragged the rest of her crew through. Gentle whispers—no louder than a breeze—confirmed the return of her friends to their bodies. All of them exchanged glances.

Cavern marched ahead, unaware.

It was Indira who set a finger to her lips to silence the wide-eyed kingswolf. It was Indira who quietly gained a few steps on Cavern until she was right behind him. And it was Indira who brought her hammer across his temple, spinning him into unconsciousness.

An hour later, Indira's tutor device was starting to get annoying. It kept telling her—and all the others—to run off into the mountains. Worse, it was taking points away from them every time they disobeyed. This was supposed to be the part of the story where they escaped the bad guy's first attack, counted their lucky stars, and joined the waiting revolution.

But things had changed.

The first order of business had been tying up Cavern while he was knocked out. Gadget had offered a corded wire that looked flimsy, but the girl promised it would work as well as the thickest ropes. When Cavern finally woke up, he found himself thoroughly bound. Gadget had forced a pair of her work gloves over both his hands and even went as far as taping his fingers together so that he couldn't take them off. Cavern narrowed both eyes directly at Indira.

"You won't get away with this," he began. "The Howling King will send more of the Stained. We will not stop until we find every dragon—"

Indira held up a hand. "Look. You gave your speech. Can you let us give ours?"

He leaned back, firelight bright across his face. "Fine."

"The scenario has been interrupted," Indira began. "We arrived at that crossroads and were supposed to be attacked by kingswolves. I assume you were trailing us. We were supposed to fight and defeat the kingswolves in those towers. You would have found them, rallied to the mountains, and hunted us down. Right?"

His eyes tightened. "As if I'd tell you the king's plans!"

Indira groaned. "The king's plans don't matter right now. Didn't you see that gigantic ship back at the crossroads? Didn't you notice the puppies running around?"

She pointed back to their campfire. The remaining kingswolf had shifted into her full wolf form and curled up with all the little golden pups, doing her best to keep them warm in the cold night. "Do those look like kingswolves?" she asked. "Did that pirate ship look like it belonged in the forest?"

Cavern hesitated before shaking his head. "I suppose both are strange."

"Great. Now we're getting somewhere. Gadget?"

Their tech genius stepped forward. She had a tutor device balanced delicately on one finger. "The Plot sisters gave us a few extra devices. I've uploaded our footage," she said. "I know you won't believe us without seeing this for yourself. I'm going to slide it into your left eye, unless you already have a device like this one implanted there?"

He shook his head. "Devices? No, we have demon advisors."

Indira and Gadget exchanged a glance.

"Demon advisors," Gadget repeated. "Right. Well, you

can borrow this one for now. Watch the playback I have cued up for you. It'll give you a good idea of what we're facing."

Cavern looked annoyed but eventually nodded. "Fine."

As gently as possible, Gadget slid the lens into their antagonist's left eye. He braced himself, jaw clenched, like this was clearly an attempt to poison him. Indira watched him blink and guessed the second vision of the device was layering itself over what he saw in their world.

"If you stare long enough at the video, it will . . ."

But she trailed off as Cavern's eyes went wide. Indira guessed that his vision of the forest had vanished, replaced by the footage of their encounter with Joey. She'd just watched the same video, analyzing every angle of the recording. She knew from experience that they would need to know everything they could to beat someone that powerful. When Cavern finished watching, Gadget helped him remove the device.

"See what we're up against?" Indira asked.

"Who was that strangely clothed wizard?"

Indira couldn't help laughing. "We're not sure. We just did our first analysis while you were knocked out. All of us watched that same video. Phoenix, why don't you catch him up?"

Phoenix stepped forward. "We know he's not a part of our scenario. The clothes were the first giveaway. The boat was a second. Not to mention our tutor devices don't even recognize him. He's crashing the tutorial. Finally, we know he's powerful. What he did wasn't exactly magic. Magic leaves traces. It tells a story. When we went back to the boat he summoned, I tried to follow the trail, but it's not an illusion. It's not an enchanted item that he transfigured. It's an actual boat. He pulled a boat out of thin air. We studied this in our history classes. There hasn't been a wizard that powerful in a really long time."

Cavern was nodding. "Perhaps he is ancient? An elder wizard, reborn?"

Indira had slowly been convincing herself of a different answer. There had been one too many worrisome clues: the too-sharp colors, the stunning power, the overall oddness. Indira didn't like where the clues pointed, but that didn't make her conclusion any less likely.

She cleared her throat and offered her own guess. "I think he's an Author."

19

Enemies to Friends

Even if she wasn't completely convinced that Cavern was on their side, Indira knew their best choice was to trust him. It would have been easy to tie Cavern up and leave him behind. But the more she thought about Joey, the more she realized they were going to need all the help they could get. Having someone with Cavern's abilities? If it came to a fight, that cave trick might just come in handy. As Gadget removed the antagonist's bindings, Indira grinned. She didn't think this was a step in the typical Hero's Journey.

Cavern flexed his newly freed hands.

Phoenix leaned close to her and whispered, "Are you sure about this?"

Indira shrugged. "Never hurts to have more firepower."

Cavern actually cracked his neck before grinning at them.

"Tell me. How did you escape the cave? I have always thought that was impossible."

Indira waved her hammer. "I've got a few tricks up my sleeve."

"Magical weapons," he scoffed. "Protagonists always have unfair power-ups."

"Seriously?" Indira asked. "You have a magical cave that traps people's consciousnesses and cuts them off from their bodies and their abilities. Are you really pretending that's not superpowerful?"

"I only have that ability because I traveled through the darkspring for seven—"

Indira shook her head. "Yeah, yeah, yeah. You went into the darkspring—whatever that is—and you came out the other side. This isn't the time for more backstory. There's someone out there wreaking havoc. Now is the time for action. Let's get moving."

It was the middle of the night, but Indira knew they'd be able to follow the road well enough to make up time. She found herself hoping that Joey had stopped some-where to rest. Did Authors sleep the same way characters did? She'd never thought to ask any of her teachers. As they started, she could hear Squalls whisper a question to their new friend.

"Hey. So, as the resident bad guy in the story, you

wouldn't happen to know how I was supposed to die? Is there some kind of accident? Pirate attack? Maybe a flock of rogue owls? Just wondering if your advisors gave you any extra information. . . ."

But Cavern just shook his head. "We were not given plans. I have only my instincts."

"Right," Squalls replied. "Yeah. Makes sense. Sorry to bother you."

Indira couldn't help grinning at that. The group continued walking. It didn't take long for Gadget to prove her usefulness again. She managed to hack into their tutor devices and change some of the operating functions. A few minutes was all it took to coordinate their devices so that now the messages were slightly muted. Notifications kept popping up—most of them instructing Indira to head for the mountains—but they were easier to ignore now.

Phoenix constructed a makeshift torch, lit one end, and handed it to Indira. She thanked him with a smile as they continued to march. The kingswolf did her best to lead the puppies in a ragtag row. Every now and again they'd resort to their designed instincts, going after Allen's ankles, but for the most part they walked along behind the group on their unsteady little legs.

After a while, Joey's trail became easy to follow.

About thirty minutes down the road, Cavern pointed to a distant building. It was not one that Indira and her crew had passed. "I stopped here earlier," he said. "It was a tavern. And it was full of citizens from the neighboring village."

The building was no longer a tavern. It looked more like a bulge growing out of the earth. The doors were reinforced with steel. There were no windows, or people for that matter.

"It kind of looks like a bunker," Gadget said. "You know? Like the military uses . . ."

Indira nodded. "We might want to keep a list of what Joey has summoned. So far we've got a pirate ship and a military bunker. Not sure I see the connection, but let's gather the clues. . . ."

They kept marching. Indira knew everyone must be exhausted, but she could feel it in her gut that they needed to make good time. There was no telling what trouble a rogue Author could cause if no one else knew he'd entered their world. It didn't take long to find more ominous signs.

Indira was thankful that most of the clues were along the roadside. So far Joey hadn't stumbled off toward any of the larger villages. She didn't want to think about what might happen when he encountered more people. That silver lining didn't make the changes they discovered any less disturbing. They found a military-style barracks, followed by a massive treasure chest that was full of onions. That little detail had Cavern cracking up.

"It's funny. Because you are expecting gold. But it's onions. Clever guy."

Eventually, they stumbled across the same carriage they'd crossed paths with earlier. It stood abandoned in the middle of the road, the driver gone. Indira searched the back of the cart and found it empty. Only a colorful bird remained, fluttering from the roof to the driver's seat and squawking unintelligibly. The group was trying to figure out what exactly had happened when Gadget's eyes narrowed.

"Don't you see? It's got the same mustache! That's the driver we met on the road. The one who was going to turn us in. Joey magicked him into a parrot!"

Indira squinted. There was a strange curling line right beneath the parrot's beak. Gadget's eye for detail was impressive. "Fits the theme," Indira agreed. "Pirates have parrots."

The group vowed to help the man—who merely squawked in return. All they could do was keep on moving. The next bend in the road showed off more of Joey's handiwork. Indira led her crew toward the same monument they'd passed the night before. It seemed like that had happened ages ago. Their crew had been in danger ever since.

The great monument that honored all the characters who'd come before them, all the characters who had crossed the threshold in their own famous stories . . .

Phoenix whispered, "He destroyed it."

Destroyed was too small a word. Pieces of stone had scattered in every direction. Joey appeared to have used the monument as target practice. Huge scorch marks overlapped along the center of the road. The famous sword—Excalibur—had been cast aside, warped by the fire. Each of the digital displays had fallen or shattered in what looked like a series of explosions.

Indira was trying to process the destruction when the air around them shivered with movement. There was a bright flash, and Indira turned, her hammer raised.

But it wasn't Joey.

It was the girl with the pigtails. Last night she'd been a projection. Now she appeared before them as a flesh-and-blood character. She took in the sight of their crew. They all watched as she clutched the little dog tightly to her chest and broke into tears.

Indira finally remembered her name. "Dorothy? Are you okay? What happened?"

Her choking sobs made her first responses difficult to understand, but she kept repeating the same sentence until they understood.

"My Story House," she gasped. "He *destroyed* my Story House!"

20

The Broken Journey

Have you ever felt unlucky, dear reader? The one night you didn't do your homework is when your teacher decides to call your name for the answer? Or the candy bars in the vending machine only get stuck when *you* try to buy them? That was how Indira was starting to feel about the world of Imagination. It was almost as if it decided to glitch whenever she was around.

First she'd been the target of an unfinished character disguised as one of the school's trusted brainstorms. Ketty had been using dark magic to force her way back into a story, all while forcing Indira out of it. That adventure had nearly broken the entire city of Fable.

Now she was right in the middle of *another* breakdown.

The province of Plot was clearly under attack. Dorothy from the *Wizard of Oz* was soon joined by dozens of other characters. There was King Arthur, clutching the broken sword to his chest, asking if anyone knew a good local blacksmith. The boy in overalls—Huckleberry Finn—was trying to keep Dorothy calm. She kept clicking a pair of ruby heels together and looking at the sky.

As the noise and chaos grew, Indira decided enough was enough. She found the largest stone chunk from the broken memorial and climbed atop it. Cupping both hands, she shouted.

"Hey! Everyone! Calm *down*. I need everyone to be quiet for a second!"

The swirling mass of characters paused long enough to look her way. She didn't exactly have a plan, but she didn't want to lose the momentum. "Let's figure this out *together*. Dorothy. You were the first one who appeared. Tell us what happened."

Hearing her name, the famous character finally looked up from her glittering red slippers.

"I woke up in my Story House," she replied. "I was going on a little walk through my first scenes—basking in the glow of my adoring fans, as usual—but there was no door. The story had changed. I didn't ever go to Oz. My—well, I stayed in Kansas. I never left."

Huck Finn nodded. "I never took to the river."

"And when I went to pull the sword from the stone," King Arthur added, "I failed."

More characters shared their stories, each with a common thread. The destroyed monument had been a celebration of crossing the threshold. It was the beginning of nearly every character's adventure. Moving on from the ordinary and into a world of unknown. As the noise started growing out of control again, Indira waved for silence.

"Raise your hand if your story changed."

Every single hand went up.

"So none of you actually *went* on the adventure?"

There was a muttered agreement. Indira's mind was racing. She'd thought at first that Joey had simply destroyed the monument. Somehow, though, his powers had echoed deeper than just into the physical stones. He'd actually broken a crucial step in the Hero's Journey. Authors were powerful, she knew, but apparently walking into the world of Imagination increased that power to something dangerous.

"If you can't cross the threshold . . ."

Phoenix was nodding. "No adventures. A whole lot of stories that never begin."

"That makes this puzzle simple to solve," she replied, raising her voice. "There's a rogue Author out there. All we have to do is find him and defeat him. If we can do that, we can return all of this back to normal." She looked around at those gathered. There were centuries of famous protagonists with them now. Joey would regret that. "And with a team of heroes like this? No chance in the world we lose."

Indira leaped down from her makeshift pedestal. She signaled for the rest of her crew to gather their knapsacks and get moving. There was a churning excitement all around them. She'd known the speech would work. Inviting old heroes to fight in a new story? Who could resist?

Every single one of them joined Indira's march. She'd made it about fifty paces down the road, though, when there was a resounding pop. She flinched as more pops followed the first. Turning, she watched the characters vanish one by one, expressions full of terror.

They were not gone for long. Back at the monument, the characters reappeared. Indira started jogging toward them.

"I don't understand. What's happening?"

Huck Finn called back, "Hey! S'pose I give another direction a try."

He turned the opposite way and sprinted downhill. As he reached about the same distance, another pop split the air. Huck vanished, only to appear right beside the monument yet again. "Well, ain't that somethin'," he said with a frown.

"We're *stuck*!" Dorothy groaned. "On a road. And it's not even a *pretty* road."

King Arthur collapsed dramatically, tossing his sword onto the ground like a broken toy. He lowered his face into his hands. "All my kingdom," he wept. "Reduced to this."

Indira tried to put on a brave face. "Hey! We're going to fix this. My crew and I can go. We'll find the Author and we'll fix this. Don't worry! We'll be back."

"Wait! Peasant!" King Arthur stumbled to his feet. Indira resented the term *peasant,* but Arthur looked so desperate that she said nothing. He lowered his voice so only she could hear. "If a deal must be made with this dastardly foe, consider freeing me first. I'm a king, after all."

Indira resisted knocking him on the side of his armored head. "Unbelievable." She made an effort to look past him and at the other characters. "We're going to fix this! I promise!"

Turning, she marched back to join her crew. Gadget and Allen watched her carefully. Even Cavern was looking at her with something close to respect.

Phoenix whispered, "So, what's the plan?"

"No idea," Indira admitted. "But step one is finding Joey. Gadget, can you get that carriage back there working?" The girl nodded. "Good. Let's start moving."

If they wanted to save Plot, there was no other option.

It was time to fix the world of Imagination. Again.

Different Kinds of Bravery

Gadget had the borrowed carriage up and running in no time. Unlike their stolen carriage, it was not designed to fail halfway through the trip. The batteries still had plenty of charge.

At first the transformed parrot wasn't eager to leave his vehicle. It took some effort to get him to flap out of the driver's seat and back onto one of the shattered stones of the monument.

Their kingswolf ally agreed to stay behind with the trapped protagonists. Indira was glad to have something of a base. The magic of Imagination was fickle. It was possible the characters might disappear again, or worse. And they'd need someone who knew what was happening to report. It also helped that the puppies would remain there. Indira thought their presence would lighten the mood and keep the trapped characters from going stir-crazy.

A few minutes later, Gadget had them moving. The voices died away. Now it was just the whipping of the wind in their faces and the roar of the engine beneath them. Indira told the others to be ready for battle. All the clues were leading down the main road. It wasn't hard to figure out where Joey was heading. Indira just hoped they'd catch up to him before he got his hands on the town of Ordinary and all the characters there.

When they reached the farming outskirts, Gadget slowed the carriage to a stop. It was agreed that they should leave the vehicle in a safe location and approach on foot. Easier to keep the element of surprise that way. Everyone climbed down, except for Allen.

"I want to go back to the monument."

Indira shook her head. "Back at the monument, you said you didn't want to be left behind. . . ."

He nodded nervously. "That's because I thought maybe there'd be a secret attack on the monument, and I'd be the guy who got left behind . . . but now I'm thinking I'm the one who gets blasted as soon as we enter the city. You know? Sacrificial death. Lets all of you know where the bad guy is hiding or whatever. . . ."

Indira was about to say something when Phoenix spoke. His voice was steady.

"Hey, Squalls. I've been thinking about something."

All the nervous muttering died away. Phoenix waited

until Allen looked at him. Not with fear, for once, but with curiosity. "About what?" he asked.

"All this time," Phoenix said patiently, "you could have just run away. Right?"

Squalls shrugged. "I mean . . . I guess . . ."

"You could have left," Phoenix confirmed. "Fable is to the south. All you would have had to do was start walking away. But I noticed . . . you're still here. You stuck with us. You kept going. You never left. Do you know what I call that?"

Squalls considered his answer. "Lack of awareness of my options?"

"Bravery," Phoenix corrected. "I call it bravery. You can go back to the monument if you want. None of us will stop you. You can even head back to Fable. But I have a feeling we're about to face something really powerful. And I'd feel a whole lot better if you were with us."

Indira watched Phoenix nod once to the boy before turning and walking away, as if he was certain that Squalls planned on joining them. Allen took a deep breath before sliding out of the carriage. He didn't say anything. No one else spoke either. But he walked beside them like there had never been any thought of leaving. Indira caught Phoenix's eye and winked at him. He was pretty good at finding the best in each of them. She liked that.

The group doubled back to the road and nearly ran right into yet *another* person. Indira gasped at the sight. The figure was barely standing. It took Indira a second to recognize the old-fashioned business jacket. "Minerva? Are you all right?"

She swept forward just in time to catch her pretend mother. The catch was a little awkward, and she did her best to ease the woman safely to the ground. They sat there in a heap as the others gathered around. Indira had a feeling this wasn't a part of the scenario either.

"Don't go," Minerva gasped. "Too dangerous."

Fear cut through Indira. Her words confirmed the worst. Joey had arrived.

"Tell us what happened."

Minerva shook her head. "Something wrong about him. He wasn't—he didn't follow any of the normal rules. None of the guards could stop him. He was too powerful."

Indira nodded. "He's not from our scenario. That's why we came back. We're here to stop him."

"Wait." Minerva shook herself. "No. Wait a minute. There's a protocol. If an outside force interferes with the scenario, there's a protocol for reporting it back to the Editors. I thought he was just an antagonist getting carried away. You're sure he's crashing the scenario?"

Indira and the others nodded.

"Come on, then." Minerva struggled to her feet. "I know where to go."

22

The Editor Hotline

Following Minerva proved difficult. She was almost too weak to walk. Indira roped one arm around the woman and they made their way together. Minerva directed them to an abandoned barn at the southeastern end of the valley. There were massive gaps in the siding, and the paint was peeling from every surface. Minerva led them up to the front door—which barely hung on its hinges—and knocked a distinct pattern.

Her touch rippled along the very fabric of the building. Indira stared as the wooden panels warped and twisted. The entire building shrank down, kicking up great puffs of dust, and reshaped itself into a polished wooden desk. Minerva sat down in the lone chair that appeared. Indira thought it was an odd sight, an office desk like this out in the middle of a cow pasture.

Minerva picked up a phone and dialed. She tapped a button to switch the setting to speaker, and all of them listened as the call went through. There was a brief click, then the sound of someone rummaging in the faraway background, followed by an incredibly bored voice.

"This is the Editor Hotline. How may I direct your call?"

Minerva spoke. "Hi. I'm out here with the Hero's Journey tutorial in the southern province located in Plot. Identification number is 91719. We're encountering some outside interference from an individual known to us as Joey. He is not assigned to our scenario. We are requesting assistance. The unwelcome party has taken over the starting town."

There was a loud thump. Indira thought she heard a trace of excitement in the voice now.

"I'm sorry, but did you say someone *took over* the starting town?"

"Yes," Minerva answered. "Our scenario does have a climactic scene involving the starting town, but this individual is from outside the scenario. I repeat: we require assistance."

The person on the other end of the line squealed. "That's a Plot Twist violation! This is seriously the best thing that's happened all day. What is your location?"

Minerva frowned at the idea that this could be the best part of anyone's day.

"Sorry, but is there a supervisor we could talk to?"

"I mean, sure, if you want some big shot to put your request on a stack of other files they might not get to right away," the voice answered. "But if you want results, you're talking to the right girl. Coordinates, please."

Minerva sighed. "We're just to the east of Ordinary."

Their assisting Editor couldn't keep the excitement out of her voice now.

"And that's the town in question?"

"Yes," Minerva answered. "He's taken it captive."

Indira couldn't help thinking there was something familiar about the conversation. There was the slightest touch of déjà vu about it. "I'm scanning your area now," the voice said. "And . . ."

There was another loud squeal of delight. Indira startled. She *knew* that noise.

"I'm seeing some serious fluctuations," the voice said giddily. "The first spike was recorded two days ago, with steady growth since then. Definitely an imminent threat. This is so legit. . . ."

Indira couldn't stay quiet. She knew the voice, the mannerisms, everything.

"Maxi?"

There was a brief pause. "Sorry? What was that? I don't think I ever identified myself—"

"Maxi? Is that you?!"

There was another explosive squeal. "*Indira?* What in

the worlds? Are you—oh! You got assigned to a tutorial. You were telling me about it before you left! Is Phoenix there too?"

He sighed. "Hi, Maxi."

Maxi burst into laughter. "Best. Day. Ever!"

"Um, excuse me," Minerva cut back in. "You used the phrase *imminent threat.* As in we're all in danger. Right now. Is that correct?"

Indira could imagine Maxi with a headset on, one eyebrow raised.

"Imminent threat," she repeated. "Right. I'll report this straight to the higher-ups. Could you do me a favor and describe what's happened so far? I'll need everything documented."

The group patiently filled Maxi in on the last few days. Minerva—who'd only seen a brief glimpse of Joey—was shocked as Indira recounted their own introduction. When she added her educated guess that Joey was a rogue Author, her pretend mother shook her head in disbelief.

Maxi finished her notes before replying. "Got it," she said. "Hmm. Now, we might have a *teensy* problem. Let me look something up right quick. It'll be just a second." Indira heard her rummaging through her desk space. "This department still hasn't heard of databases, apparently. So I've gotta search through this massive law book with its dusty pages. The worst."

Phoenix and Indira exchanged a glance, half smiling. She hadn't realized how much she'd missed Maxi.

"Okay," Maxi said, thinking out loud. "So we want to look at intervention policies. Hmm. This falls under the category of *in-world heroes*. And here we go. . . ." Maxi made a thoughtful noise, and Indira could almost see her tracing a finger down the length of the page. "Ah. I hate when I'm right. So here's the sitch, Indira. You are known as an in-world hero. That means you're not *just* a protagonist in a story. You've actually taken on heroic status here, in the world of Imagination."

Indira's cheeks went bright red. She avoided the stares she was getting from the others.

"Sure, so what?"

"So that changes the rules," Maxi replied. "Do you remember last year?"

Indira almost laughed. "Do I *remember* last year? Maxi. We were involved in a dark plot that almost destroyed the entire city of Fable. Of course I remember last year!"

"Sass!" Maxi exclaimed. "I love you with a little bit of attitude. Keep that going, girl! But that's not what I meant. Last year, we called the Editors, right? Remember they gave us a full day to figure it out ourselves? That protocol is built into the way Imagination works. The whole goal is to give characters a chance to learn how to be heroes, blah blah blah. . . ."

Indira nodded. "Got it. So we just have to survive for

one day. That shouldn't be a problem. We'll do what we can to contain Joey until you get here. Is that all?"

"See, that's the thing," Maxi answered. "It's a week now. You have to survive for a *week*."

Indira's mouth opened, but no words formed. Her brain felt scrambled. An entire week? That didn't make any sense. The others were looking nervously between her and the phone.

"Hello?" Maxi asked. "You still there? These hotline phones are the worst. . . ."

Minerva jumped in. "Still here. Sorry. I think we're all a little shocked. Why would it take the Editors a week to get here? I thought you just said the rule was one day."

"That's the catch," Maxi said. "It's a one-day protocol for *first-time* heroes. Indira's already done this before. That extends the policy to seven days. She's proven herself, or whatever, so the world of Imagination trusts her enough to give her even more time to solve things this round."

Indira finally found her voice. "Seven days is forever, Maxi. This is a serious situation. We've got an Author wreaking havoc. He already destroyed a crucial part of the Hero's Journey. Characters are literally being pulled out of their Story Houses. There has to be some way to get around the policy."

"Girl, I got you," Maxi replied. "I'm going to fast-track all the paperwork. And we'll keep an open line of communication. But for right now? That's our policy. I've been with the Editors for a few months now. It's all rules all the times, girl. Trust me. They're not going to override their precious policies, but there are a few ways I can help."

Indira sagged until she was leaning fully against the desk to stay upright. This was unthinkable. Joey was out there ruining Plot. He'd already disrupted one of the most famous story styles in history. If he did more damage now, it would all be her fault.

Seven full days.

How bad could things get before the Editors showed up?

"First, I'm going to run a comprehensive check," Maxi was saying. "I'll search the database for Authors named Joey, narrow it down with his general age, narrow that down with kids who play lacrosse, and then with kids who are number twenty-three. If you can get any more specifics, that'd be great. For now, I'll work with that and get as much dirt on him as possible."

Maxi took a deep breath before forging on.

"While I do that, you can do some reconnaissance. I'm going to need an exact location, a report of what he's been doing, and a report on current damage levels. Oh, and Indira, I know you. You're going to want to take this guy head-on, but it makes the most sense to combine what we all find out and *then* form a plan of attack. Got it?"

Indira felt the slightest annoyance at how right Maxi was. She had definitely been planning on rushing into battle at the first chance. She took a deep breath. It was a good reminder of why Underglass had assigned her this tutorial in the first place. Learning to trust her team. She looked around at her crew before nodding.

"Got it," she replied. "We'll start our investigation."

"This is so *fun*," Maxi squealed. "I've been dealing with boring stuff all day."

Phoenix shook his head. "The world of Imagination is in danger, Maxi."

"It is! And here we are to save it *again*. No big deal. Go, *us*."

He couldn't help grinning at Indira. Clearly they'd both missed Maxi.

Minerva—the only adult in the group—did her best to follow up on details and logistics. Maxi gave her the number for her direct line, assured their group that the case would be given a high-priority status, and even put in some requests for extra resources.

"We can't intervene," Maxi was saying. "But I'll see if some of the other organizations in Fable can send anything helpful your way. It might take me some time, though."

"Thanks, Maxi," Indira said. "We're going to get to work over here."

There was an excited hoot and then the phone went dead. Indira smiled. It was classic Maxi. Indira knew from experience that her friend would do everything in her power. But an uncomfortable feeling still sat in Indira's gut. Even with Maxi's help, seven days was a long time. It would be hard to contain someone as powerful as Joey for that long.

If only there were some way to distract him. . . .

"Minerva." Phoenix's voice interrupted her thoughts. "What can you tell us about Ordinary? Are there any secret ways into the town?"

Indira's fake mother offered a smile. "I've been running this tutorial for years. I know every inch of Ordinary, including what's beneath it. How do you think I got out?"

The rest of the crew grinned back.

It was time for some spying.

The Plot Underground

"Well, that will make spying a little harder."

Allen Squalls was pointing out the obvious, but that didn't make him wrong. They'd finally gotten a look at the town of Ordinary in the distance. It was standing right where they'd left it, but it was no longer standing *how* they'd left it. The outer wall had risen about thirty feet and Indira thought it looked larger somehow, with even more buildings than before.

That wasn't the only change. Two flags flew on opposite ends of the town. One was a classic skull and crossbones, a pirate flag. The second flag was harder to identify. Phoenix made a guess. "I'd bet it's military," he said. "There was a bunker back there. A barracks, too. Pretty sure that's what the other flag means. . . ."

Indira felt a little twisting in her gut. It was hard to

plan for someone with powers that felt as limitless as Joey's. He could change things with a snap of his fingers, and those powers didn't show any signs of slowing down. He'd transformed the entire town. Indira was scared of what they might find inside those walls. Luckily, their crew had a few tricks up their sleeves. As they circled around to discuss their plan to infiltrate the city, Gadget smacked herself on the forehead.

"The bees! Of course! The bees!"

Indira's eyes widened. "You still have access to them? We could monitor the whole town. . . ."

Gadget rolled back one sleeve to reveal a little data pad looped around one wrist. "If I had all three of them? Definitely. I'll have to reprogram the other two."

Indira winced. "Sorry about that."

"It's fine," Gadget replied, focusing on her task. "Remember? I need some of your instinct. You need some of my research and planning. I'm going to establish a new route for them around the town with new objectives. I think we'll be able to get some good data."

"But doesn't the data feed back to your dad's workshop?" Phoenix asked.

Gadget nodded. "It's synced with a device that analyzes all the information. It's kind of like a computer. If you can smuggle it out of the town, we can monitor everything without having to face Joey directly. We can even listen in on his conversations."

Indira looked to Minerva now. "I can't ask you to lead

us into the town. Not in your condition. It's dangerous. Can you map out the way through the underground you mentioned?"

Minerva frowned. "It's complicated. There's a town beneath the town. It'd be best if I go with you. I'm really fine, I promise. . . ."

But Indira could see what a struggle it was for Minerva to remain standing. She was about to ask for a piece of paper for Minerva to sketch out a rough map when another voice interrupted. Their whole crew just about jumped out of their skin as a familiar young girl joined their circle. Beginning grinned like she'd been there the whole time.

"Don't worry, I know the way."

Half an hour later, Indira found herself crawling inside a huge pipe. Thankfully, the secret route wasn't a sewage pipe, but it didn't exactly smell like roses, either. Beginning crawled in front of them, leading her chosen crew down the route that Minerva could not.

Indira had drafted Cavern and Phoenix to come with her. Gadget stayed behind to reprogram the bees. She was more important to them safe and sound in the forest. Even with his recent boost in confidence, it was easy to convince Squalls that he should remain behind as well. Indira thought it made sense to separate their wizarding powers, just in case. He promised to summon a little rain in an effort to cover their movement in the city.

"Squalls seems to be doing a little better," Indira whispered to Phoenix as they continued crawling. "More confident now. You've done a great job helping him."

Phoenix grunted. "Thanks. I've been running him through a few drills, too. His magic . . . it's like he's separated from his powers. That's why he keeps nodding off. It's almost this hidden part of him that has to wake up, while the scared part of him falls asleep."

"Is that normal?"

"No," Phoenix answered. "It's not. I'm pretty sure it's the result of what Brainstorm Ketty did. She broke him last year. Bullied him into thinking he'd never be a good character. It will take a little time to get him back to who he was. If he regains his confidence, he'll regain his control over it. . . ."

"So it can be fixed?"

Phoenix nodded again. "Of course. He's going to be really powerful, too. You've seen some of his magic. Imagine how he must have been when he first came to Protagonist Prep with power like that. I doubt he was the kid we know, always so nervous about everything."

Indira tried to imagine that and couldn't.

"If there's anything I can do to help, just let me know."

Phoenix's eyes were like little rings of light in the otherwise dark passage.

"Keep believing in him. The way you believed in me. He'll come around."

Ahead of them, Beginning was lowering herself out of the pipe. Indira was not ready for the sight that greeted her at the tunnel's end. She'd been expecting some kind of abandoned underground. Instead, it was buzzing with life. Lanterns glowed in every direction. Huge factories stretched as far as the eye could see. Indira saw Marks moving in and out of the buildings, their voices chorusing with the constant machine noises.

Cavern and Phoenix leaped down, shaking the platform. Cavern's eyes went wide.

"What is this place?" he asked.

Beginning favored him with a smile. "Wonderful, is it not? Fable and Fester train characters, but Plot gives birth to the actual stories and journeys those characters go on. What you saw on the surface? That's more of a pretty costume than anything. Down here is where the real magic happens. In Plot, we like to say that it's all about the details. Come on, I'll show you what I can as we head to Minerva's tunnel."

The grinning girl led them forward. Seeing all the workers, Indira couldn't help asking the obvious question that came to mind. "Should we tell them there's an emergency? Joey took over the town right above them! Maybe there should be a temporary evacuation?"

Beginning shrugged. "The enemy is a relatively young Author. I suspect he'll have a hard time making his way this deep into Plot. Don't get me wrong. Any Author who enters the world of Imagination is *powerful*. But this particular area is less about power and more about experience.

Joey is likely to do his damage to the most basic elements of our world, which is no less frightening.

"Besides, this place is very well hidden. And an evacuation would set back production. These crews are fueling every single story that's currently being written in the Real World. Can you imagine all the Authors out there suddenly not knowing where their story should go?"

She let that question linger in the air.

"Ah! Here's our World-Building building. Say that three times fast!"

The crew sidestepped a few Marks who were taking a water break. The front entrance of the nearest building confirmed the name of the factory in bright letters. Beginning opened the door wide enough for all of them to get a glimpse inside. A huge conveyor belt was churning through the main section of the building. Indira squinted.

"Are those . . ."

"We're currently making a batch of dystopian societies!" Beginning confirmed. "We ship them to the Authors in miniature form."

Sure enough, each of the little squares contained a perfectly scaled miniature world. Indira couldn't believe what she was seeing. There were futuristic space stations, abandoned planets, ghostly small towns. Each one had been reduced to about the size of a microwave.

Beginning explained, "This factory is responsible for every dystopia that's ever existed. Societies run by massive spiders. Communities controlled by genetic code. There was even one society that forced teenagers to fight to the death because of food!"

Cavern shook his head. "How barbaric."

Beginning ushered them out. Indira followed her down catwalks, ducking to avoid a sudden burst of steam from one building. A turn brought them around to the front of a smaller factory. Indira noticed that the building was strangely designed, its sides narrowing like an hourglass halfway up.

"What's that one?" Phoenix asked.

"Plot Twist," Beginning answered. "Always working overtime in there. The current crew are the ones who came up with He Was Dead the Whole Time. It was an instant classic."

As they approached the center of the massive underground city, the noise became deafening. Indira saw signs for the FLASHBACK FACTORY, the RED HERRING REDISTRIBUTION CENTER, and an entire building dedicated to POETIC JUSTICE. Hundreds of questions came to mind, but she left them unasked. As curious as she felt, she realized her job was waiting for her in Ordinary.

She needed to stay focused.

Beginning seemed to sense her urgency. The young girl dropped the tour-guide act and quickened the pace. Indira was thankful she'd come, as the winding route would have certainly been difficult with just a map. Eventually, they passed through the main section of factories and out the other side. Beginning led them up a final catwalk before gesturing to a latched gateway.

"This leads to Ordinary," she announced. "I wish you luck."

Indira frowned. "You aren't going with us?"

The girl shook her head. "It's far too risky."

Phoenix snorted at that. Indira understood how he felt. It was risky for *all* of them. She kind of thought the person who ruled over Plot would be willing to go with them at least.

"We know it's risky," Indira pointed out. "But we're still going."

Beginning frowned. "Perhaps I have been unclear. I do not mean that I fear for my own personal health. It's the same reason you did not see Middle when this rogue Author first appeared. She did not want to take the risk either. Sometimes our appearance can be deceptive. It is easy to think of me as a child. But do not be fooled. I am as old as time itself. I am the first line in every story ever told. I am the opening image. I am the sound of pages turning, the quiet sigh that can be heard whenever someone sets their feet in a new world. I am BEGINNING."

That word echoed louder than even the distant machine noise.

"Our mutual enemy has already broken steps in the Hero's Journey," Beginning reminded Indira. "His dark magic has tainted hundreds of stories. Middle and End have already suffered significant injuries because of it.

Can you imagine, though, if he found me? The beginning of all? No, I cannot risk entering the city."

Indira took a deep breath. "But we can."

Beginning grinned. "Precisely. Onward, my champions."

They weren't going to get a better pep talk than that. Taking a deep breath, Indira worked the entry hatch open. A ladder was waiting. She exchanged nods with Phoenix and Cavern, and started the ascent.

24

The New Scenario

As she climbed, Indira repeated Maxi's advice. Every bone in her body wanted to take on the threat directly. She didn't want anyone else to get hurt, anything else to break. Beginning's fear only confirmed the danger that Joey posed to their world. But she knew Maxi was right. It would be best to combine their strengths, make a plan, and face him together.

Above, slats in the ceiling cast little slashes of light along the upper walls of the tunnel. They'd arrived. Indira reached up and gave the hatch a healthy shove. It swung upward and then hit something with a resounding bang. All three of them froze.

"Nice stealth," Cavern hissed.

No one moved for a full minute. When no response came — and it seemed as if the noise had gone unnoticed —

Indira pulled herself carefully into a dimly lit basement. Another stairwell led up the opposite wall. She couldn't tell if they'd arrived in a business or a home. It struck her that she'd forgotten to ask Minerva.

Indira turned to help Phoenix. Instinctively, she reached for Cavern next. His skin grazed hers, and the lights in the room vanished. Indira felt the sudden gusting of a cold and violent wind . . .

. . . before blinking back into the basement.

"I'm so sorry!" Cavern was saying. "I forgot! I marked you earlier. You've been inside the cave. All it takes now is a touch to pull you back. I'll be more careful next time."

The room was spinning a little. Indira shook herself.

"Marked me? So creepy. When we're done with this, you're going to do whatever it takes to remove that. Come on. Let's keep moving."

Up the flight of stairs they went, through a creaking door, and out into what appeared to be a sitting room. Indira's eyes were still adjusting to the light when she realized where they were.

"Of course!" she said. "This is my house."

As if to confirm the statement, Indira's pet chicken came marching out of the next room, clucking at them. The creature strutted forward and pecked her hand affectionately.

"You have a chicken?" Cavern asked.

"His name is Peck."

Cavern barely heard her as he walked around the spacious room, eyeing the decorations. "And you live here?"

"Just for the scenario," Indira explained. "This was my assigned home."

"It's so nice," he replied. "I was assigned to live in a dark cocoon."

Indira decided not to ask any follow-up questions to that. "Let's keep the lights off for right now. And be careful looking out the windows. I don't want to give Joey any reason to notice us."

Outside, the rain was coming down hard. It wasn't exactly dark, but the absence of the sun definitely cast a grayness over everything. Phoenix made his way over to the nearest window and glanced outside. "Just an alleyway," he announced. "Where's the front door, Indira?"

Peck lifted his head and darted toward the front of the house.

"Follow the chicken," Indira suggested.

All three of them crept down the hallway and crowded around the front entrance. Glass panes ran down both sides of the door, and Indira edged out far enough so that she could spy on the street without being seen. The sight left her breathless.

"How long were we in the tunnels?"

Phoenix gasped. "What was Squalls thinking?"

The entire street was flooded. Thankfully, Indira's house was slightly elevated. That morning she'd descended a stoop to get down to street level. It had likely saved the house from what was outside. Every street and alleyway had been transformed into a canal. Indira even noticed a pair of neighbors, farther down the street, gliding away in some kind of motorized boat.

Cavern's voice sounded doubtful. "It could not have rained this much."

"Are you sure?" Indira asked.

"We weren't in the dark for long. Even torrential rains wouldn't cause such flooding."

Something else caught Indira's eye. Down at the bottom of her house's entryway, a small boat was tied to one of the handrails. Indira didn't remember it being there the first day.

"Why would we even have a boat?" she asked herself.

Phoenix glanced over. "What?"

She pointed. "That boat right there. This town isn't near a lake or an ocean. Why would there be a boat tied to the front of our house? There were people down the road in a boat too."

"You're right. It doesn't make any sense," Phoenix said. "Which means it connects back to Joey. Anything that doesn't fit the scenario has his handwriting all over it. I mean, if he can make the outer walls higher, he's powerful enough to turn the streets into canals."

Indira shook her head. "But what's the point? Why canals?"

Cavern let out an annoyed noise. "Is that what you

good guys spend all your time doing? Talking about every little detail? No wonder our books take so long. Come on."

He opened the door and crept out onto the stoop. Indira and Phoenix followed, pulling their cloaks tighter as the rain started to soak them from above. Peck darted out ahead of them and leaped into the boat. Indira's eyes traced up and down the street that had been transformed into a canal. It looked empty for now.

Cavern gestured to the chicken. "Not exactly a stealthy animal."

"We can't just leave him," Indira replied.

Cavern nodded. "You're right. He might be a valuable food resource."

Indira shot him a scandalized look. "You don't *eat* the lovable pet. That's like the most basic rule of Sympathetic Characters. What's wrong with you?"

He shrugged. "I'm usually the bad guy."

Luckily, the waiting boat was big enough for all four of them. Indira climbed in and forced Peck to the front of the boat, carefully away from Cavern. The boat came with more surprises. Instead of the typical control system she'd expected to find . . .

"Is that a video-game controller?" Indira asked.

A black cord connected the handheld controller to the central console. Phoenix picked up the controller like it was second nature. "Speaking of Sympathetic Characters class, I did a whole side project on video games last year.

It was my choice for the 'skill readers can identify with.' Let me take a look. Pretty sure I can figure it out."

He eyed the buttons for a second before jamming his finger down on a brightly colored *B*. Their boat lurched forward so quickly that Indira almost went toppling over the side. Cavern caught her—barely avoiding skin-to-skin contact—and the two of them settled back into their seats as Phoenix guided them out over the water.

In any other situation, Indira would have thought this was pretty cool. They were in a town with canals for streets, driving a boat using a video-game controller. It was harder to enjoy when she knew each new detail led back to such a dangerous source.

Joey was here somewhere. She shivered as their boat picked up speed. Phoenix guided them to the far right side of the road, carefully moving them into the shadows of the nearest buildings. Every few seconds, Indira thought she spied movement down adjacent streets or back alleys, but no other boats appeared.

When they reached the end of the road, Indira remembered this was the same route she'd taken to school a few mornings before. She'd made the same turn, walked up the street, and bumped right into Ledge Woods. She wondered if he was still here somewhere.

Phoenix slowed the boat down, idling it against the nearest building before making the turn. Their position offered them a view of the main strip. There were a few boats, but they looked like they were well down the road.

For the first time inside the city, Indira heard cannons firing.

"What is he doing to them?" she asked nervously.

"I don't know," Phoenix whispered back. "But let's focus on the mission for now. Get to the workshop. Get Gadget's recording device. Get out."

Indira nodded. "Do you think we can cross without being seen?"

Phoenix watched the distant movement. When one of the final boats rounded a corner, he punched the accelerator again. Their boat darted forward like a fish, stuttering only slightly before picking up speed. "Which building is it?" he asked.

"The fourth one. Up ahead. Go into the alley there."

There were shouts behind them, but Indira thought they sounded distant. A glance back showed an empty waterway. Phoenix nosed them around a half-drowned oak tree before slipping into the quiet of the workshop's alleyway.

When Indira had passed it the first time, the shop had been busy with customers and shopkeepers, all dancing around a slew of whizzing inventions. Now the front doors were shut and the entire store appeared unlit. Indira tried to glance through the windows, but all she could see was the reflected thunderheads above. It was still raining lightly.

"The window there." Cavern pointed. "I think even I can fit through it."

Indira had forgotten how massive their antagonist ally was. She squinted before nodding. "I think so too. Stop right there, Phoenix. We'll have to tie up the boat."

Peck squawked a little. Indira reached out and stroked the bird's head gently as the nervous seconds stretched. Phoenix idled against the wall nearest the window, killed the engines, and reached for the same rope that had been used to tie the boat to her house's stoop.

Fresh cannon fire shook the buildings a few streets away. Closer this time. Indira could only guess what kind of mayhem Joey was creating. It was a small relief to remember that any town resident who was hurt badly enough would reappear back at the Ninth Hearth.

At least no one would die for real.

Cavern let out a little grunt as he pried the stubborn window open. It groaned, but the sound of the rain was louder. It was a tight squeeze, but Cavern managed to wedge himself inside. Indira was impressed by the soundless descent he made entering the building. She did her best to channel the same stealth. It took some effort to twist her body and land lightly at the same time.

The drop was surprisingly short. Just a few feet. New smells and sounds greeted her. Some kind of shaved-wood scent. The echo of silence. Cavern helped Phoenix inside. Indira stared at him for a second. "Where's the bird?"

He stared at her. "In the boat?"

She glanced back out the window. To her surprise,

Peck had curled up in the very front of the boat. She shot Phoenix a look. "If we lose him, it'll be your fault."

"If we lose him, that means we lost the boat. We'll have bigger problems if that happens."

Cavern hissed at them. "Quit wasting time. Where's this device?"

The window had dropped them on a landing inside the workshop. It was the turning point in a set of stairs. The staircase on their right led down, and the one on the left led up. Indira considered both options before remembering what Gadget had said the day they first arrived.

"She lives above the workshop. This way."

Phoenix gestured. "There's a switch here. We could use a little light."

Before Indira could protest, Phoenix shoved the massive switch upward. A blast of noise and light thundered around them. Their jaws dropped as the entire workshop came to life. Circuits fired; engines spun. She watched an electric train begin chugging around a track. Some kind of espresso machine huffed smoke as it poured a steaming mug of coffee. Little helicopters buzzed into the air, circling the room.

Indira snapped, "Shut it off!"

Phoenix slammed the switch back down. Most of the room went quiet, the lights flickering out, but the remaining charge forced a few of the devices to finish whatever action they'd been performing.

"Move." Indira shoved Phoenix up the stairs. "Now."

Cavern led the way. Indira was blinking—still blinded by the flash of lights—but Cavern seemed unaffected. He marched down a hallway, checking doors as he went.

"How can you see anything?" Indira hissed.

"I've been through the darkspring," he replied. "It gifted me with night vision."

Indira raised an eyebrow. That could be useful. For now they needed to move quickly. Phoenix's mistake would definitely draw attention to this building. She was dead certain that the thunderous noise—however brief— had been loud enough to turn some heads.

Cavern opened a final room. "Ah. Your scientist lives here."

He was right. Indira saw abandoned projects and half-finished sketches. All the devices would have fit Gadget's personality well. "Okay. The computer is inside a brief-case. Gadget said it has a brown handle that's slightly faded."

All three of them spread out. Cavern went for the closet. Phoenix headed straight for a distant bookshelf. Indira searched a pair of nightstands before checking under the bed. It reminded her of searching through Brainstorm Ketty's house with Maxi last year. That had been her first taste of real detective work. It had also gotten her into trouble with the Grammar Police.

She coughed, trying to fight off the swirling dust, when Cavern made a satisfied noise.

"Found it."

He turned to them, holding up a brown briefcase. Indira saw the edge of a computer sticking out of one corner. "Nicely done. Let's get—"

A burst of light.

Indira flinched. All the thunderous noises downstairs clicked to life again. Someone had turned the switch back on. Footsteps sounded too. An intruder was approaching. Cavern tightened his grip on the briefcase. Indira lifted her hammer expectantly. She watched a gloved hand push open the door.

It wasn't Joey. It was Ledge Woods.

His eyes widened. "What are you doing here? Are you out of your minds?"

Indira could only stare. It wasn't the same aggressive tone he'd used before. Ledge stared at her like she had three eyes, then caught sight of Cavern standing in the corner.

"Cavern? You're here *with* them?"

The giant antagonist waved. "What's up, Ledge?"

Ledge looked on the verge of a panic attack. "I don't know how you got into the city, but you need to get out now. He's coming. He's coming here! I'll do my best to stall him."

"Wait," Indira said as Ledge turned. "Tell us what's happening. We need to know as much as we can about what Joey's been doing."

Cannon fire boomed outside. Indira thought she could

hear the faint sound of laughter. Ledge actually shivered. "It's a game. He took over the town. I don't know. It's strange. He makes us fight. We're either marines or pirates. And he just keeps making us play the same game over and over again." Another boom sounded. "You need to leave now! Get help!"

Indira nodded, storing that information. The group descended the stairs together. Ledge had thrown the same switch that Phoenix had as a diversion. The entire workshop hummed with life. When they reached the landing, Indira saw movement near the front entrance.

A voice called from outside. "Come out, come out, wherever you are!"

Ledge whispered, "He thinks I'm his scout. Hurry up. Get back in your boat and go!"

Indira thanked him. Cavern went first, wedging himself up and out. Phoenix went next. Indira hadn't exactly liked Ledge earlier that day, but at least he was helping them now.

She felt bad leaving him.

"Come with us," she whispered. "It would help to have someone who was on the inside."

He took a deep breath. "Fine. Just hurry up. I'll come with you."

Indira nodded, pulling herself through the open window. Phoenix helped her silently into the boat. Peck gave a happy shake of feathers seeing her, but thankfully didn't make more noise.

Indira turned back to help Ledge.

But the window was closed. She frowned. Ledge Woods was grinning out at her.

That was her only warning.

A pair of boats floated into sight at the back end of the alleyway, cutting them off. Phoenix reached for the controller and started up the engine, but a third boat appeared on the main street. It was a superior model to the one they'd commandeered, and captained by a very familiar figure.

Joey had found them.

An Unexpected Rescue

The rogue Author's clothing had changed.

Gone were the navy-blue jersey and shorts, replaced by some kind of military battle armor. Indira thought he looked a little ridiculous, like a toddler trying to walk around in his parent's shoes. Even with the wardrobe change, he was still wielding the lacrosse stick from their first meeting. Indira's eyes narrowed on it. That had to be the source of his power.

Joey laughed obnoxiously. "Told you, Ledge!" he called. "This is way more fun than facing them head-on. The story is *always* better when the heroes have hope. Nothing like an unexpected betrayal!"

Indira glanced back. Ledge offered a proud salute before disappearing down the stairs. Indira's eyes swung back to Joey. Up close, the features she'd noticed during their first encounter were even more intense now. His eyes were shockingly blue. His blond hair was so bright it stung to look at it for too long.

"You have to stop this!" Indira shouted. "You don't belong in this world."

Joey frowned at her. "You can't tell me what to do!"

It was such a surprisingly bratty thing to say that Indira almost didn't notice him thrusting his lacrosse stick into the air. Indira flinched, but no cannons fired. Nothing exploded. Instead, magic swirled around them. She blinked a few times before looking down.

Her clothing had changed. The light pink tunic was gone. She looked at Phoenix and Cavern. All of them were wearing pirate clothing now.

"A shame you had to join the *losing* team," Joey said in a mocking voice. Indira was still trying to process the fact that he'd changed her clothes in less than a thought. She felt paralyzed by fear. This kind of power was unlike anything she'd ever seen.

Phoenix came to his senses far faster than she did. He summoned a fireball into the air. His eyes glowed bright as he shoved the spinning flames in Joey's direction. Indira's heart leaped hopefully as the flames darted over the water, casting out shadows in every direction.

But the Author just smiled at them.

He lifted his lacrosse stick. The fireball halted in midair, hanging between both boats like a miniature sun. Another flick of Joey's wrist drowned the flames. Indira's jaw dropped as the deadly fireball transformed into hundreds of bubbles floating harmlessly into the air.

Joey laughed again. "Surrender your boat, pirate scum!"

Phoenix looked helpless. Indira still couldn't move. Even Cavern stared in awe. All three of them saw the truth. There was no beating someone *this* powerful. Joey's boat started closing the distance between them. Indira knew they'd lost.

Until an unexpected hero took flight.

Little Peck had been strutting back and forth in front of her. She watched as he fluttered onto their boat's front railing. The rooster took a running start, angled in Joey's direction, and leaped off the prow of the boat. Indira hadn't known chickens could fly.

Maybe they couldn't.

But Peck soared through the air like a superhero. Joey's expression twisted, almost in slow motion. Cruel grin transformed into pure shock. Peck made contact, driving his beak right into Joey's face and forcing the rogue Author to stumble back. Feathers puffed into the air. The chicken and the Author went down together.

Indira shouted, "Let's go!"

Phoenix had already lunged for the controller. He jammed a finger down on the right button and their boat shot forward, barely scraping against Joey's before getting clear. Indira caught a brief glimpse of the Author rolling around, shouting wildly, as Peck continued his assault. She was briefly tempted to join the fight, thinking for a fraction of a second that this might be Joey's only moment of weakness. But the moment passed like a strike of lightning.

As their boat roared out of the alleyway, Indira saw a new threat approaching. Ledge Woods had climbed into his own boat. He took in the sight of their escape with wide eyes.

And Indira had the drop on him. She threw her hammer.

Magic tugged her through the air. Her feet landed hard in the back of Ledge's boat. He was still staring at the place where she'd been when she caught the spinning weapon. Before he could turn, Indira brought her foot up and kicked his backside. The traitor went sprawling into the water.

Her eyes darted up as Phoenix and Cavern passed.

"Don't stop!" she shouted. "I'm coming!"

Another throw. The hammer arched out over the water and Indira found herself shoulder to shoulder with Phoenix, facing the way they'd come. She caught the hammer a second time, grinning back at the damage she'd caused. She felt bad for abandoning Peck, but as they rounded the corner, she knew he was the only reason they were still alive.

"Back to the tunnel!" she ordered.

Phoenix was already whipping around the turn. There was cannon fire behind them. Engines revved and echoed over the water. Indira thought she even heard Joey's furious shouts chasing them. Clearly, he wasn't used to losing. The thought had her smiling as Phoenix rammed the boat up against her house's front stoop. They disembarked quickly.

Her eyes flicked back. The water behind them churned with movement, but no one saw them slipping inside the house. She closed the door carefully behind them and began the descent. No one spoke as they crawled back through the pipes. Beginning was waiting anxiously at the bottom. She saw their weary faces and made a quick but necessary decision.

"I'm shutting down this tunnel," she said. "We can't risk him following you."

Indira watched the land's representative set a hand against the tunnel. Magic shivered up its length and the tunnel became just another part of the wall itself. Indira knew they'd need to get back into the town, but she guessed that Beginning had other ways in. The emissary was right. They couldn't risk Joey finding the underground factories. There was no telling how much he'd destroy.

By the time they'd navigated the underground and reached the exit tunnel, it was nearly dark outside. Phoenix summoned a flame into his hand, allowing it to flash in the air and flicker. After a moment, he extinguished it. That was the signal. Indira saw a matching flame appear in the forest off to their right. It glowed for only a few seconds before gasping out.

"That way," she said.

They crossed the distance to find the rest of their crew. Cavern was still clutching the briefcase with the device to his chest. She was honestly just thankful they'd all survived, even if she felt guilty for leaving Peck behind. The others stood at the shadowed edge of a forest.

Gadget looked thrilled. "You got it. This is huge."

"That's the good news," Indira replied. "The bad news is that Joey is even more powerful than we thought. And he's going to be *really* mad that we beat him. He'll be looking for us now. No more element of surprise."

"We know," Minerva replied. "Look."

Her pretend mother pointed toward Ordinary. The town's massive walls loomed in the distance, but now massive banners were unfurled over the sides. It took a second for Indira to realize they were *wanted* posters. Joey had used his powers to produce house-size images of each of them, dressed in their pirate gear. Underneath, he'd attached absurd rewards for anyone who assisted in their capture. Her first thought was that other characters would never dream of helping someone like Joey, but Ledge was living proof that some of them would.

Sighing, she turned back to the others.

"At least we look cool," she said. "Time to go check in with Maxi."

26

Breaking Ordinary

"I've got so much juicy info for you guys, it's not even funny."

Maxi's voice had more energy in it than the rest of their crew combined. Indira glanced around at the others. Phoenix and Squalls were running through a few magical practice exercises. Gadget had finished programming her bees and was leaning over the computer, analyzing incoming intel with bloodshot eyes. Minerva and Cavern leaned on opposite sides of the call desk, looking like a pair of mismatched bookends. Indira answered when no one else spoke.

"Let's hear it."

"Well," Maxi went on excitedly. "First, I think I know how Joey got here. There was a brief opening in the dimensions between the Real World and Imagination. I'm talking less time than it would take to snap your fingers. Your team took Group Port B Thirty-Three. Did you experience any issues?"

Gadget looked up sharply. Indira saw horror written on the girl's face.

"We teleported to the wrong location," Indira answered. She didn't want to make Gadget feel bad. It had been an accident. "The machine was missing one of its location sensors."

"Which created a tiny crack in space and time," Maxi replied, as if that were an everyday event or something. "It just so happened that Joey fell asleep at the *exact* moment the gap opened. His subconscious slipped through the opening. He basically dreamed his way into our world. It had like a .00004 percent chance of happening."

"Great," Indira said. "How he got here doesn't matter. Let's focus on how to *stop* him."

"I'm two steps ahead of you," Maxi continued. "Let's start with other examples of Authors entering our world. It's happened three times before in the written history of Imagination. I researched all three—and let me tell you, I'm still coughing up dust from those books. Someone needs to copy those over to digital files like yesterday—"

Indira cleared her throat. "Focus, Maxi."

"Right, of course. All three Authors dreamed their way into our world. It always happened that way. An accidental crossing of the borders, so to speak. All three of them were slightly more . . . mature than our current opponent.

The method for returning the Authors was always the same. You have to *scare* them awake. It's kind of like any dream, right? If you fall off a cliff or something super spooky jumps out, it startles you awake."

The rest of the crew was paying more attention now. It was the first time they'd been offered a direct strategy for fighting someone like Joey. Phoenix was nodding.

"So we have to scare him," he said. "Easy enough."

"Pretty much," Maxi answered. "But there are other factors involved. The longer they've been in this world, the harder it is to frighten them. I mean, one Author was in the imaginary world for about fifty-three years. . . ."

Indira's heart skipped a few beats. "Did you say fifty-three *years*?"

"Right? That's like forever," Maxi replied. "Anyway, let's talk about Joey. It took some digging, but I located his file. He's super new to writing. Our profile doesn't have a ton on him. He's eleven years old. He's been writing for the past few months. He writes fan fiction based on video games that he's playing. His current favorite is this battle thingy called *Pirates versus Marines*."

Indira felt like she'd been hit in the head. Understanding echoed through their group. All the signs made sense. "That explains so much!" she said. "The pirate ship. The city's streets being canals. That bunker. The parrot! Everything he's summoned so far is either a pirate or marine theme."

Maxi squealed with excitement. "Wait! Did you say canals?"

"Yes," Phoenix answered. "Every street in Ordinary is a waterway now."

There was a flurry of movement on the other end of the line. Indira imagined Maxi flipping through a messy desk of papers before surfacing victoriously.

"There's a stage like that in the video game. It's called Not Your Mother's Venice. I'll see if I can send over the schematics. According to the file, Joey spends hours playing this game. If he knows the maps, you'll need to know them as well as he does. . . ."

"Maxi," Phoenix jumped in. "What's the point of the game? Like, how do you win?"

"It's a battle zone," she replied. "Here's the description: 'Contestants are sorted into two teams: pirates or marines. Both teams start at a home-base location. When the game begins, players are able to travel throughout the map, with the goal being to eliminate the other team. Points and power-ups are awarded for sinking opponents' boats, taking over key bases, or eliminating opponents. Each round ends when all members of the opposing team have been defeated.'"

Indira's stomach sank. "That's what Ledge told us. He said that Joey was making them play the same game over and over again."

"He could have been lying," Cavern pointed out. "He lied about helping us."

Indira shook her head. "Maybe, but I'm pretty sure he thought we were walking into Joey's trap. He didn't actually think we'd escape with any information. I'd bet that Joey is playing this game over and over with the citizens of Ordinary. Forcing the townspeople to fight each other."

"And I'll bet he never loses," Phoenix said. "Not with his powers."

Minerva asked the one question Indira hadn't thought to ask. "Have any of Ordinary's citizens appeared at the Ninth Hearth?"

Indira knew that at least death in their world wasn't permanent. She'd been through the process once herself. After tackling Brainstorm Ketty off the highest ledge of a tower, she had appeared at the Ninth Hearth and had been slowly restored back to life by that magic. It wasn't an experience she wished on anyone, but at least the citizens might escape from Joey that way.

"We've seen fluctuations," Maxi said. "But instead of appearing in the Ninth Hearth, they're returning to a starting point in Ordinary. It looks like Joey set up his own regeneration center. There's a respawn zone. It must be a part of the video game he plays. And as an Author in our world, he's powerful enough to do something like that."

Indira grimaced. "So he really can make them fight over and over."

"He's basically torturing them," Phoenix whispered. "We have to stop him."

Before Maxi could relay her own advice, another sound echoed. Indira looked across the clearing and saw Beginning sitting by the fire. "It isn't me this time!" Beginning announced.

Leaves crunched underfoot and twigs snapped.

A figure approached from the road. All of them turned as the kingswolf they'd left back at the memorial appeared. She was slightly out of breath. Indira guessed she'd run the whole way there in wolf form.

Half gasping, she said, "We've got a problem."

Joey's powers were making things worse.

"All the waiting characters transformed," the kingswolf explained. "At the exact same time. We were all hanging out, trying to stay positive, when their clothing changed. About half of them are wearing pirate outfits. The other half have some kind of military armor. I wasn't sure what was going on, so I wanted to come update you."

"*Pirates versus Marines*," Minerva said. "His game."

The kingswolf frowned. "What game?"

"That's not even the most important part," Phoenix pointed out. "He's breaking another step in the Hero's Journey. Ordinary is supposed to represent the starting point, right? It can be anything. Authors can start their story in a city or on a farm or under the ocean. It can be wherever! Joey's magic is forcing this theme to be the start of *every* story. Everything is *Pirates versus Marines* now."

Beginning's voice was a whisper. "So not only do the stories *stop* for no reason, but now they all start in the exact same place. If this magic holds, it will make for very boring stories. It won't take long for the readers to abandon us entirely."

"Unless they're really into pirates," Gadget noted. "Or marines."

Indira considered her own attire. She wasn't sure anyone could deal with a world that was *only* pirates all the time. "Maxi. What happens next? If we keep him distracted until the Editors can take action against him? What will the consequences be?"

"Well, I was running through some scenarios earlier," she replied. "And—not to freak you out—but there's a possibility he destroys all of Plot. The effects would echo into every story that's ever existed. . . ." She paused. "But that's like worst-case scenario. The Editors will arrive and perform a reset. All the new stories will be fine after that."

Indira's stomach dropped. "But every story that existed *before* now?"

"Would be broken, yeah."

"Thanks, Maxi."

Indira hung up the phone. Her mind was racing. Every story that existed *before* now included *her* story. It was bad enough to think of all that Joey had already ruined, but now his presence in their world was personal. Indira looked around at the others.

"We need to get some sleep. In the morning, we can take a look at Gadget's intel, make a plan, and wake Joey up before he can do more damage."

Cavern nodded. "What's the scariest thing we can show him?"

The others looked around, deep in thought. Indira's eyes settled on Phoenix. An idea had been forming slowly over the last few hours. "I'm sure we'll come up with something."

27

Intel

If they had not been so exhausted, it would have been very difficult to sleep. Indira's dreams were a mixture of cannon fire, pirate attacks, and howling. It helped that she was curled up, back to back, with Phoenix and the others. That source of warmth was the only thing that kept her comfortable enough to actually doze off.

Before morning had dawned, Indira woke. She slid free of the others, careful not to wake them, and shook Phoenix's shoulder. He looked up and she held one finger to her lips for silence. Quietly, he slid free and joined her. Indira led him off to the opposite end of camp.

Gadget was there, still awake, analyzing her data. Indira knelt beside the girl and lowered her voice to a whisper. "Show me what you've found."

"On the first page, I've mapped out Joey's movement,"

Gadget answered in a whisper. "He never stops. No sleeping at all. There's another scent signature at his side almost ninety percent of the time. I've compared it against earlier data. The signature is from Ledge Woods.

"The rest of the town is kind of scattered. I'm pretty sure you three infiltrated at the end of one of his games. He finished off a few more groups before restarting everything. You can see here." She pointed to the upper corner of the screen. "All citizens returned to life."

There was a sudden spark of heat signatures. A flood of voices being recorded too. Gadget paused to play some of the snippets her bees had logged. They heard townspeople complaining about the game. Some asked why the Editors hadn't come to save them.

It was also clear that Joey had run them through several games already. That fact was creating another problem. "When he transformed the town into a map from the game, it removed the food. All the townspeople are exhausted. Which means that every new game, they're less active. Which leads me to the last important piece of data. . . ."

Gadget spun another graphic onto the screen. It was a recording. A voice filled the air, and Indira shivered, hearing Joey. It was almost like he was sitting right next to them.

"I'm starting to get bored."

Another voice answered. Ledge. "We could go somewhere else. . . ."

"Yeah?" Joey again. "Where else is there to go?"

"There's a bigger city. It's called Fable."

Gadget cut the audio, frowning. "The bee rotated position, so I didn't hear the rest of the conversation. But it sounds like the town is no longer presenting him with a fun challenge. It's good news, I guess, that he'll leave them alone. But it's really bad news for Fable."

Indira nodded. "Where he can do even more damage."

"He's already broken the Hero's Journey," Phoenix whispered. "We have to stop him."

"Gadget," Indira asked. "What's the highest point in the town?"

The girl squinted a little, focusing on the statistics. Indira watched as she navigated several different screens. "Hmm. There's a bell tower. It's the highest location."

"Thanks," Indira replied. "How about you get some sleep? You deserve it."

Gadget looked down at her feet for a moment, and Indira could only guess what the girl was thinking. Ever since Maxi had revealed *how* Joey had arrived in their world, Gadget had been working overtime to try to make up for her mistake. After watching Phoenix treat Squalls like a brother, Indira realized that maybe it was her turn to play the same role for Gadget. She reached out and set a firm hand on the girl's shoulder.

"It's not your fault. You heard Maxi. What happened was an accident. Less than a one percent chance. Last year . . ." Indira took a deep breath. "I messed up a *lot* last

218

year. Mistakes happen. It's what you do next that matters. All this research? It's going to help us beat him, Gadget."

That brought the briefest smile to the girl's face. After a long and stretching moment, Gadget glanced at Indira's hand on her shoulder. "Okay. Too much touching. Thanks."

Indira smiled as the girl closed the device and quietly returned back to the others. Gadget had admitted earlier that she liked machines a little more than people, but Indira couldn't help noticing that it was the fact that she'd endangered other people that was bringing out the hardest-working version of the girl she'd seen so far. Gadget nestled underneath a blanket and drifted off to sleep. Indira whispered a promise the others couldn't hear.

"Don't worry. We're going to fix it."

She turned back to Phoenix. He was watching her closely. An unspoken agreement was reached. Both of them turned and started walking to Ordinary.

Instincts

It's a rare moment, dear reader, when someone can be right and wrong at the same time. Indira and Phoenix were leaving behind their loyal friends, to protect their loyal friends. Both of them felt the weight of guilt and honor, right and wrong. In such moments, we can only do our best to make sense of our own hearts.

They made an effort to approach unseen, but realized halfway to the gates that no one was actually standing along the watchtowers. The eyes of the town—and all its residents—were turned inward. Indira could hear cannons firing on the other side of the looming barricade. Another game, another round of torture for Ordinary's citizens.

It was time to save them.

The Hero's Journey was broken. Plot was on the verge

of destruction. Fable could be next. Indira took her place at the base of the town's outer wall and locked eyes with Phoenix again. "So my plan . . ."

". . . is to use my dragon form," he guessed. "I saw you looking at me when Cavern asked how we might scare Joey. And you asked about the highest point because you want Joey to fall. Falling always wakes people up. The roof is exposed, so we can attack from above. We'll just have to make sure he doesn't see us until the very last second."

Indira was staring at him. He'd pretty much read her mind. She couldn't help grinning.

"Right. Yeah. That's the plan."

He grinned back at her. "Let's get going."

The walls were high, but not high enough to keep out someone with a magic hammer. After locking arms with Phoenix, Indira took aim and launched the silver weapon in a measured arc. It spun upward and the magic snatched them both. She caught the hammer, feeling Phoenix's weight against her, before ducking down along the ramparts.

"I'm not sure I've said it before," Phoenix whispered. "But I love when you do that."

Indira grinned at him as they crouched over by the wall, careful not to be seen. Their raised position offered a solid view of the rest of Ordinary. Indira saw a few buildings that stood higher than the outer wall, but none as high as the distant bell tower.

"There it is."

Indira nodded. "Come on. We need a view of the front doors."

The two of them circled until they were directly across from the building's entrance. It was a gray stone structure with glass windows that reflected back the morning light. The streets surrounding them were silent and empty. She guessed that Joey had already come through this area.

"Time to lure him in," Indira said. "I was thinking fire might do the trick. How's your aim?"

Phoenix grinned. A slash of heat filled the air as he summoned a fireball. It spun to life between his palms. He took careful aim before shoving the flames forward. They spiraled out over the water, shooting like a rocket, and collided with the uppermost section of the bell tower in a burst of bright sparks. The two of them ducked back down as the flames began to spread.

"No way he misses that," Indira whispered.

Every second felt like a minute, every minute like an hour. But eventually they heard the faint hum of an engine. She held her breath as Joey's boat nosed into the intersection.

He was armored the same way he had been the day before, still gripping his lacrosse stick tightly. Ledge Woods hovered at the back of the boat like a shadow. Indira watched Joey point up at the visible flames. Indira's heart leaped. Joey directed the boat toward the front of the building. The trap had been set. And he was taking the bait.

She smacked Phoenix's shoulder excitedly as both Ledge and Joey disembarked, climbing up water-slick steps. They shouldered through the engraved double doors at the front of the bell tower. Indira knew they'd head straight for the roof.

Timing was important. She knew Joey could easily teleport, or summon an elevator out of thin air. She hoped, however, that he'd take his own game seriously enough to follow the rules. The building was five stories high. Indira knew it would take him at least a few minutes to reach the roof if he was taking the stairs.

"Ready?" she asked, backing away to give Phoenix space.

He summoned his fire again. "Let's go over the plan one more time. I transform into a dragon. You climb on my back. We use the cloud cover to hide our attack, and then we both dive at him from above."

Indira nodded. "Our attack forces him to the edge. He falls. It wakes him up. We save the world."

"Don't you mean we save the world *again*?"

He smiled at her before the flame in his hand began to spread, consuming his entire body. Indira backed up a step as the transformation burst to life. Great gasps of smoke poured into the air, and she could only hope there were no windows in the stairwell Joey was using.

She knew the element of surprise would be crucial.

In that sudden brightness, Phoenix had taken his new form: a great, sprawling dragon with twisting reptilian limbs. She stood there admiring the burnished scales until he lowered his front shoulder in invitation. Grinning, she said, "Don't mind if I do."

Indira climbed his foreleg easily and settled into a comfortable nook behind his neck. Her stomach turned a little as she remembered what Brainstorm Underglass had told her about there being two competing romantic interests for the role in her next story. It was hard for her to imagine anyone she could like more than a boy who transformed into a dragon.

"Let's go scare this kid back into the Real World."

Indira tightened the grip of her knees, settled in low, and still nearly tumbled off sideways as Phoenix swept into the sky. His wings stretched out like a pair of smoke-black blades. It took great effort not to shout wildly with the sheer thrill of the wind rushing past her. Instead, Indira hovered against his neck, doing her best to focus on the watery streets below her.

Phoenix pressed higher into the sky, fighting gravity with each beat of his wings. She saw that their flight was getting attention. The citizens who had survived the game so far all stopped to stare. She wondered if perhaps they thought the Editors had finally sent someone to save them.

And she hoped she *could* save them.

The citizens weren't the only people who noticed.

Indira's tutor device suddenly spun to life. There was a little message on the center of her screen that had just been delivered:

What are you doing? What's the plan?

Indira guessed that was Gadget, hacking into her device. She pushed away the guilt. Now wasn't the time for hesitation. She needed to trust her instincts. Indira and Phoenix had made this decision to keep their friends out of harm's way. She could only imagine how it looked from outside the city to see Phoenix rising up above the clouds. With a swipe, she dismissed the message. She needed to stay focused and calm.

She tucked herself against Phoenix's neck as he leveled off. Below them, the bell tower looked like a giant fist raised to the sky. She saw that it was a narrow building with a roof that connected the doorway and the part they'd set aflame. Phoenix circled slowly, waiting for signs of movement, and Indira had to wipe away the tears that formed in those cold, sweeping winds.

Several seconds passed. She was nearly shivering, her hands growing colder.

And then movement.

Indira and Phoenix saw it at the same time. She tapped the side of his neck. The very second her hands resettled in their grips, the great dragon began a hurtling dive. Indira saw the two figures edging out onto the roof. Naturally,

Joey was in the lead. Ledge followed. Neither of them saw the great beast approaching from above. She realized Joey would not look up. Why would someone with his powers ever look up?

Indira pressed into Phoenix's neck and whispered the command. "Now!"

Phoenix's wings swept wide. The sudden gust finally got Joey's attention. He looked up at the exact moment Indira had hoped he would. Phoenix opened his terrifying dragon jaws and loosed an earth-shattering roar. The sound thundered. Indira's heart leaped as she saw Joey's reaction. It was going to work. The rogue Author stumbled back, eyes wide with fear. Indira knew he was only a few paces from the edge of the building. Just a small, hip-high barrier. It couldn't have been more perfect.

"Fire!" Indira commanded.

Phoenix took in a breath; then fire raced out in bright streaks toward an already startled Joey. Indira knew they needed that first startled reaction to become fear, and they needed that fear to drive through Joey deep enough to wake him from his slumber in the Real World.

Ledge shouted something, but too late. The burst of flames forced Joey against the hip-high wall. His back-pedal was fast enough and frightful enough to send him toppling over the edge. Indira roared her triumph at the final look on his face.

Eyes wide with fear, Joey tumbled out of sight.

Phoenix swept overhead.

Indira whipped her head around to get a look. There were strange ripples in the air and near the water. She didn't see a splash, though. "It worked!" she shouted. "He woke up!"

If he hadn't, she knew he would have hit the water for sure. Indira was still shouting triumphantly as Phoenix circled back around for another look. She couldn't believe it had worked. She was about to shout a command for Phoenix to land when something heavy fell on her shoulder. The grip tightened.

"I've always *wanted* a dragon!"

She spun instinctively, but Joey was faster. He used her own momentum to give her a shove. The force of the blow sent her sprawling off Phoenix's back. Her hands grasped desperately at scales and missed. She was falling.

The breathless, pit-in-the-stomach feeling was not new to her. She'd experienced a drop just like it during her auditions. And again when she'd fallen over the ledge with Brainstorm Ketty. Only this time it wasn't part of the plan.

Indira screamed as the ground swallowed her whole.

29

On the Run

A sequence of chaotic thoughts flashed through Indira's brain.

Joey survived.

And now he has Phoenix.

Oh, and I'm about to drown.

The third thought pulsed loudest. Her limbs responded. She clawed upward, fighting toward the surface. Her lungs felt like they were on the verge of bursting.

She came gasping out, legs kicking to keep her afloat. Her eyes darted to the sky. Phoenix's form was sweeping through the clouds. She saw him spiraling and lashing his neck and guessed he was doing his best to resist Joey. It wouldn't last long. The Author had proven his ability to bend the rest of the world to his will. He'd overpower Phoenix soon enough.

There was a shout. Indira braced herself for a blow until she saw the source. Across the canal from her, one of the townspeople was calling to her. It was the baker who had handed Indira a pastry that first morning. "He's coming back! Get moving! Take cover!"

His warning shocked her back to life. Indira looked up and saw that the baker was right. Phoenix was circling around. He let out a great roar, and Indira imagined the fury he must have felt at being forced to follow Joey's commands.

Her mind raced. She had to escape somehow. "The boat!"

She'd landed in the canal on the backside of the building. There was an abandoned boat on the other side by the front steps. Kicking her legs in the water, she turned. Her eyes landed on a back corner of the building. There was a door there. She started swimming.

Another roar sounded in the sky. She looked up in time to see Phoenix pulling out of a dive. "Keep fighting!" she whispered. "Keep fighting him, Phoenix."

Indira climbed up the slick steps and lowered her shoulder. The bell tower's bottom floor looked like a church. There were rows for seating. Great stained-glass windows brightened the path ahead of her. She wasted no time as she darted across the main room and out through a pair of double doors.

She was trying to get her bearings when a location pinged in her second vision. Did Gadget know what had happened? Was this her escape route? Indira didn't have any other options. She leaped into the back of the waiting boat and grabbed the controller.

The location pinged again. Indira hoped her friend was smart enough to lead her on an escape route. She punched the same button she'd seen Phoenix use, and the boat jolted forward. At least the location wasn't far. One more turn and then down a long straightaway.

Another shout caught her attention. Indira whipped around in time to see a body arching out over the water. Angling toward her. In all the chaos, she'd forgotten about Ledge.

His upper body collided forcefully with the back of the boat. The whole thing shook. Indira barely kept her footing, punching the accelerator again as he dug his claws into the ship's hull. The boat kept picking up speed, but Ledge clung on desperately. The back half of his body dragged through the water. Indira reached for her hammer. Ledge shouted something as she turned and attempted an awkward one-handed swing.

He slid his hand to the right along the railing, dodging. Overhead, Phoenix had swept lower. She could tell Joey was winning that battle. Indira took another distracted swing with her hammer, but Ledge dodged again. This time the movement cost him. His right claw slipped a little and he nearly went under. She was about to swing a third time and finish him off when she looked up. Her boat was heading straight for a wall.

She shoved her hammer into her belt and dove for the controller. A quick pull on the joystick brought the boat into a hairpin turn. It still slammed into the side of the nearest building, shaking a little before darting forward again.

Indira glanced back. Ledge was barely hanging on now. She found herself on a final straightaway. Gadget's pinged location was just a few hundred paces in the distance.

It took effort to keep one hand pressing the *B* button down as she used the other to reach for her hammer. Ledge shouted louder and louder, and finally Indira understood. He wasn't shouting at her. He was making noise, trying to get Joey's attention.

Indira reached for her hammer again. As she straightened, Phoenix came flying around the corner ahead of them. Those beautiful wings swept outward to block her path. They were wide enough that the tips grazed the buildings on either side of the road.

Even at a distance, she could see the pain in his eyes. He was no longer controlling his own body. Joey sat on his back, lacrosse stick held up like a sword. It wasn't hard to figure out what would happen next, what someone like Joey would force Phoenix to do in this moment.

Indira's boat was hurtling straight at them. She saw the flex of neck muscles, the jaw opening wide. Joey's intentions were clear. Indira clutched her hammer tight and leaped over the side. Fire sprang out of Phoenix's open jaws.

She felt the heat of it press against her neck before she broke the water's surface. The bolt hit her stolen vessel and she heard wood crack, exploding in every direction from the pressure. All the sound and heat, however, was cut off by the water around her.

Her feet touched the bottom. Looking up, she saw that everything was chaos. Wooden pieces scattered. Ledge floated to one side of the wreckage, unconscious. Flames licked over the surface of the water. Above all of that, she saw a darker form hovering, waiting for her to surface. Indira felt like she was having a panic attack. There was nowhere to go. Eventually, she'd run out of air. Forced out of the water, she'd be captured by Joey.

And then she saw it.

The ping on the map in her second vision. It glowed as bright as a guiding star. She realized she was nearly standing in the right spot. Her eyes were drawn ahead. The dot was there.

Gadget had marked an exit for her.

It was not a typical grate. Indira swam forward carefully, staying as close to the canal bottom as she could, and trying not to make sudden movements that might stir the water. Each stroke brought her closer to a massive drainage grate. There must have been a creek that ran through the town, flowing out below this section of the outer wall. Indira reached it, lungs protesting, and realized the gaps were too small. Why would Gadget highlight this for her?

Even a child couldn't fit through the openings in the

grate. She glanced up. The great shadow was still circling, wingbeats stirring the surface, searching for her.

Indira was running out of time.

But there was no latch on the grate. Nothing at all.

And then a bright line of text flashed across her vision:

Your hammer!

It was a message from Gadget. Indira's vision was starting to blur. Her hammer? How would that . . . ?

. . . The idea took root. Of *course*. She'd thrown her hammer plenty of times, but only ever through the air. That didn't mean it couldn't work underwater. Indira pressed herself against the grate and—with great care— slid her hammer through an opening.

If this didn't work, she'd drown.

She released the weapon. It floated downstream, and she felt the familiar tug. The hammer's magic dragged her across the barrier. She was still underwater, however, and it took all her remaining strength to reach out and seize the hammer's grip. She nearly fumbled before grasping it again. Indira held the weapon as tightly as she could.

And then the dark undertow claimed her.

30

Consequences

Indira opened her eyes.

The sky was bright and blue; it was well past morning. Her entire body felt like it had been picked up by a giant, shaken soundly, and then tossed aside like a forgotten doll. She was lying on her back in the mud of a riverbank. Trees crowded around her like nosy neighbors. Her first efforts to sit up sent pain firing down her right side.

She lay there for a while longer, taking in deep breaths, trying to remember what had happened. It was the sound of the river that connected those missing links in her memory. She knew the river led back to the underwater grate. Before she'd reached the grate there had been an explosion. Joey had survived their attack.

Indira groaned with the effort it took to stand. She had

several burns, a few cuts. The fall from Phoenix's back had painted bruises down her right side. That final image of Phoenix pulsed back into her head. His eyes had been so sad and lost as Joey forced him to fire on her boat.

She remembered that the river ran *away* from the city. Backtracking through the forest, she did her best not to make too much noise. The town came into view through a gap in the trees. At this distance, she heard no cannon fire. Nor was there any sign of Phoenix and Joey soaring through the open sky.

Indira used the cover of scattered farms and barns to circle south. She hoped Gadget and the others would be waiting for her. She was sure they'd feel betrayed by her decision to attack without them, but that didn't matter now, not with Phoenix in the hands of their enemy. They'd have to make a plan. "I have to save him," she whispered to herself.

Every step was its own punishment. Not just the bruises and the sore muscles, but the absence at her side. The smiling red-haired boy who'd been through so much with her already. The boy she liked so much. She'd taken him into enemy territory *again* and let him get captured *again.* Why hadn't she thought through the risks of what they were doing? When she'd imagined the showdown with Joey, she'd never imagined them failing.

A small part of her still didn't understand how Joey had survived. He'd been standing almost within arm's reach of her. She'd seen the look on his face. He had been *afraid*. The wide eyes and the gaping mouth. The fall from the building. Why hadn't he woken up?

As she navigated the final hill, Indira's concerns doubled. The curtain of forest that had kept their base of operation out of sight had been reduced to char. Indira waited in the shadow of a battered shed. Her eyes were drawn past the still-burning stumps. Through all the smoke she could just make out the call desk they'd been using to contact Maxi.

It had been destroyed.

Joey had found their camp and he'd used Phoenix's fire to destroy it.

Indira eyed the city and the sky before picking her way forward. She half hoped someone would appear, that Gadget or Squalls would wave at her from the nearby forest to signal that they'd survived. But the only movement came as she was circling the grounds one final time.

A familiar strutting.

"Peck?" Indira called in surprise. "How'd you make it out?"

She couldn't have said why, but it was a huge relief to see the pet rooster. She didn't know how the chicken had escaped the city, and she didn't care. She collapsed to her knees and hugged the little creature, realizing Peck's survival was the first thing that had gone right in days.

"It's so good to see you."

He ruffled his feathers pleasantly against her neck. The

moment she released him he made a series of sharp noises before darting straight into the forest. Indira hesitated at first, but she remembered that this was the way stories worked. Strange events weren't simply coincidence.

Besides, she had no idea what to do next. It was easier to follow the chicken.

Peck found a forest trail and took it. Indira did the same. It was almost pleasant to walk without knowing where she was going, without thinking of all that had gone wrong. Peck continued on for nearly an hour before stopping suddenly to nip at a few specks in the road.

"Hello there, Indie."

If you've ever moved away—or been gone for a long time—and heard the voice of a good friend, you'll know how Indira felt in that moment, dear reader. There was only one person in the world who called her by that nickname. And it was the one person she needed to see, even if she didn't know it. Deus came striding forward. He was more commonly known as Deus Ex Machina, the provider of convenient solutions. She'd been lucky enough to have him as a mentor during her first year of school, even if the two of them had gotten off to a rocky start.

He greeted her with a grim smile. "One of these days," he said, "we'll meet in far more average circumstances. Perhaps for a cup of tea? An afternoon snack? Anything that doesn't taste like the end of the world."

Even in the darkest hour, Deus could always make Indira smile.

"That wouldn't exactly be our style," she replied.

"No, it wouldn't. Shall we go for a stroll?"

Peck made a little noise before continuing down the path. Deus offered his arm and Indira looped her own through it, feeling safe and comfortable for the first time in days. Her mentor had that effect. He was the provider of convenient solutions, after all. It was his job to enter the plot when all looked lost and give characters the slightest nudge in the right direction. Indira found herself hoping that was the reason he was visiting her now.

"Are you here to give me a pep talk?" she asked.

"Would you like me to? I've got a few speeches about how the night is darkest before the dawn and all of that. . . ."

She waved the idea away. "I just need to know how to beat him."

"That's a tad more difficult," he admitted. "My talents are in keeping you *alive*. Daring escapes. Last-minute rescues. That sort of thing."

"Some help you've been so far," Indira complained. "He captured Phoenix."

Deus threw her a stubborn look. "I've clearly spoiled you if you don't see all the ways I've been working to turn the tides in your favor so far. Have my efforts really gone unnoticed?"

Indira frowned. "You've been helping me?"

"Of *course*!" he exclaimed, a little annoyed. "You're up

against a rogue Author! I've been pulling strings since the moment you set foot in Ordinary. Where do you think Peck came from?"

Now Indira was really confused. "The rooster?"

"The rooster who saved you once already!" Deus corrected. "He wasn't part of your original scenario. I sensed you would need him, though, so I smuggled him in. Not to mention that first encounter with Joey. Who do you think was responsible for his cannon misfiring?"

Indira nodded. She'd forgotten about that first encounter. Everything Joey had done since then had worked like a charm. "It was a little convenient the first cannon didn't fire."

"My specialty." Deus grinned. "I also provided the bee schematics for Gadget. Those certainly came in handy — and will continue to come in handy. But that's the extent of my tricks, Indie. I sensed you would face a great threat, but I'd never imagined someone like Joey was on the way. I thought you were preparing to square off with some particularly nasty antagonists." His grin faded. "Clearly, he's more than that. Our entire world is in jeopardy."

"The Editors won't come," she said. "But what about the brainstorms?"

Indira knew they possessed some of the most powerful magic in the world, but Deus shook his head sadly. "Their powers were altered after the Brainstorm Ketty incident. It was agreed that they should be brought under the same governance as the Editors. Now the two groups follow the same rule book during any crisis that occurs in the world of Imagination."

"Meaning they have to wait before they can help too?"

"I'm afraid so."

Indira took a deep breath. "So I'm on my own. Again."

"That was going to be my *next* topic of conversation." He flipped a silver coin up into the air. Indira caught it instinctively. "You've fallen into the same trap you fell into last year."

She scowled. "No I haven't. What trap? I didn't fall into a trap."

But as she looked down at the face of the silver coin Deus had given her, she saw herself. The engraved image was of her standing triumphantly over a fallen bad guy, hammer raised in the air, all alone. It wasn't hard to see what was missing on the coin: the rest of her crew.

"You most certainly have," Deus replied. "You are pretending—once again—that you must face every battle as the lone hero. Even though this whole training scenario was designed to teach you otherwise. You were not alone last year, Indira. You are not alone now."

Another glance at the coin showed all the other characters who'd come on this journey with her. They crowded around the victory scene like quiet reminders. Indira frowned.

"I know I wasn't alone," she said. "Phoenix came with me."

"As you snuck out on the rest of your team," Deus reminded her. "Just think about how you've approached every problem. Who led the first spy mission into the city? Who thundered down from the sky atop a dragon?" Her mentor sighed softly. "It is in your bones to play the hero, and there's nothing wrong with that. I'm simply here to encourage you to make heroes out of everyone else on the next attempt. Let them shine beside you, rather than hover in your shadow. You made the mistake of thinking you and Phoenix could defeat him alone. It wasn't a bad effort, all in all, but I promise you it will take the entirety of your crew's combined talents to defeat this enemy."

For a few minutes, they walked in silence. Peck went on strutting ahead of them, winding through the forests, clearly with some distant location in mind. Indira's initial annoyance had faded. She was starting to realize how right Deus was. Brainstorm Underglass had sent her here to learn how to be a good teammate. Her tutor device had even warned her every time she'd tried to play the hero without including the other members of her squad.

Sneaking off with Phoenix to save the day? It was hard to admit now how foolish she had been. If she had just waited for the rest of her team, they might have formed an even better plan. It was time to actually take the lesson to heart. She needed to be a new kind of hero.

The forest path wound on until they reached the main road. Indira recognized the location. It wasn't far from the memorial they'd left behind. Indira realized that if her team members had survived Joey's attack, they would have come here. This was where Peck had been leading her. Deus paused at the edge of the clearing.

"One more piece of advice. I am not allowed to interfere. I can only nudge. So let me give you a polite shove in the right direction. The key to defeating Joey is to figure out what he fears. You must wake him with something he's *actually* afraid of in the Real World. Savvy?"

That sent Indira's mind racing through possibilities. She looked Deus in the eye and nodded. "See you when I need you," she said with a smile.

Her mentor gathered up Peck in his arms, winked once, and vanished into the shadows. Indira wasn't completely sure what needed to be done, but she had a feeling her crew would know. They were going to rescue Phoenix. They were going to defeat Joey.

And they were going to do it as a team.

31

A New Plan

Indira followed the road.

Around a familiar turn she saw the monument. She hadn't quite been prepared for just how *many* people would be there. Characters of all shapes and sizes had been kicked out of their stories. Far more than when Indira had last seen the location. It looked like some kind of awkward costume party, too, as all of them had been refitted in marine gear or pirate attire.

Thankfully, her crew was waiting near the front of the gathering.

"Indira?" Minerva rushed forward, all motherly instinct, and embraced Indira in a huge hug. Her pretend mother couldn't have known how much she needed it. "We were so worried."

"I made it out." Indira's eyes found Gadget. "Thanks

to you. Good job with the underwater grate. It's the only reason I didn't get captured."

She swept forward and hugged the girl. Gadget went stock-still in her arms.

"Hugging. Right," she said, trying to wiggle away. "Not my thing."

Indira pulled back and nodded. "Sorry about that. I just—I wanted to say thanks for saving me. You were amazing."

Gadget looked a little embarrassed. "I thought you might do something more . . . *instinctive*. So I made a backup plan in case you did. It's the only reason I had that location ready. We're just glad you made it out alive. The plan was to come collect you downstream, but Joey attacked before we could rendezvous. Thankfully the radar gave us enough time to escape."

"We watched the footage," Cavern said in that deep voice of his. "We were a little surprised the scare didn't wake him. It looked like you succeeded to us."

Indira shook her head. "Wait. Before we talk plans, I just want to apologize. Phoenix and I snuck off because we thought we were doing all of you a favor. We wanted to end this without anyone getting hurt. Now he's been captured. The clock is ticking. We're running out of time to save Phoenix, to save everyone. It wasn't smart of me to go in there without the best possible plan. I'm sorry we didn't wait. Leaving you all out of the loop . . . it just made our effort weaker than it could have been. We're stronger together. I know that now. And I'm sorry."

Some small part of Indira hoped they would argue with that, tell her that none of it was true. But the crew stood there in silent agreement, avoiding eye contact, and it felt like a punch to the stomach. Deus had clearly been right. She'd neglected her team. That wasn't the kind of hero she wanted to be. One by one, Indira looked her trusted teammates in the eye.

"Squalls, you've got some serious magic. We're going to put your storms to good use this time. And what Phoenix said was true: You could have left a long time ago. You're here because you were brave enough to stay. Brave enough to go where other people wouldn't go."

He took a deep breath. "I want to stay. I know Phoenix would stay for me."

Indira nodded. "And Cavern, I've never seen anything like your cave magic. I should have realized that would be useful. Gadget, you're pretty much a tech genius. You're half the reason we're still alive. And Minerva? You're as fierce as any of the mothers I've had since arriving in Fable. I promise that when we take Joey on this time, we'll all play our parts. No more of the Indira show."

The silence stretched a little longer. Indira felt heat creeping up her neck until Squalls broke into a smile. "Consider it water under the bridge."

Indira winced, remembering her near-death experience in the river.

"Not my favorite metaphor right now."

The others laughed.

"We all made mistakes," Minerva agreed. "Time to fix them. I forgot to mention that more help arrived while you were gone. Our team has a new member."

Indira watched the crowd part. A tall girl with dark skin and thick sunglasses strode forward. It had broken Indira's heart to lose Phoenix. The arrival of one of her other best friends thundered through the empty spaces his absence had left behind.

"Maxi?" She ran forward and embraced the girl. "When did you get here?"

Maxi tilted her sunglasses down slightly. "What? You think this is a face for radio? The Editors had already approved sending me before Joey destroyed the help desk. I've got a mobile command center in place now. We're coordinating everything."

Indira's heart leaped. "So the Editors are going to handle Joey?"

"We're going to help *you* handle, Joey," Maxi corrected. "We still can't intervene. They're sticking to the rule book. The countdown continues. But I have resources and I have information. I'm going to help your crew stop the Author from doing any more damage. I'm under strict orders not to take action against him directly."

Indira nodded. "We can use all the help we can get."

Maxi gestured back to the massive gathering of characters. "We've got hundreds of heroes from hundreds of stories. I've been organizing them into teams. We're hoping we can come up with a few potential strategies for facing Joey."

Indira definitely noticed that the heroes looked more organized. King Arthur was nearby, cradling his sword like a broken toy, but the others were all deep in conversation.

"Smart thinking, Maxi. We're bound to get a few good strategies that way."

There was a loud snap. Indira watched another hero from another story arrive. The man shouted something about a white whale before looking around, confused by the new setting.

"We get a new arrival every few minutes," Maxi explained. "Which brings me to our next problem. Thousands of heroes have arrived. We're pretty sure the first few characters came from books that Joey's read before. Characters he was familiar with. But now his power is going back through the entire *history* of stories. It's chaos. He's undoing every plot that's ever existed. All the Story Houses are shrinking. And characters are being summoned back to this location."

"Our newest theory is pretty straightforward: when the magic finishes, it will be permanent. Imagine this as a massive, ongoing spell."

Squalls added in a nervous voice, "Phoenix, uh, said

something about that. He said spells can be . . . interrupted more easily when they're still in progress. It's a lot harder to undo them after they're completed."

Indira was putting the pieces together. "So we have to wake Joey up before the spell finishes, or else all these stories will be permanently broken. Any idea how long it will take for that to happen?"

Maxi frowned. "It's hard to know for sure. Based on the last few heroes to come through, we're somewhere in the Romantic period? I'm pretty sure you've got at least a day. Maybe two."

Indira was trying to remember to involve the whole team. That had been the advice that Deus had given her first and foremost. Be a new kind of hero. She looked to Gadget first.

"You've watched the video of our last attempt, right?" The girl nodded.

"What do you think? Why didn't it work?"

Gadget looked a little surprised. "I—well—the whole point was that we needed to wake him up, right?" The crew nodded in agreement. "Look back at the video. He's not actually afraid. His eyes widen. His heart rate increases. He stumbles backward. It *looked* like he was afraid. But all those reactions can also come from another emotion: excitement. Think about the profile we have on Joey. He plays a lot of video games. We know his current obsession is *Pirates versus Marines,* but I'm sure he's played other games. Any way to access that info, Maxi?"

Maxi nodded. "I've got a full list of titles. Most of the games involve armies and fighting and strategy. And it seems like he gets *super* into certain games for long stretches of time."

"Any dragons?" Gadget asked.

Maxi scanned the data. "Actually, yes. Fifty-five percent of the games have dragons."

Gadget nodded knowingly. "That confirms my hypothesis. You did everything right, Indira. But it's like you used a pruning saw instead of a socket wrench!"

Indira frowned. "A what instead of a what?"

"The wrong tool," Gadget explained. "You were using the wrong tool. It didn't matter how effectively you used it, either. Phoenix could have been the most frightening dragon in the history of the world. It wouldn't have mattered. Joey *likes* dragons. So when he saw Phoenix, he wasn't afraid; he was *excited*. That's where your plan went wrong."

Cavern made an annoyed noise. "Well, my second plan will not work either. A boy who likes dragons will not fear the dark of my caves."

Indira's mind was racing. The second piece of advice that Deus had given her echoed in her mind. The key to defeating Joey would be figuring out what he truly feared.

"He doesn't like losing," she said, thinking out loud. "He showed up in that lacrosse jersey. So we know he plays sports. And video games. I'd bet he's afraid of losing."

"But we can't beat him," Squalls pointed out. "The only way to scare him would be to actually beat him at something. What are the odds of doing that?"

Indira frowned. He was right. Based on what Maxi had told them about the other Authors who had dreamed their way into the world of Imagination, it had been a particular moment that frightened them awake. A sudden scare that dragged them back into the Real World.

Gadget cut back in. "Hey! I was watching footage while we waited. I stumbled back on something that I'd forgotten. Do you guys remember going into the Foreshadow Forest?"

Everyone but Cavern and Minerva nodded.

"I don't actually remember what happened, though," Squalls answered.

"That's how it's supposed to go," Gadget replied. "Foreshadowing in stories usually occurs early on. Most of the time, you forget the clues unless you're paying really close attention to them. Or unless you have tutor devices that record the clues for you."

Gadget pulled out a device that she'd used to take notes.

"I watched all the footage. Indira, a tree told you that you'd have to lose to win."

She nodded. "I've already covered that."

"Phoenix touched a branch," Gadget continued, and Indira felt a heaviness in her heart just hearing her best friend's name. "The leaves turned into dragons that whispered something about powerful weapons falling into the wrong hands."

Indira frowned. "Already covered that, too."

"Squalls saw the word *pirate* in a spiderweb," Gadget continued. "That one is pretty obvious. Joey's whole pirate theme fits that clue. But there's one clue that I'm still not sure I understand. I tripped over a log that stood up and said, 'You can't tell me what to do!' Then it stuck its tongue out at me. It has to be an important clue! It's the only thing we haven't figured out yet. . . ."

Their crew discussed the possibilities for a while. Even though Indira admitted there was something strangely familiar about the words, she couldn't remember *why*. The crew spun their wheels on the topic for a while until everyone felt like they were right back where they'd started.

"This feels impossible," she whispered.

All the momentum she'd felt walking here with Deus was starting to vanish. How were they supposed to face someone this powerful? The rest of the crew looked drained. Except for Minerva. Indira watched her pretend mother set both hands on her hips. She had a determined look on her face and spoke in a voice that only a mother could summon.

"We're not giving up." Every syllable was sharp as a knife. "People are counting on us. Everyone has something they're afraid of. All we have to do is figure out his."

Minerva looked at each of them in turn. Indira instinctively lowered her eyes. She knew Minerva was right, but . . .

. . . you can't tell me what to do. . . .

Lightning struck. Not actual lightning. But the first flicker of an idea. It began with Gadget's foreshadowing clue. Listening to Minerva, though, was like a flash that illuminated a dark sky. Indira watched her thought take shape, branching out like lightning often did. It would take every single one of them to pull this off, but she knew the plan was their best shot.

If they all played their parts, it would work. It had to work.

"Gadget, you're a genius," Indira said. "I know how to beat him."

All in the Details

Indira found herself surrounded by heroes.

After she'd explained the plan, Maxi had rounded up a crew of characters she thought would have the best advice for Indira. There was Penelope—queen of Ithaca—who had dealt with all sorts of powerful people in a story titled *The Odyssey*.

Next to her sat Wendy Darling, who knew a thing or two about traveling between worlds with a boy named Peter Pan. Indira's favorite of the bunch was a young girl named Juliet. It surprised her to learn that the girl had costarred in a story with Indira's least favorite professor, Dr. Montague. The four of them sat around a fire, discussing strategies.

Penelope was working a loom as she spoke, her fingers guiding the thread along, nearly done with the piece of cloth Indira needed for her task ahead. "I've plenty of experience with gods. Not to mention unwelcome guests. I always found that the key to facing someone more powerful than myself was to distract them. Set them a task, or else invite them to a competition. Powerful people cannot resist a challenge."

Juliet nodded in agreement. "I think that is how you can lure this Author of yours. Pretend that beating him at his own game would be the easiest thing in the world. No one can resist the temptation to prove their own ability. He'll take you up on it, surely."

Wendy smiled. "And then the real game will begin."

The three advisors laughed. Indira had been mentally working through her role in the plan. She was doing her best to take their advice to heart, too. There were still so many ways it could all go wrong. The first part of the plan was one domino that would topple hundreds more. If just one was out of place . . .

Indira stood. "Any final words of wisdom?"

Penelope's eyes shone. "Aim true."

"It sounds like an awfully big adventure," Wendy said. "Do not forget to have some fun."

Juliet smiled. "Defy the stars."

Indira grinned back. Adrenaline was pumping through her chest as she circled around the rest of camp. She felt like a general overseeing operations. The entire camp hummed with nervous, excited energy. All hands were on deck for preparation. Indira paused at each station to check in. "Gadget, how are those tutor devices coming?"

She glanced up. "I've coded them so they perfectly match Maxi's description of the room. The only tricky part will be what happens when Minerva walks inside. The device will take a second to account for her presence. It'll probably look like a glitch. Just a quarter of a second. She's going to have to play her role convincingly if we want him to forget that detail."

Indira nodded. "And we know she can do that. Great job, Gadget. There's no way we could pull this off without you."

She was surprised when the girl held out a fist. Indira reached out to bump knuckles. A second later, Gadget was back to crunching numbers and analyzing data, but Indira felt like they'd just become real friends finally. She smiled to herself before checking on the others.

Across the clearing, Minerva was hunkered down with a set of headphones on, staring at a screen on Maxi's mobile console. Maxi had hijacked the necessary footage from the Editors' databases, confessing she wasn't sure how legal that was. So far none of her superiors had showed up to interfere. Maxi was busy analyzing the same footage as Minerva, providing pointers here and there.

Down the hill, Allen Squalls and Cavern were practicing their parts. She saw they were using a toppled oak tree for test runs. Allen's new confidence had given him a little more control over his gift. As Phoenix had predicted, he no longer had to fall asleep to summon his powers. It was a huge step for him, and it couldn't have come at a more crucial time.

She watched him use a practice gust to lift Cavern into the air. For such a massive character, Cavern's landings were surprisingly graceful. There was one particular technique Indira had wanted to know more about. She'd asked him to explain the shadow-teleporting trick he'd used on them when they first met. He'd explained that he had to be within ten to fifteen paces to use it.

Indira had grinned back at him and said that would work just fine.

Characters kept appearing. Maxi's best guess was that they had until sundown the next day before all their stories would be permanently altered. Every single story that involved the Hero's Journey would be ruined permanently. No more adventurous quests. No more portals to other worlds. It would just be a bunch of characters—all dressed as pirates or soldiers—who remained in the Ordinary World. Every reader would be bored to death.

Indira knew that meant her own story would be corrupted. She also knew there was a chance that Joey's magic could run deeper, destroying all of Plot. This was their last opportunity to stop him.

When all the pieces of the plan had been worked out, Indira found an empty blanket and lay down. The others eventually joined her, but there was a noticeable gap where Phoenix had been the night before. Indira could not help imagining him forced into flight, roaming the skies to the south, enslaved by their ruthless enemy. She whispered to the stars.

"We're coming for you."

33

The Beginning of the End

The next morning dawned cool and clear.

Indira's team gathered their materials before climbing into a carriage. Juliet and the other advisors waved as Indira's crew started down the road, ready for one final effort.

"Update," Gadget announced. "We've got audio confirming that Joey is prepared to move on. Ledge has been telling him all about Fable. It sounds like he's ready for a new game. We can't wait until the afternoon. Indira, you'll have to make your challenge as soon as we get there."

She nodded. That first meeting would be the part where things had the highest likelihood of going wrong. Indira kept rehearsing in her head all the advice she'd been given. But like anything else in life, knowledge wasn't enough. Now she actually had to perform the task.

"Is everyone okay with that timeline?" Indira asked.

There were nods all around.

"And everyone feels good about their role?"

More nods. Their crew was ready. The sun had barely risen over the distant hills when the carriages slowed to a stop. Indira leaped from the back and landed with a thud on the road. In one hand she carried her hammer; in the other, a flag that Penelope had woven for her. It had two skulls staring in opposite directions. The rest of the crew stayed inside the carriage. Indira met their gazes, head held high.

If you've ever been on a team, dear reader, you'll know how Indira felt in that moment. She was preparing to face the impossible, but she was doing so shoulder to shoulder with people she loved. Each one of them felt like a piece of armor. All linked together, Indira knew they had a strength that Joey would not be expecting. A strength that Joey couldn't understand.

Indira cleared her throat, preparing to give a speech, but Gadget spoke first.

"I've been running the numbers. We have about a 1.7 percent chance of succeeding if all of this goes right." The others exchanged glances. It was a pretty depressing number. "Not the best odds. But you know what? Everyone else has a *zero* percent chance of stopping Joey. We're the only ones who can do this. Our plan is as good as it can be. Now it's time to take action."

Allen Squalls nodded at that, his eyes already glowing with power.

"This whole time, I've been imagining all the ways I might die," he said. "Wild turkey attacks. A vending machine falling on my head. All of them sounded so awful. . . ." His eyes roamed the walls of the distant city. "But dying to save everyone else? To rescue my best friend? Well, I guess that wouldn't be the worst way to go."

Gadget glanced at him. "Best friend?"

"Well, yeah—I mean, Phoenix hasn't made it official or whatever. But I'm pretty sure we're best friends. Haven't you noticed? A fire mage and a water mage? It's like the perfect combo. So, yeah, best friends . . ."

Indira found herself grinning at that. She knew Phoenix would be proud that Allen had decided to stay and fight. Her eyes flicked over to Cavern next. The antagonist had been shifting uncomfortably as he listened to their speeches. After an awkward pause, he shrugged.

"It's been kind of fun being good. Whatever. Let's go hit something."

Indira laughed. "I couldn't have asked for a better crew. The only way that we beat Joey is by doing it together. See you all on the inside. Let's go save the world."

The crew echoed her words. Turning, Indira started the long march to the city. As the carriages parted and the town came into view, Indira felt another presence walking beside her. She glanced that way. The only Plot sister who Indira hadn't spent time with was finally making an appearance. End's crown glistened in the bright sunlight. Her queenly dress flowed elegantly behind her. Indira nodded in her direction.

"So this is the end?"

End nodded. "What kind of ending remains to be seen."

Indira took a deep breath. She was thankful not to be alone. She shifted her vision, squinting at the second sight of the tutor device, and located Joey's glowing dot. Thankfully, he had not decided to depart for Fable yet. Indira approached the town, doing her best to remain visible. When she was in shouting distance, she raised her voice.

"Joey!" she shouted angrily. "Come out! Face me!"

The shouts echoed. End paused well behind Indira. She watched the scene unfold from the front porch of an abandoned farm. The towering walls of Ordinary loomed. The town was silent. No one came at first. All Indira could do was keep screaming her challenge to the sky. She raised her voice, shouting, until her throat grew raw and tired.

Finally, the glowing dot on her radar flickered with movement.

She heard the sound of wings first. Great gusts of wind rose. And then Phoenix's clay-and-charcoal form launched over the walls. Indira lifted the flag up as high as she could. It was a challenge in Joey's video-game world, one that he would understand.

Even at a distance, she could see Joey sitting on Phoenix's back, squinting down.

"I challenge you!" Indira shouted. "Come and face me!"

Her chest was heaving. So much depended on what happened next. There had always been a small chance that Joey would take one look at her and open fire. She let out a held breath when he began his descent, leading Phoenix in a loop before touching down on the open road.

The Author still looked strange to her eyes. His features were so sharply real that she had to squint. The gold-glinting hair, the apple-red lips, the glacial eyes. Energy crackled dangerously around him as he disembarked. Indira shivered a little when she noticed that his footsteps left no trace on the dusty road. He was not truly part of this world. It was frightening to remember that.

"You're that girl," he said. "The one who brought me my dragon. Thanks again for that. He's really awesome. There's no dragon in the world as loyal as Vesuvius."

Indira gritted her teeth. "His name is Phoenix."

"He told me," Joey replied, smirking. "Phoenix? That's such a stupid name! He's not even a phoenix! He's a dragon! That's why I renamed him. Vesuvius is a lot cooler."

The dragon lifted his head at the sound. Indira had to swallow back her anger at the idea that Phoenix could be anyone other than who he was. She needed to stay focused. This moment could still go very wrong. She fixed her eyes on Joey.

"Do you recognize my flag?"

He grinned. "It's the head-to-head emblem."

"And? Do you accept my challenge or not?"

"Challenge?" Joey considered her. "From you? Is that some kind of joke or something? I've been running games in here for hours. No one can touch me. And the last time you faced me, you had a dragon and you *still* lost. I wouldn't exactly call that a challenge."

Indira recognized the patterns in his speech. Maxi's research had been useful. She'd dug up old files of Joey talking smack to his friends and opponents. A lot of his early writing included similar dialogue. Indira decided to use the advice Juliet had given her. Make it seem as if beating him at his own game would be nothing to her.

"You're right. It would be too easy." Indira let the words float into the air. "For me."

Joey's attention sharpened. "Wow. Are you even serious?"

"I am serious. It's okay if you're afraid. Don't worry. I won't tell anyone."

The calm expression on Joey's face melted away. Indira knew she was walking a narrow tightrope. She needed to lure him into battle without making him mad enough to attack her here and now.

"I want a head-to-head," she said. "The Venice map.

You can choose what the power-ups are. No other play-ers. No extra lives. First one to eliminate the other person wins."

Maxi had spent nearly an hour going over all the rules with Indira. The surprised look on Joey's face made her feel that that hour had been more than worth it. Joey looked impressed that she knew the rules at all. He considered her offer before shrugging.

"Wins *what*?"

"First place."

Joey frowned. "That's not enough. I've already *proven* I'm the best."

Indira swallowed. She wasn't prepared for this. What could she possibly offer someone like Joey? She knew it didn't really matter. She wasn't actually here to beat him. She was just here to lure him into playing one more game. What did he really want?

"If I win," she said, "you go back where you came from. Free Phoenix. Free all of us and go back home. Leave us alone once and for all."

Joey considered that. "And if I win?"

"I'll take you to Fable."

His eyes narrowed. "Ledge already told me about Fable. I can go whenever I want."

Indira took a risk, inventing wildly. "Without the se-cret password to get into the city? Ledge clearly isn't from there if he doesn't know about that. If you want access to the best game—the biggest city—in our world, you'll have to beat me to get it."

Indira kept her face as calm as she could. Joey was watching her closely, and it felt like he could see right through her lie. A second passed and Indira decided to dig the knife in a little deeper, pulling out a line that would have made Juliet proud.

"What? Afraid to lose?"

He snapped back. "I'm not going to lose."

"Prove it."

The anger on his face was a good sign. Her taunts were working.

"Deal."

Indira felt such intense relief that she nearly forgot the other instructions, the other dominoes that needed to topple for their plan to work. Joey was holding out his hand to shake on the arrangement, but she had a few more requests.

"I don't want any of the townspeople in our way," Indira said. "And we start on even footing! You can make Phoenix one of the power-ups if you want, but we both start in boats."

Joey considered that request. Indira flinched a little when he raised one hand. She thought he was about to attack, but instead he snapped his fingers. A great slash of power cut through the air. Indira was forced back a few steps by the blooming energy. There was movement on her right. Indira looked over and found that the entire populace of Ordinary had appeared on the nearest hillside. All of them looked as shocked as she did.

"Back inside, Vesuvius."

The command scraped through the air. Indira watched Phoenix take flight, and she had to resist reaching for her hammer and hitting Joey right then and there for trying to rename her best friend. Joey held out his hand again to seal their pact.

"You're going down," he said.

Indira reached out. "Bring it on."

As their hands touched, there was an answering flash. Indira's entire world spun and spun. When it righted itself, she was sitting inside a boat, floating on the canal.

She'd teleported inside Ordinary.

A great booming voice counted down. "Three! Two! ONE!"

And the game began.

34

Head-to-Head

A thundering shot rang out.

Indira didn't hesitate. She snatched the controller and directed her boat to the nearest building. Maxi had explained the rules of the game and all the various strategies for a head-to-head match. Indira knew power-ups would be waiting on the roofs of certain buildings. She wouldn't survive five minutes against Joey without them.

And that was the goal. Indira wasn't the hero this time. She was the bait.

Indira's boat skidded to the front of a familiar building: the courthouse. She leaped out, sprinted up the wide steps, and shouldered through the entrance. The interior was dimly lit. She assumed Joey had started on the opposite end of the map. It was likely he was doing the same thing that she was.

As she started up the main staircase, her eyes flicked briefly to the radar in her tutor device. Indira was in the western corner. Sure enough, Joey's dot glowed at the eastern end. She noted that it wasn't moving. Maybe he was going up through a building like she was?

Indira opened the door that led to the courthouse's roof. As expected, an icon hovered in midair, glowing orange. Training had included Maxi teaching Indira about each power-up. Fortune was on their side—and Indira wondered if maybe Deus was out there pulling a few strings—because the first icon would be very useful. The image was a pair of feet splashing across the surface of a river.

"Water walking," she whispered to herself. "Exactly what I need."

The second her outstretched hand made contact, the power-up glowed, spiraled into a smaller form, and attached to her shoulder. It glowed there like a little blue pendant. Indira knew that a touch of that button would activate the power-up.

As she turned around, the sight of Joey's glowing dot made her pause.

It still hadn't moved. "What is he up to . . . ?"

Her eyes scanned the distant building tops. Power-ups twirled here and there. It was far too quiet. Indira was moving silently back to the stairwell when a pair of military jets screamed overhead. Indira gave a shout of surprise as the two planes swung back around and took aim.

She slammed down the steps, leaping four or five at a time. The explosions came a few seconds later, shaking the entire building. Indira took the last flight of stairs as the entire ceiling caved in. Debris came spiraling down in dangerous shards, and she barely dove through the front entrance in time. Her boat was waiting right where she'd left it.

"Nice try, Joey," she said through gritted teeth.

The jets continued firing on the building as Indira pulled out into the canal. She'd read about that power-up too. It was an air strike. The player picked a random section of the city to fire upon. Eventually, the jets would vanish from sight. She had to keep moving.

The second building she climbed was empty. The third—a small apothecary shop—produced another useful tool for the showdown to come.

"Explosives," she whispered.

On the icon, there were three cannonballs with lit fuses. The power-up settled onto her shoulder beside the water-walking one, a glowing red dot waiting to be activated.

Now she just needed to find Joey.

Another glance at the radar had her worried. The Author's dot on the map still hadn't moved. She was starting to get the feeling that their tracking system wasn't working. The realization sent a shiver down Indira's spine. She'd been counting on that advantage.

Indira made her way to the next building as quietly as

possible. Another icon waited there, and her heart beat faster at the sight. It showed an image of two parrots entwined with one another. She remembered that Maxi had thought the two birds looked totally adorable. Indira knew the birds would fly in the direction of her closest enemy.

She activated it immediately. Red light swirled as the two parrots appeared out of thin air. They flapped and fluttered, turning in circles. Indira watched them land on the edge of the building. Indira stared in confusion as they fluttered once before settling down on the ledge.

"Seriously? A glitch?"

But then she realized both birds were looking *down*. Indira darted across the roof, and slammed against the raised ledge, eyes searching below. Her boat was there.

Another had joined it.

Both rocked gently in the breeze. Indira panicked. Joey was here.

She turned in time to see the roof entrance blast open. Joey stepped out, thrilled by the sight of her trapped on the far end of the roof. Indira pressed her back to the ledge of the building, instinctively positioning herself. She raised her hammer slowly and put both hands above her head in fake surrender.

"You caught me. Nice work."

He grinned. "I thought you said this would be a challenge."

Indira took a deep breath. It was all guesswork, but

she held the hammer out behind her head, over the water, and prayed that her aim was true.

"It's not over until it's over," she called back.

Joey activated one of his power-ups. An actual turret — complete with rotating weaponry — blinked to life in front of him. He was about to open fire when Indira let go of her hammer. Magic dragged her through the air, from the roof to a boat in less than a breath. In that dizzying moment, she barely had time to look up, locate the falling silver hammer, and lunge for it.

She caught it just before it could splash into the canal.

Breathless, she turned back to the boat's controls. There was shouting above and the sound of Joey's turret scanning for a target it no longer could see. But Indira was already on the move. She slammed down the *B* button on the controller, grinning as the boat thundered away.

"Come on," she whispered. "Let's have a little chase."

It was time for phase two. Their chosen location was halfway across town. Indira didn't waste even a second. She knew Joey would have tricks up his sleeve that he'd use to catch up with her. She just needed to reach the right spot on the map for the rest of their plan to work.

She darted down the first alley she saw, swung through a side street on the lower end of town, and thundered back up one of the main drags. Buildings and houses whipped by, and there was enough noise from her engine that she almost didn't notice the great gusts of wind pressing down from above. Her eyes flicked up. Joey had found Phoenix.

"Fly, Vesuvius!" she heard him shout. "Faster!"

Wings spread. Indira took a narrow side street, ducking into a space where she knew they couldn't follow. Her destination wasn't far now. She just hoped she'd given the others enough time to get in position. A bolt of fire hit the roof of a nearby building. The explosion shook the frame, light dancing across the water, but Indira just kept speeding away.

She took a final turn and found herself racing down a familiar road.

A glance to the skies showed that Joey had been forced to swing higher into the air. She watched as he climbed up, trying to get her back in his sights. She had ten seconds at the most.

Indira cut her engines. Momentum carried her boat to the very center of the street. Indira tried not to look at the familiar house on her right. She needed to focus. She reached instead for the two power-ups on her shoulder. Blue and red lights swirled to life.

A trio of cartoonish explosives appeared in her right hand. In the same second, a pair of winged shoes molded over her current pair. Indira chanced another look at the skies. Joey's flight had him wheeling back in her direction, preparing for an attack.

Now was the time.

Indira dropped the explosives inside her own boat. The fuses were still sizzling as she leaped over the starboard side. Her feet landed, but instead of splashing down into the water, she stayed atop it, the water-walking power-up carrying her across impossibly. She picked her angle very carefully, running in the direction of the sun, remembering their crew's very carefully designed plan. She darted into the alley there and waited.

From that hiding spot, Indira turned. The explosives in her boat detonated first. As the smoke rose, Joey descended on Phoenix's back. It was the most beautiful sight. The wooden shards of her boat had flown in every direction, leaving only a smoking pile floating over the water. Joey pulled Phoenix up sharply, hovering in the air, searching.

"Where'd she go, Vesuvius? Sniff her out."

Indira waited.

Her water-walking power-up had thirty more seconds left before it ran out. The beating of Phoenix's wings cleared away some of the smoke. Joey directed the dragon lower, still searching for some sign of her in the wreckage. The moment was coming. Phoenix kept turning until he was at exactly the right angle, directly opposite the house that Indira had marked. Indira tightened her grip, raised her hammer, and sprinted forward.

Twelve paces. That was all that separated her from Joey.

Each lengthy stride swallowed that distance. Indira bellowed a war cry, her footsteps gliding impossibly over the water's surface. Joey's face twisted in surprise. His body turned instinctively. He brought his lacrosse stick swinging around as Indira leaped through the air to strike him. Her hammer swung back, and Joey did exactly what their team had expected him to do.

Faced with the prospect of losing, he cheated.

Indira hung in the air, immobilized, her hammer halfway to its intended target. She gritted her teeth for show and pretended to be surprised.

"Hey!" she shouted. "This isn't one of the power-ups!"

Joey grinned. "You thought you could beat me? Seriously?"

Indira faked her resistance. She let out a snarl as if she were trying to throw that invisible weight from her shoulders. All her effort, though, was intended to keep Joey's eyes fixed on her. Keep him distracted, no matter what.

"I escaped you before," Indira grunted. "I'll escape again."

She tried to finish the swing of her hammer. It only moved a fraction of an inch. Joey saw her effort and started laughing louder. Phoenix's wings beat steadily to keep both him and Joey airborne. All that movement and sound was likely the reason Joey didn't notice a gust of wind rising up above the rooftops. His eyes were fixed hungrily on her instead. That was also why he didn't see the other figure float through the air and land farther down Phoenix's back.

Indira had chosen her angle of attack very specifically.

Joey was squinting at her, the sun directly in his face. That was by design. It cast his shadow along Phoenix's clay scales.

"Admit that I beat you," Joey taunted. "I want to hear you say that I'm better than you."

Indira couldn't help grinning.

"You are better than me, but you're not better than *us*."

A frown stretched across Joey's face as Cavern appeared in his shadow. The antagonist roped one arm around him, pressing that ink-black hand to the Author's cheek.

Dark magic blossomed.

They hadn't been sure of this part. Would the magic work on someone as powerful as Joey? But Indira watched the black handprint appear. Joey's bright eyes darkened. His shadow vanished with a whiplike swish. It worked. Indira didn't know how long the spell would hold, but for now Joey's spirit was trapped inside Cavern's dark cave.

Allen Squalls glanced down from the opposite rooftop. In the house on their right, Minerva and Maxi peered out from the windows. Cavern set a firm hand on his captive's shoulder. "We've got him," he said with a grunt.

Indira nodded. "Take him inside. It's time to send him back to the Real World."

35

The Perfect Plan

Cavern lifted Joey and leaped from Phoenix's back to the waiting porch. Indira searched the rooftops and canals, wondering if Ledge Woods would make an appearance. They were challenged instead by an unexpected roar. Phoenix had lifted his head. Indira thought Cavern's magic would have broken Joey's control over Phoenix, but it didn't look like it had.

Phoenix looked furious, thinking they were kidnapping his master.

Indira leaped across the distance to stand between Phoenix and Joey. Cavern had turned, backpedaling warily. Phoenix shifted his reptilian head, snapping sharp jaws.

"Wait!" Indira locked eyes with him. "Look at me! Phoenix! Remember who you are."

Cavern used the distraction to slip inside the house. Phoenix's eyes were starting to glow. If he unleashed his fire and burned down the house behind her, there was a good chance their plans would be completely ruined. Indira had to break Joey's control of him. Instinct told her that the hammer wasn't going to work this time. She needed to use a different kind of power.

"I have a secret."

His head was still tossing angrily from side to side, but she noticed that those words had snagged his attention. Both of his coal-burning eyes fixed on her.

"Brainstorm Underglass told me why you were assigned to this tutorial," she said. "It was a test run to see if you'd make a good . . . romantic interest. For me."

Heat rushed over her cheeks and down her neck. Phoenix's entire body had gone statue-still. Those great marble-like eyes watched her, unblinking.

"You're one of my best friends. I'm sorry that I risked your life. I'm sorry that Joey did this to you. But your name is not Vesuvius." Indira felt the truth tremble out of her. "Your name is Phoenix. You're my favorite person. And I like you so much. And your story—our story—is only just beginning."

There was a hiss of smoke. Indira watched as the great form twisted and shrank until there was an ordinary boy with dashing red hair standing in water up to his chest. She smiled down at him. "Want to help me save the world?"

He looked confused for a second, as if he'd just woken

up from a dream, but then his eyes flickered with flame at the sight of her. "I thought you'd never ask."

Above them, one of the second-story windows was flung open. Maxi leaned out with a scolding look on her face. "Could you two quit flirting and get up here?"

Indira grinned as Maxi vanished back inside. Reaching down, she helped Phoenix out of the canal with a splash. The two of them walked forward, shoulders pressed together, ready to face the final part of *this* adventure together. Indira led him to the very top floor, to the same room she'd woken up in when all of this had started.

A strange scene greeted them.

Cavern stood at the center of the room with one hand set on Joey's shoulder. His other hand was pressed to his stomach. Every few seconds he grunted in pain. The spell appeared to be holding Joey captive for now, but Indira could see he was fighting with all his strength to keep the Author trapped. That was expected. In all their planning, they'd only hoped for ten minutes.

Meanwhile, Gadget was leaning down in front of a seated Joey. Indira watched as the girl carefully slid two of the prepared tutor devices into his eyes and then blindfolded him.

Maxi wielded an item that Indira initially mistook for a wand. A closer look showed that it was a red pen. Every time she slashed the air, something in the room transformed. The farmhouse dresser became a flat-screen TV.

A pair of overalls shimmered into lacrosse gear. Item by item, Maxi slowly edited the room until it looked like the one Joey actually lived in.

The stairs behind Indira creaked. Minerva was there. Indira could hear the woman practicing her lines. She had traded her classic outfit for something a bit more modern—a pair of flowy sweatpants and a brightly colored sweater. In her right hand, she held a pair of pristine scissors. Gadget eyed them for a second and laughed.

"All this tech, and the most important thing in the room is a pair of scissors."

Everyone smiled. All the details had been chosen with great care. Allen Squalls stood by the window, his eyes unfocused. The light in the room was dimming as gray clouds formed outside. Little dots of rain were already streaking down the window. That had been Allen's idea. They didn't want to risk a chance of breaking the illusion. Better to obscure the surrounding town with a little bad weather. Not to mention, it would hide the fact that it was still noon in their world, when they wanted him to believe it was night. Indira didn't hear Allen muttering about all the possible deaths that awaited him, either. He was focused instead on doing his job.

"He's getting close to escaping," Cavern announced. "Move faster."

Maxi circled the room, dedicating her attention to the gaming systems she had summoned. Indira knew she was carefully going back through a detailed list, making sure every title and controller was exactly the way it would appear in Joey's room in the Real World.

"How is this going to wake him up?" Phoenix whispered.

Indira explained. "We realized he's not afraid of dragons. Which makes sense. He plays video games with dragons all the time. But there is one thing that *every* eleven-year-old boy fears. Come on, I'll show you."

She led him across the room to an empty closet. Gadget was already pressed into the back corner, staring down at a screen, making minor adjustments to the tutor devices she'd programmed. Indira crawled into the right side of the closet. Phoenix followed her. Maxi had carved a hole in the wall there, and the back of Joey's favorite video-game system was pressed against it.

"Can you make smoke?" Indira asked Phoenix. "Without setting everything on fire?"

He snorted. "Of course."

"One minute," Cavern announced. "Final preparations."

Allen Squalls put a few final touches on his storm before joining them in the closet. He surprised Phoenix with a quick side hug. "Bestie! Welcome back!"

Maxi was still whipping around the room, making minor adjustments. There were dirty socks on the floor now and cups half filled with soured liquids. The whole place looked a little disgusting. Cavern carefully repositioned Joey in the chair. Maxi set a controller in the boy's lap. She was heading for the closet when she remembered something. "The clock!"

She darted back across the room to adjust the time. Now it read 4:37 a.m. She sprinted back, slid into the closet beside Squalls, and closed the doors behind her. The group fell silent.

All their careful planning was about to be put to the test.

"I'm going to release him," Cavern announced. "Ready?"

Minerva called a confirmation from the stairs. Indira leaned forward. She could just barely see the room through a crack in the wall. Cavern carefully removed the blindfold from Joey's eyes. Silently, the antagonist darted toward the stairs.

Joey was staring blankly ahead.

The door opened and closed. For a few seconds, the only sound was the gentle patter of rain on the window. And then the television turned on. The explosions on the screen sounded exactly the same as all the cannons Joey had fired on them.

The Author blinked back to life.

He glanced around the room, clearly confused.

His eyes settled on the controller in his hand. One of his thumbs traced the joystick. There was another explosion on the television. The noise drew his eyes up. He frowned at the screen. Indira could see his confusion growing. He was asking the same question that every dreamer asks. Where was he? Had any of what he'd just experienced been real?

As he glanced around the room, all the details he saw would fit his memories of the Real World. Maxi's careful design guaranteed that. And the tutor devices Gadget installed would color his vision, too, enriching it until it matched the intensity of the Real World.

Joey was still looking a little lost when Minerva burst into the room.

It was a classic scene. The mother catching her son staying up too late playing video games. She threw him a scandalized look, features brightened by the glow of the screen, and crossed the room like a strike of lightning. Indira saw Joey actually flinch backward.

Gadget's programming would be rewiring the image in his head. Minerva's features would be blending with the images Maxi had researched of Joey's mother. The image was more than a woman wearing clothes similar to hers or acting the way she acted. Joey would actually see his mother standing in front of him.

"Joey!" Minerva exclaimed. "I thought I told you to go to bed by eleven!"

Indira saw him flinch again. That voice was the most frightening thing Joey could imagine. Minerva pressed forward until she was towering over him.

"It's almost five a.m.! You're still awake? Playing these *video games*?"

Joey swallowed. Indira thought she saw the bright colors of his hair and eyes fade just a little bit. He opened his mouth. "But I wasn't—I don't know what—"

"No excuses," Minerva cut in. "You're *grounded*."

The room actually trembled with that pronouncement. The ground started to shake. Outside, Allen Squalls brought down a strike of lightning to punctuate the threat. Joey's calm expression twisted a little as the nightmare kept getting worse.

"Mom," he begged. "I promise—I wasn't—"

Minerva ignored him. She marched across the room, and this was the part they'd spent so much time practicing. It was always messy trying to figure out which cord connected where and did what, but any real parent would know *exactly* which one to take.

Everything needed to happen at once.

Indira's voice was barely a whisper in Phoenix's ear. "Summon the smoke."

At the same time, she lifted her hammer. And Minerva yanked out a very specific black cord. She held it in the air for Joey to see, swinging her pair of scissors around. All it took was one snip. Indira swung her hammer. It crashed into the back of the machine, shattering crucial pieces. Squalls brought down another bolt of lightning. Gadget scrambled the tutor devices so that the entire room would look like it was shaking violently. Phoenix's smoke floated out from the back of the machine. All of this happened in less than a breath.

And then Minerva delivered the final, crucial line. "You'll *never* play this again."

Horror echoed across Joey's face. He pointed at the smoke as his features twisted and a scream echoed through the entire room. The boy who didn't fear dragons or dark caves or zombies most certainly feared *this*. Really, it was a string of his greatest fears, all chained together. The fear of being caught doing something he wasn't supposed to do. Followed by the fear of actually being punished for it. And, finally, the fear of never getting to play his favorite games again. It was an unthinkable fate.

All that fear cut through Joey like a knife. Indira could imagine him waking up in the Real World with sweat on his forehead, breathing heavily. In the same moment, Joey vanished from the world of Imagination in a bright flash.

Minerva slumped to her knees. Maxi pumped her fists in the air. The crew rushed out of the closet, joined by Cavern from his hiding place on the staircase, and their shouts of joy were likely heard all the way in Fable. Indira looked around at the others, knowing each one had played their part perfectly.

She'd never felt more like a hero.

36

Back to Normal

Joey's disappearance rippled through the rest of the world.

Indira and her crew emerged from the house to find the streets of Ordinary as they'd been that first day when they arrived. The canals were gone. Even the scorch marks from cannon fire had faded. Indira's challenge had already secured the safety of Ordinary's citizens. She just hoped defeating Joey would fix all that had happened beyond the city walls. Had they saved the rest of Plot from his magic? And what about the Story Houses?

Their crew piled into a carriage and shot back down the country roads, Gadget at the wheel. When they reached the crowd by the monument, Indira saw the changes immediately. All the pirate gear had vanished. All the military armor, too. And all the characters had been restored back to their original costumes and roles. She saw Dorothy's glinting ruby heels and Huck Finn in his dirty overalls.

Men and women in dark suits, wearing dark sunglasses, wove through the gathering. The Editors had finally arrived. Indira saw them wielding the same powerful red pens Maxi had used. Each swipe drew pieces of the monument back to where they had originally stood. Indira also spied Ledge Woods sitting off to one side in their custody. She could only guess how much trouble he was in. He'd gone far beyond the role of an antagonist. He'd actively worked with someone capable of destroying their entire world, and he'd laughed his way through the whole thing. Indira suspected Ledge would not be returning to Fester anytime soon.

Indira felt a final weight lift from her shoulders when the last piece of the monument settled back into place. It immediately began to glow, its restorative magic bright. Then the trapped characters began to disappear, one by one in the reverse order of their appearance, as they were returned to their Story Houses.

It had worked. They'd won. Indira's heart soared.

Her advisors crowded forward, eager to get in a word before vanishing.

"Never a doubt you'd return," Penelope whispered confidently. "Never a doubt."

"And I suspect it was a grand adventure," Wendy chimed in.

Juliet took Indira's face in her hands. "If you want the job done right, send a woman."

Indira couldn't take all the credit, though. She gestured back to the rest of her team.

"It was all of us. We all played our parts. Thank you so much for your advice."

Other characters crowded forward. King Arthur graciously thanked them at first, but ruined the kind words by pointing out he'd have finished Joey off much faster. Indira didn't mind when he disappeared. Huck Finn simply tipped his straw hat to them before vanishing.

Only when the final characters had been safely restored to their Story Houses did Indira allow herself to collapse onto the grassy hillside. Maxi was farther down the road, reporting to some of the more senior Editors. But the rest of Indira's crew stayed with her, lying back against the grass, their eyes tracing the clouds.

"A 1.7 percent chance of success," Gadget said aloud. "I'm going to have to adjust some of my predictive algorithms. Pretty sure the computer wasn't accounting for how *awesome* we are."

Everyone laughed.

Phoenix added. "Minerva, that was some *serious* mom power."

She was grinning. "Your smoke effect was a nice touch."

"Not to mention Squalls with those perfectly timed lightning strikes," Gadget said.

Allen's cheeks brightened. "We couldn't have done it without your programming."

Gadget sighed. "Speaking of programming, I returned the devices to their original settings. I know our scores impact our grades, maybe even our placement in a story someday."

Phoenix groaned. "Don't remind me. We basically broke the whole quest tutorial."

"Well, there's good news and bad news," Gadget replied. "First, we actually accomplished a lot of the steps in the Hero's Journey by accident. The bad news is that our scores are all in the negative. There's a message waiting on each device that says, 'You have failed to complete your mission. Return to Fable and report to Brainstorm Underglass.' The word *failed* isn't promising."

Minerva pushed up to her feet. "I'm planning on writing up a full report. I'll even go back to Fable with you if it will help. There's no way you should be punished for what happened. No one would have been expected to complete the tutorial with a rogue Author on the loose. You're all heroes in my book."

"Whatever happens," Indira said, "we report to Fable together."

As the silence stretched, Maxi returned to the group.

"The Editors have this under control now. I'm being sent to Fable as your representative. I'll do my best to explain to the brainstorms what happened. Come on. It's time to get you home."

288

Rather than risk another group portal, they traveled home in a larger version of the motorized carriages they'd been using. Indira guessed the Editors could have probably snapped their fingers and sent all of them back to Fable, but as she looked around the carriage, it was clear how much everyone needed rest.

Allen Squalls fell asleep in a pile of blankets in one corner, no longer afraid of being attacked by a family of wild owls. Gadget fiddled with a few of her inventions before drifting off too. Maxi settled her head in Indira's lap and started snoring. Even her friend's snores were kind of adorable. Indira was enjoying the rumbling lull of the road beneath them when she realized only she and Phoenix were still awake.

His eyes were steady flames, even as he frowned. "My memory is a little fuzzy. I don't remember everything that happened when Joey turned me into Vesuvius. It's kind of like he temporarily erased me and my thoughts and personality. So how'd you break me free?"

In all the chaos, she'd forgotten that this moment was coming. There'd been so many things to discuss after Joey's disappearance. She'd set aside what had happened right before their victory, when she'd been staring into the eyes of a mind-controlled dragon that she just so happened to have a huge crush on. Phoenix hadn't mentioned anything about the speech she'd given. She'd thought he was embarrassed, but now it was clear he'd forgotten it all.

"You really don't remember?" she asked.

He shook his head. "Joey was controlling me. I know that much. And we flew around the city looking . . . for you. I remember that. I remember trying to fight against him, but there wasn't anything I could do. And then . . ." He frowned, looking down at his own hands. "I remember you were there and suddenly I was standing in the canal. Looking up at you."

His eyes found hers. She took a deep breath to keep her voice from trembling. It was terrifying because she didn't actually know what would happen. She liked Phoenix. She'd been certain—staring up at him in his dragon form—that their story was only just beginning.

But her gut feeling didn't change the fact that their team was returning with negative scores on their Hero's Journey. Brainstorm Underglass had mentioned they'd be assessing Indira's connection with Phoenix, not to mention his own abilities. Had he done enough to earn a place in her story? Even if Indira felt certain they were a good fit, that didn't guarantee his spot. She couldn't bear the idea of making a promise only to break it later. Better to tell him the truth she could control.

"I said that I had a crush on you." Indira blushed.

The sparks in his eyes became flames. Phoenix was looking at her like she was speaking a different language. He smiled after a second. "Even though I'm part dragon?"

"Even then," she answered. "I like you because you're . . . well . . . you're just you! I don't know! You're always trying to do the right thing. You bring out the best in people, like you did with Squalls. I've liked you since the very first day we met. When you were just a weird kid in a robe with no last name."

The sudden confession made her blush. She looked away, watching the hills rise and fall around them. It took a few seconds for her to find the bravery to look back. She smiled.

"But, yeah, the dragon part definitely doesn't hurt."

An awkward moment passed. Indira did not know what to say or what to do, and the awkwardness was only made worse when Maxi spoke.

"If you're going to kiss, at least let me move."

Indira blushed a rather violent shade of red. Phoenix looked ready to transform into smoke so that he could escape through the cracked window.

"We're not going to kiss," she said quickly.

Phoenix shook his head just as quickly. "I wasn't—we weren't—come on, Maxi!"

The girl grinned a little before snuggling deeper in between them. Indira was both thankful and slightly annoyed. She didn't know the first thing about kissing. But it was a relief when Phoenix reached across to set his hand next to hers. She slipped her fingers over his, and the two sat there in a comfortable silence, pretending a whole new world hadn't just formed for both of them.

Phoenix broke that quiet nearly half an hour later and asked the one question she was dreading. "How is that supposed to work?" he whispered. "If we're not in the same story, even though we like each other? Could we ever have a happy ending?"

Indira tried to sound confident. "I think we'll find out soon enough. Until then . . ."

She laced her fingers through his and closed her eyes.

"Until then," he whispered back.

37

Heroes?

"Ready?"

Indira stood at the front of the group. They'd paused briefly outside Brainstorm Underglass's office. Everyone had taken a second to smooth collars and tuck in shirts. Gadget double-checked to make sure her devices wouldn't go off in the middle of the meeting.

None of them knew what to expect. The urgent message that they'd failed and should report back immediately was still glowing in each tutor device. Indira took a final look at the crew. "I'm proud of each of you," she said. "Keep your heads high."

She knocked. A voice called back, asking them to wait a moment. Indira looked around at the others, feeling more nervous than she was letting on, when the door opened. Maxi exited the room first. She'd spent the last thirty minutes inside, arguing their case to Underglass.

Behind her, three familiar sisters exited as well. End graced them with a smile. Middle smirked as she passed. Beginning was far more emotional. The young girl gave each of them a hug, except Gadget, who she briefly bumped knuckles with. "Thank you," she said, over and over. "For saving Plot. For being heroes! Remember that every end is just a new beginning."

As she said those words, the three figures merged back into one, striding down the hall and away from them. Indira thought she saw the emissary of Plot grin back before vanishing around a corner. Indira swallowed once — unsure how to interpret their presence — before glancing in Maxi's direction. "Well?"

Maxi's sunglasses hid her expression. "I did my best. Time to face the music."

Underglass called for them to enter.

Indira gulped again and led the crew inside. As always, the brainstorm's office was immaculately clean: every piece of furniture, every single folder, in precise order. Underglass looked up as they marched inside, an unreadable expression on her face. Indira stood front and center. The rest of the crew fanned out on either side. Maxi hovered in the background.

"Indira," Underglass said in her crisp voice. "Welcome back."

Indira cleared her throat. "We've prepared a full report."

Minerva moved across the room. She set an unnecessarily large binder on the desk. She and Gadget had worked well into the morning hours preparing every detail, supplemented with saved footage from the tutor devices. Underglass turned to the first page with a sigh.

"I've learned much of what happened from the Plot sisters and from Maxi," Underglass explained. "However, the facts still remain. You did not complete the assigned mission. What is worse, your points combine into the lowest total of any group we've ever sent on the Hero's Journey."

Indira's heart sank. Was that really what mattered? After all they'd been through, they were going to be measured by some useless scale? The brainstorm continued.

"Indira, you struggled with teamwork at the beginning. Gadget, you were so distracted by the devices that you missed your first few scenes. Phoenix and Allen, you did well together at the start. But, Allen, you kept getting distracted, and Phoenix ended up being a little headstrong. At the end of the day, every one of you ignored your directions, even going so far as hacking into your devices and changing them! While you did accidentally accomplish some of the Hero's Journey, none of you hit your target goals, you left an entire rebellion out of the scenario, and you never even faced the Howling King!"

Their speechless crew stared at Brainstorm Underglass. The Plot sisters had surely explained everything that had happened. Maxi must have argued in their favor too. Who cared about the Howling King? Indira was trying to figure out how to respond when Underglass continued on mercilessly.

"You also took the assigned antagonist and made him into one of your teammates. You ignored several crucial steps. And you did all of this . . ."

Her gaze swept across the whole group, sharp as a knife.

"To save the rest of us. For the second time."

A smile carved its way across those serious features. Maxi burst out laughing behind them, clearly in on the joke. The others looked around in confusion. Indira pointed at the brainstorm. "That was *mean*," she said. "Seriously? After all we went through?"

Underglass smiled. "Maxi suggested it. I couldn't resist. And, frankly, I could not be more proud of each of you. Trust me. There's plenty of good news to go around. I do hope you know that our hands were tied. We were limited to the same waiting period as the Editors. Ultimately, we were relying on your talents, your teamwork, and your ingenuity to see us through. You performed beyond all expectations. Indira is familiar, I think, with what happens when you act heroically in the world of Imagination. Accomplishments such as these tend to find their way back to the Real World. The Authors always take note when someone performs admirably."

The brainstorm cleared her throat. Now her voice took on a different tone.

"Gadget, step forward."

Their teammate obeyed, her rocket-shaped earrings swaying with the movement.

"One of our chief desires for this mission was working on distraction. It was your old habit that started this whole mess. We monitored your progress after that, however, and were delighted to see you using your talents to push the story forward. Not only that, but you focused on using your ability with *machines* to help *people*. I loved seeing you make a plan and take action. All of these represent serious improvement. I am so proud."

Underglass reached beneath her desk and pressed a button. On the far right side of the blackboard behind her, slanted handwriting appeared: *The Tinker's Daughter.*

"How long have you been with us, dear?"

Gadget did not answer at first. Indira looked over to see that the girl was crying. She wiped away the tears before nodding. "Four years."

"A long time," Underglass confirmed. "The wait is over. Your story has arrived."

Gadget wiped more tears away before turning around

to rejoin the group, but not before offering each of them a quick fist bump. She whispered a brief but sincere thank-you to each of them before taking her spot at the end of the line. Indira couldn't resist leaning over to whisper. "What are the odds of that?"

Gadget grinned at her as Brainstorm Underglass's attention swept to the other end of the gathering. "Minerva Deacon," she announced. "Step forward."

Indira's surprise was mirrored on the face of her pretend mother, who'd only come to Fable as moral support for them. All along, however, Indira had thought Minerva a brilliant actress. Her final effort playing the role of Joey's mother had been award-worthy.

"After what happened with Brainstorm Ketty, we've made a habit of keeping better track of the unfinished characters who play such vital roles in the world of Imagination. We've also made a better effort to monitor which connections might still be viable."

A second story title appeared on the screen: *Mother's Magic.*

"You will train in our graduate program," Underglass informed her. "The story is still in its developmental stage, but it seems as if your Author has not forgotten you quite yet. If you're willing to put in the work . . ."

"Of course," Minerva said quickly. "I'll do whatever it takes."

There was nothing playacted about the giddy look that she shot back at the rest of them. It was the perfect surprise, and it couldn't have happened to a more deserving person.

"Allen Squalls, step forward." The young wizard stumbled to the front. "This school owes you a great debt. We were ashamed that one of our own targeted you last year. It was a relief when you chose to join this Hero's Journey tutorial, and even more of a relief to see you perform so admirably. We hadn't considered before just how . . . funny you are. It wasn't one of the talents you displayed at your auditions. But with magic like yours, and a clear knack for gallows humor, I've no doubt there's a story waiting for you. Would you consider enrolling at Protagonist Preparatory again?"

It wasn't lost on Indira how closely Allen's life was tied to hers. She'd ended up in the very story that Allen might have starred in. Indira watched the nervous boy who'd dreamed up a thousand deaths stand tall, his voice brimming with confidence now.

"I'm ready. I want to try again."

Underglass looked like a proud mother as Squalls returned to his place in the line. Phoenix threw an arm around him, whispering quiet encouragements. Gadget held out a hand to bump knuckles. The room fell silent again, however, as Underglass stood.

"I'm afraid I only have one more story to announce."

Indira felt her stomach tighten. Her eyes darted over to Phoenix. He was looking at her with a surprising amount of fear. She hated the idea of leaving him behind again. Both of them turned to nervously watch Under-glass press a final button. The bold-faced font appeared on the board:

Indira Story and the Infernal Sun

The words struck her like a blow to the chest. All the excitement she'd felt when she'd seen her first title swung in the opposite direction. A glance showed that Phoenix's face had fallen. His fiery eyes were pinned to a tile on the floor. He was going to be left behind again.

"The good news is you'll both head out immediately," Underglass said casually, like it wasn't the biggest news in the world. "The Author already started on the first scene. I believe it involves a certain someone transforming into a dragon during math class."

Phoenix's eyes lifted. The smile that flashed across his face was so bright that Indira thought he might burst into flames. His eyes swung to her. "Did you know?"

She shook her head. "I knew you had a chance, but I didn't want to make any promises I couldn't keep. That's actually what I told you to break Joey's spell. That we were destined to end up in a story together. I can't believe it actually came true."

Underglass nodded. "Your performance in the tutorial confirmed what we already suspected. You'll join Indira's series and play a prominent role. As I told Indira the first time around, I could not be more proud. You are worthy of this, Phoenix. You always have been."

Maxi rushed forward and put an arm around each of them.

"Best. Day. Ever!"

38

Celebration and a Secret

I t would have been enough, Indira knew, that they had saved the world. These rewards were extras, cherries on the top of an already delicious sundae. Once it was clear Underglass was finished, the crew turned to each other, hugging or smiling as they finally tasted the fullness of their victory. Before they could leave, however, Underglass cleared her throat.

"Indira," she said. "Wait a moment."

The others slid out into the hallway, led by Maxi's bright encouragements. Indira promised she'd catch up with them before closing the door and facing Underglass.

"I figured it couldn't *all* be good news," she said.

Underglass lifted an eyebrow. "It's not *bad* news, exactly. Phoenix earned his spot, but he did not earn it at the expense of your other potential romantic interest."

"But I thought . . ."

"So did we," Underglass confirmed. "One or the other. That was our expectation. But it appears the Author plans to include *both* of them. I wanted to give you a head start, time to think about it. I know Phoenix is fond of you, and that you are fond of him. I thought the two of you performed wonderfully. However, the reality is that you will also have another character assigned to your story who likes you just as much as he does."

Indira swallowed. It had been hard enough figuring out how to hold Phoenix's hand without making her palms sweat. The idea of some other boy smiling at her was just too much to handle. Underglass gestured up to the board. There was a shiver of light, and her title adjusted slightly, adding a plural *s* to the final word:

Indira Story and the Infernal Suns

"As I said, not *bad* news. For now, I'd like you to enjoy your victory." The brainstorm made a shooing gesture. "I've sent for David as well. Why don't you all head over to the Talespin? I'm sure the crew could use a few celebratory white mochas."

Indira thanked the brainstorm before ducking outside. The others were waiting farther down the hallway, discussing their new roles excitedly. Indira started walking that way before noticing that someone else was waiting outside Brainstorm Underglass's office.

"Cavern?"

The antagonist looked wildly out of place, but that did not stop him from grinning.

"Indira! Weird seeing you here. Weird."

She nodded, a little confused. "I didn't realize you'd have to report to Underglass."

He shook his head. "We don't usually."

It took Indira a minute to notice what he was holding. There were a bunch of forms attached to a wooden clipboard. "Wait a minute. Are you . . . transferring?"

He looked around nervously. "Keep your voice down. I . . . maybe. We'll see."

She laughed. "Your secret is safe with me."

Before he could reply, Underglass called his name. He straightened like a soldier, adjusting his collar slightly. Indira caught his eye before he walked inside.

"You know, I think you'll be pretty good at being *good*."

He rolled his eyes. "*Pretty* good? I did not enter the darkspring for seven years so that I could be *pretty* good at anything. You good guys always think you're the best. . . ."

Indira kept smiling long after he'd vanished into the office. Up ahead, David had joined up with the others. Her brother looked taller and sharper than when she'd left him. Training had suited him well. He let out a laugh at the sight of her. Ducking past the others, he wrapped her in a huge hug. "Baby sister. It's felt like ages."

Indira laughed at that. "You have no idea. How was training?"

It looked as if he'd grown a few inches, carved muscles onto his slender frame. There was also something in the way he stood, like he'd practiced being confident long enough that he actually *was* confident now. David smiled at her appraising glance.

"Woke up every morning before dawn," he said. "I've never run so much in my life. Every hour we had a new class. Lunch breaks if we were lucky. I'll admit there were a few times I thought about giving up. A bunch of kids dropped out. It was the hardest thing I've ever done." He paused to look around at the others. "How about you? Was your Hero thing fun?"

Their crew exchanged glances before bursting out laughing.

"Fun," Indira repeated. "That's one word for it."

Their crew headed back through the halls of Protagonist Preparatory. Indira ran a hand along the wall. She missed the old school. When they reached the front entrance, Maxi heaved a huge sigh, taking in their crew one more time.

"Well, it's been fun. I'm so glad you guys called me, but I've got to get back to headquarters. No rest for the weary and all that . . ."

Indira could tell she was stalling. She smiled at her best friend.

"Maxi. How about white mochas first? On me?"

That was greeted by a squeal of delight. "Thought you'd never ask!"

Naturally, they headed straight for the Talespin coffee shop.

———

Mr. Threepwood quickly wiped down their permanently reserved table. Indira was a little embarrassed when he said, in a voice loud enough for other nearby tables to hear:

"I feel like you should get a new table every time you save the world!"

Indira smiled back. "We're fine with just the one. How about some white mochas?"

Gadget leaned in. "Could I actually get an iced, sugar-free vanilla latte with soy milk?"

Squalls added, "And please don't poison mine. Thanks."

Threepwood blinked in confusion before noting those requests and rushing off to fill their order. Phoenix grinned at Indira as David started pelting the group with questions, having finally figured out they'd saved the world a second time. He kept shooting astonished looks over at Indira as they told the story, and saying things like "Well, of course, she's my baby sister after all"—which had Indira laughing.

It was the kind of day that could only be spoiled by the fact that it eventually had to end.

39

The Sequel

Indira stood in front of her first Story House, feeling shocked and honored. The sprawling gray house looked nearly the same. Three levels high, a pair of balconies, storm-gray bricks. The only notable difference now was the thousands of little strings attached to the roof. Indira had started counting them and quickly given up. David stood beside her.

"I told you the readers would come. Just look at all of them!"

There were a few golden threads. Indira knew what that meant—for those readers, the story had become one of their favorites. A treasure they'd keep with them their entire lives. Other colors—like silver and green and cerulean—coordinated to other emotions. Maybe it was the first book a reader had picked up in a long time, or the funniest book they'd read that year.

The fact that there were any threads at all warmed Indira's heart.

"It's their story now," she whispered. "Come on. Time to get to work on the sequel."

When she'd left, her first Story House had been on the very edge of a new neighborhood. It had seemed a little lonely. Now it felt like it was the middle of a busy town center. There were coffee shops built into the lower floors of certain buildings and even a market square.

Indira knew these were good signs. Healthy stories and healthy characters made up a healthy neighborhood. All the new readers would keep the place blossoming with life.

She whispered goodbye and started down the nearest hill. A new neighborhood had sprouted there on the edge of the constantly growing township. There were buildings of all shapes and sizes, all in different stages. Indira and David made their way through crowds of characters, many taking breaks between scenes, and came to a stop before a rose-red home that looked more like a shed than a house at the moment. It had a gleaming black door that shivered with light depending on where they looked. An unfinished porch wrapped around the front like the beginning of a dragon's tail. Indira's eyes settled on Phoenix.

Her friend sat cross-legged between their house and the neighbors', quietly studying the Author's directions for the first scene. *His* first scene. Indira crossed the square and stood at his shoulder.

"Nervous?" she asked.

He looked up at her. "Weren't you?"

"She kept going to use the bathroom," David remembered. "Classic delay tactic."

There was a little commotion as someone pushed through the crowd. Indira recognized the dark sunglasses, but Maxi had set aside the official Editors' attire for a more fashionable vest today.

"Maxi?" Phoenix asked. "I thought you had to go to headquarters or whatever."

"And miss your first scene?" Maxi smiled. "As if! We started this whole thing together. I was here for Indira's first scene. I wanted to be here for yours. What's the point of having best friends if we don't celebrate all the little things? Now get in there and don't mess it up. I brought popcorn!"

She waved a bucket that Indira hadn't noticed until that moment. Something about this felt right. Phoenix stood. He'd traded the wizarding robes for a pair of jeans. Indira watched as he brushed dirt off them before striding to the front door of *their* Story House. He looked back with the same nervous grin he'd had that first day they met. There was still a taste of mystery in that smile. Indira couldn't wait to see what was waiting for them.

As he gripped the doorknob, the entrance brightened. From black to fire bright in less than a breath. Phoenix did not take his hand away. He opened the door, drinking in the scene that was waiting for him. Indira watched with a mixture of a hundred feelings that she couldn't quite name. He took the first step inside and Maxi let out a little whoop.

Any guesses at what happened next, my dear reader?

Let me spoil it for you.

The Story House came to *life*.

40

Back in the Real World

The rain started at lunch.

Joey West had been sitting with his buddies at the table, eyeing the coming storm. He'd spun his lacrosse stick a few times before a teacher told him to put it away. Brandon, one of his teammates, had elbowed him as the rain started coming down.

"Looks like video games today," Brandon said. "Want in on some *Pirates versus Marines*?"

Joey watched the rain. "Maybe."

For some reason, that particular game no longer interested him. Months ago, he'd been playing twelve rounds a night. Sometimes with his friends, sometimes with strangers. But the game had started boring him. He wasn't sure why. It made things a little awkward at school, though, because that was all any of his friends ever talked about.

They herded into Mrs. Dailey's class after lunch, only to be herded right back out.

"We're going to visit the book fair in the library," Mrs. Dailey announced. "Don't forget to bring your money down with you."

Joey had forgotten about the book fair. He kind of wished he had some cash on him as the class stumbled into the library. Sprawling displays of new books waited. Hardcovers decorated with bright colors. Glinting stacks towered like treasures. Joey paused in front of the first display. It was a *Pirates versus Marines* book. He flipped through the first few pages before setting it back on the shelf.

The librarian danced around the room, offering advice. Joey thought she'd have worn a superhero cape if the principal had let her. She was kneeling down at that moment, running a finger along the spines of books before choosing one for a girl from the grade below them.

"I think you'll like this one," she said with a knowing smile.

Joey wandered deeper into the book fair's displays. A few titles caught his eye, but he'd read the back of the book and get bored halfway through. Most of his friends were still crowded around the front entrance of the library. Brandon grinned before bouncing his lacrosse ball as high as it could go. Mrs. Dailey swept over that way like a hawk.

As Joey circled back, movement caught his eye.

He blinked a little before squinting. *What on earth . . . ?*

The cover of one of the books was *moving*. The sight dragged him a few steps closer. Was he seeing things? He frowned. There! It moved again. The image on the cover looked like an ocean. As he squinted, the dark waves were clearly rising and falling.

"Cool . . . ," he whispered under his breath.

A student nearby looked over. Joey didn't notice, though. His eyes were pinned to the figures that had appeared on the dark horizon. He watched them grow in size and shape until they were close enough to be seen over the towering waves. The red-scaled dragon almost seemed as if it was flying right at him. Joey stared as the dragon approached, becoming more and more prominent on the book's cover. And then he saw her.

A girl with light brown skin, unruly dark hair, and a silver war hammer at her hip. Joey wasn't sure why, but something about the girl looked so familiar that he actually stopped breathing. The dragon swept forward, wings stretching out, until the two of them were front and center on the dark cover. Joey's heart hammered in his chest.

The same girl who'd been helped by the librarian paused beside him, a few books clutched to her chest already. "Are you okay?" she asked.

Joey pointed foolishly. "The cover is *moving*."

She stepped a little closer. "This one?"

Joey flinched as she reached out and grabbed the book. He thought the water of that dark ocean might splash right up in their faces. Or, worse, the dragon would take offense and breathe a great blast of fire in their direction. The younger girl held the book up and inspected it.

"It's holographic," she said, like that explained things. "It looks like they're flying, almost."

He wanted to tell her she was wrong. He'd been watching the whole time, and the dragon and its rider had not been there a moment before. The dark ocean had been empty. But that would have sounded a little weird. Joey nodded instead.

"Yeah, holographic. Cool."

He waited for the girl to move on to another section before snatching the book off the shelf. His heart continued to thunder as he flipped through the first few pages. Something about a dragon. A boy a lot like Joey was in class, bored out of his mind, when he started sweating profusely.

That was the worst. Joey had recently learned about sweat. A girl he liked named Laura had seen him in the hallway after gym class. He'd gone to offer a high five when she spied his shirt, soaked halfway through, and let out a little squeak. "Is that *sweat*?"

Joey flipped a few pages.

The next chapter switched to a new perspective. It was the girl on the front cover. Her name soared off the page, rising into the air like mist: *INDIRA STORY.*

Standing in the library, Joey knew it was impossible that lightning could strike him. But that was how it felt as his vision briefly blurred. He imagined himself on the back of a dragon, staring directly into the eyes of that girl, and it was almost like he was there.

Almost as if he had lived another life.

The vision vanished. He was back in the library, clutching another world to his chest like a waiting promise. He crossed the room and could not have explained what was happening to him. Only that he needed to read this story about this boy who was a dragon and this girl with the magic hammer. He had to know what happened to them. It felt like a story he'd started writing once, a long time ago, and for the first time he was being invited to see how it all would end.

The librarian—angel that she was—let him walk out with it after he promised to bring money the next day. He ignored the calls of his friends as the group walked back to class. He realized that he'd skipped some of the beginning, so he turned back to the start and read the first line again. It thundered through him unexpectedly.

Phoenix found out he was a dragon by accident, with only the school's janitor there to witness the discovery.

Acknowledgments

Escaping Ordinary is one of the first books to reach publication without a ton of input guiding me along the way. By the necessity of deadlines and the rhythm of the publishing world, I ended up writing this story mostly on my own. But the curious thing about being a writer—and getting deeper into one's career as an artist—is that certain voices merge with your writing at some point. You are so much more than your own imagination.

Susan Letts is always at my shoulder reminding me I have a story to tell. Anne Dailey is always handing me a slip to go to the library, urging me to really dig deep into my writing for a few hours. Bland Simpson still takes time—in my head, at least—to quietly guide me back through the threads that make up a proper story. Alan Shapiro is there to remind me that while I wasn't a great poet as a freshman, some of my lines really sing now.

To anyone who might see me in the corner of a coffee shop, I would look very much alone. Working in silence. If only they knew what a talented team of people I had with me. The teachers who've guided me to this point. The writing group who knows some of my characters even better than I do. I always feel a little like Harry Potter, walking on to face his doomed end, but with a bright team of people whispering encouragements as he goes. Thanks for being my crew.

But the loudest and most impactful voice has to be Emily Easton's. *Escaping Ordinary* is our sixth book together. We've been to other worlds. We've tackled dark plots and greedy corporations. I'm especially certain on this one that your voice guided the story home. Thanks for your steady work, and for seeing the magic in this world. Our team at Crown BFYR deserves an equally large shout-out. Claire Nist and Josh Redlich are often behind the scenes, but no less vital to the success of the series. Thank you for your diligence. The art team was fantastic, and I cannot thank Maike Plenzke enough for breathing life into my characters on these great covers.

Thanks to my team at Nelson Literary Agency. As always, a special hat tip to my partner in crime, Kristin Nelson. Your initial edits righted the ship that was *Saving Fable*. Without that guidance, there wouldn't *be* an *Escaping Ordinary* for readers to enjoy. Thank you.

I'm also thankful for my loving wife, Katie. The life of an author is chaos and out-loud thinking and impromptu readings about characters I've not even remembered to introduce to you, but you're there for it every day and unwavering at that. Thanks for loving me and my books. I'm grateful, too, for Henry. You'll be three years old when this comes out. I can write playful books like this one *be-*

cause we run around the living room pretending to be lions together. Thank you for stirring my imagination and always bursting out from your room to give me a hug when I get home. I'd like to keep that little tradition going until you're sixty.

Finally, I've dedicated this book to Thomas. As I write this, we haven't even met. You're about the size of an avocado, but growing every day. I wanted to dedicate this book about imagination and teamwork and overcoming great obstacles to *you*. Because I know from experience that all I've imagined about you will fall short of the real thing. And I know that you're the newest member of a dysfunctional team, but one that always stands together, shoulder to shoulder. Lastly, I don't know what obstacles we'll face—together or apart—but I promise I'll walk you through all of it, every time, no matter what.

About the Author

SCOTT REINTGEN is a former public school teacher from North Carolina. He survives mostly on cookie dough, which he is told is the most important food group. When he's not writing, he uses his imagination to entertain his wife, Katie, and their sons, Henry and Thomas. Scott is the author of the middle-grade novel *Saving Fable*, as well as the Nyxia Triad and *Ashlords* for young adults. You can follow him on Facebook, on Instagram, and on Twitter at @Scott_Thought.